Love's Refuge

SANDRA LEESMITH

To Mary Ann,
God's love is
the best refuge

Sandra Leesmith

AMBER PRESS

Published by Amber Press
www.AmberPressPublishing.com

Cover design: *Lena Goldfinch* (Stone Lily Publishing & Design)
Cover images: *Mystock88photo* (couple), *Gnives50* (lighthouse
and beach), *Melektaus83* (girl near a tree/braid), *Suprijono
Suharjoto* (sky) | *Dreamstime.com*

PRAISE FOR LOVE'S REFUGE

"This heart-stirring romance in the beautiful island setting provides the perfect backdrop for healing and hope!"
—Ruth Logan Herne, RUNNING ON EMPTY (Love Inspired)

"LOVE'S REFUGE is a haunting story of a girl trapped by the trauma of her past. The refuge she's found has become a prison and when love finds her she must face her deepest fears in order to claim that love."
—Mary Connealy, bestselling author of the
TROUBLE IN TEXAS Series

"Put a hurting almost-hermit together with a compassionate city boy, and a sweet love story unfolds. Readers....will love this look at a tranquil island where there's no electricity but sparks still fly."
—Rachelle Rea of INSPIRING DARING

"Sandra Leesmith will whisk you away on a beautifully, heart-pounding adventure of a love that will leave you breathless, a life full of pain waiting to be shed, and a choice that is laced with fear yet promises boundless joy and lavish dreams. Your heart will be lighter, and you'll walk away with a sharper appreciation for what you have."
—Amber of THE WONDERINGS OF ONE PERSON

DEDICATION

To my uncle and aunt, Jack and Lenny Hovde
of Bellingham, Washington,
and all my Hovde cousins
who love the out-of-doors as much as we do.

CHAPTER 1

"DUMMY, DUMMY, DUMMY." Skye Larsen dove for the ground and covered her head. She didn't move. Uneven lumps of grass pressed against her stomach and chest. She closed her eyes and pounded her fists. How could she have forgotten to check for oncoming planes before crossing the island's airstrip?

A rumble came on the wind. She looked up to see a small Cessna airplane heading straight for her. The pilot gestured for her to get out of the way. The plane roared over, barely missing her. Backlash wind threw her flowered skirt overhead and whipped the tall grass against her bare legs. She plopped her cheek against the cool grass and moaned. "Great. Just what I need today."

The blue and white plane scudded across the grass runway and stopped. She lifted her head and watched the plane circle at the end of the cut-grass strip and taxi toward her. Seeing the "For Sale" sign on her favorite piece of land was bad enough. Now she was going to have to face an irate pilot, probably one of those typical city dudes who wanted to escape from Seattle but brought the city with them instead. She struggled to her feet to brush grass and dirt from her blouse and skirt.

Her world was changing, and she didn't like it.

"Unbelievable," she muttered as she stomped across the grass runway toward the approaching plane. She breathed in the scent of wildflowers and grass mingled with salt air. She loved this remote island in Washington's Puget Sound, its thick woods, quiet nights and simple lifestyle. It was safe—no drugs, no vandals, no violence. Not like in the city where she'd grown up.

The pilot taxied close, nosed the Cessna into the wind, and cut the engine. Skye braced herself as she watched long legs, clad in khaki Dockers, descend from the plane, followed by a sleek torso covered in a brown polo shirt. When his head emerged, Skye groaned. She clenched her fists and prepared for the burst of rage she saw in his expression.

Dark eyes, set in a squared and rigid face, sparked with anger under brown hair blowing in the breeze. "Didn't you see me coming?" He stormed up and stood in front of her, hands fisted. "It's only by the grace of the Almighty I didn't smack into you."

Skye pulled herself upright, jutted her chin, and clamped her teeth together. "You could have pulled up and circled around." And why hadn't he?

"Not when I'm low on fuel. My blasted fuel gauge must be off."

That explained his over-reactive anger. He was just as mad at himself as he was at her.

"Well," he demanded. "What do you have to say for yourself?"

Skye tore her gaze away from the fire in his eyes and looked past him at the whitecaps tossing in the straits of Puget Sound. What could she say? That she'd been so distracted she'd ignored caution and crossed the small island's grass airstrip without looking? "You missed me." She shrugged. "You're a good pilot."

Air whooshed from his lungs. "Don't tell me you test every pilot's ability this way?"

She brushed aside wisps of hair loosened from her braid. "Of course not. I didn't hear you." She gestured toward the choppy bay. "I didn't expect a plane today. It's windy."

"Which is why it's a miracle I missed you."

Wind whipped her skirt around her legs, the hem snapping

against the tops of her hiking boots. She tugged on her braid. "The way this day is going, I'm surprised you did."

He studied her from head to toe, causing heat to rush up her neck and into her cheeks. The anger left his eyes, replaced by a semblance of compassion. "Bad day, huh?"

Sighing, she closed her eyes, then nodded.

He relaxed his shoulders. "Know the feeling. I'm going to have to get that gauge checked. Don't suppose there's anyone here who can do it."

She gestured toward the caretaker's house on the other side of the airstrip. "I was on my way to talk to Jack. If anyone on the island can fix it, he can."

The pilot shifted. "And Jack is?"

She swung her gaze around and caught him staring. "The caretaker," she explained as she studied him from his leather Loafers to the sporty sunglasses he had shoved on top of his head. He appeared to be a businessman, but dark hair—a little too long—brushed the edges of his collar. And was that a pierced hole in his ear? "This is a private island, you know. Are you scheduled to be here?"

He nodded. "I'm glad you're headed that way. I'll follow you. Sounds like he's the one I need to see to check in and get my keys."

Skye chewed on her bottom lip. "I'm not usually so rude. I'm Skye Larsen." She held out her hand.

Strong, blunt-ended fingers wrapped around hers in a firm shake that raised goose bumps on her arm. "Danny Fraser."

She pulled her hand away and surreptitiously rubbed it on the folds of her skirt. "Go ahead and tie down your plane. You can meet me over there." She pointed to the outbuildings at the end of the dock. "I'll look for Jack and introduce you."

He nodded, opened his mouth, then closed it before pivoting on his brown Loafers and climbing back into his plane.

Skye hurried across the field. Behind her, Danny revved the props and taxied to the grassy section where Fred Davis and his father's small planes were tethered.

Another yuppie. She shook her head. Leeza Island had once been pristine and private. Unfortunately, it had captured the attention of urban professionals from Bellingham and Seattle, largely thanks to the Randalls. After building their cabin, Ted Randall had made it big in Seattle and proceeded to invite all their friends and business associates to the island. Now changes were taking place. Private airplanes, fancy houses, a salt-water conversion system. They'd be demanding electricity next. She sighed as she approached Jack's house.

"Jack! You here?"

"In the garage," he yelled. "Come on around."

Skye skirted a black pickup, the only automobile allowed on the island. Jack and his wife, Lenny, used it to haul luggage and food up to the houses for boaters when they docked. Skye still carried in her own provisions on her back—like in the old days.

She rounded the corner of the largest building near the dock and found Jack struggling with a busted crab pot. "What's up? That looks like it's seen better days."

He threw down a wrench. "Blasted poachers. Someone's been tampering with my pots."

A thread of uneasiness curled inside her. "We've never had trouble before."

He took off his baseball cap, smoothed back his gray hair, and put the cap back on. "Did before your time. In the seventies. A bad lot. Stole everything they could find. Needed money for drugs."

Another thread tightened in Skye's chest. Memories tugged, but she shoved them back.

Jack peered behind her. "Hey, where's Ace?"

Images of her black Labrador's soulful eyes pulled at her heart, easing the momentary alarm. "He had trouble getting up this morning. He's showing his age."

Jack nodded, sympathy etched in his blue eyes. "I know the feeling. Did a plane just land?"

Skye leaned against the counter cluttered with tools. "Some guy named Danny Fraser. Never seen him before." She toyed with a wrench, remembering how his long fingers sent shivers up her arm when he'd touched her. Ridiculous reaction. He was a yuppie for goodness' sake. Like she'd fit in with their concern for brand-name clothes and high-priced décor. "You expecting him?"

Jack stood and wiped his hands on his cut-off jeans. "Must be the fellow Ted Randall is sending over to stay in his cabin. Thought he'd delay his trip with this wind."

"I wasn't expecting a plane either. Almost ran me down when he landed," Skye admitted. "My mind was on other things."

Jack looked at her, his expression concerned and caring. "You got a problem out at your place?"

She smiled at Jack, appreciating his attentiveness. He and Lenny had been surrogate parents to her ever since she'd come to live on the island thirteen years ago. "When did the end lot go up for sale? Mr. Johnson told me he'd never sell it."

Jack fidgeted with his handkerchief before stuffing it back in his pocket. "Old man Johnson died last month. 'Pears his grandson is planning to sell."

Skye sagged onto a nearby wooden box. "I'm so sorry to hear that. Was he sick long?"

"A heart attack. Quick."

Images flashed through her mind of the gentle man, bent with age but always active. Johnson had a house near the dock, but he also owned the land by her place. Since his wife's death from cancer a year ago, he hadn't been to the island much. "I'm glad he didn't suffer. Don't his kids want to keep the house or the land?"

"His two sons live in Southern California. They want to sell both. His grandson lives in Seattle. He's taking care of the sale."

"Do we know him?" She rubbed at her temple. This had to be a bad dream.

"Can't say he ever came around here. Sounds like an astute businessman though. He's priced the lot and the house at its max."

"I wish I could buy it myself, but I couldn't even hope to afford the lowest price." Skye slumped, her braid dangling across her shoulder. The small stipend she received from her grandmother's estate and the money she made from the wool blankets she wove and sold to Mount Baker Arts and Crafts would never be enough.

There had to be something she could do to stop the sale. She couldn't bear to have a house built that close to hers. She could already hear the generator chugging in the silence, the loud music and laughter as they brought over guests to impress. "Do you have his address? Maybe I can convince him to donate the land for a park."

Jack came up beside her and tossed his tools on the workbench. "You're a dreamer, just like your granny." He shook his head. "I only have a realtor's name and address."

Skye stood and pulled on his shirtsleeve. "Can you give it to me? I'll write a letter. Or call."

Jack patted her hand. "Sure thing. It's at the house. But don't go getting your hopes up."

Gravel crunched outside the door. Danny Fraser stood silhouetted against the glare from the bay. The scent of his spicy aftershave drifted in, distinct from the combined smells of fish and salt air.

Skye pulled her hand away from Jack and waved the man inside. "Jack, meet the gutsy flier who just came in, Danny Fraser."

Jack shook Danny's hand. "Bet you're after some keys, young fella."

Danny nodded at Skye and smiled at Jack. "I've heard you're the man I need to see."

Heat crept up her cheeks. Why on earth was she reacting this way? He'd smiled, that was all. She toyed with the end of her braid and tried not to stare at his rugged face and dark, smiling eyes. He gestured with his hands as he explained about the issues with his plane. Now that he wasn't frowning, he looked younger, somewhere in his mid-thirties.

Jack stepped toward the door. "You staying at the Randalls' place?"

Danny fell in step behind him. "Ted's my boss. He and Barb guaranteed R and R if I came here."

Skye followed the two men. "You'll get rest and relaxation all right. No telephones or television. Just nature at her best."

Danny raised his hands. "I don't really have time for this, but they insisted." He paused. "There is cell reception, isn't there?"

Jack shook his head. "Nope."

Danny frowned.

Skye studied his back with its tense muscles playing underneath the cotton shirt. She'd noticed lines of stress around his mouth and eyes. Flyboy might not think so, but the island would be good for him.

Jack stomped the sand off his feet at the door and entered his house. He'd enclosed the back porch years ago and made it into a small office. He ruffled through a stack of papers and handed Skye one of the sheets. "Here's the info you wanted. Go ahead and write down what you need while I get the man his keys."

Skye poked her head in the kitchen and waved at Lenny,

who, judging from the smells drifting into the office, was baking cookies. She grabbed one of the loose pens off the counter and wrote the name and number of the realtor on a yellow Post-it. "A 'For Sale' sign. And a city boy. Unbelievable day," she muttered as she tucked the paper into her skirt pocket.

Jack rummaged through his desk for the key. "Do you have much gear? I can drive you over to the house."

Danny pointed to a duffel sitting outside on the grass. "I travel light." He sounded proud of that fact. "Is it far?"

Skye set down the pen. "The Randalls' place is out by mine. I can walk you over."

Jack handed the keys to Danny. "I'd appreciate that. I have some more work to do on those crab pots."

Skye walked out the door, ignoring the fact that, from his expression, Danny Fraser looked like he'd rather have the ride. "Come on, Flyboy. You'll enjoy the walk. Our island scenery is best seen on foot."

Danny thanked Jack and followed Skye. She waited while he picked up his duffel. "You must not be planning to stay long."

Danny hefted the bag over his broad shoulder and came up beside her. "A week or two."

She looked at the duffel bag. "You didn't bring much food."

"Just clothes. I figured I'd buy groceries here on the island."

Skye shook her head. "Got big news for you. There's no store on the island. Everybody brings in their own supplies."

The stress lines on his forehead deepened, highlighting his rugged features. "Ted didn't mention that. He said everything I needed would be here."

Skye shrugged and started walking toward the airstrip. "He probably has supplies stocked in the cabin. We'll check it out when we get there."

She made a point this time of looking skyward before stepping onto the runway. She didn't want another close call, especially in front of Danny Fraser.

She heard him muttering under his breath as they trekked across the grass airstrip. His breath came in gasps; obviously he wasn't used to the physical exercise. Probably worked behind a desk all day.

As they walked, she pointed out some of the sights. "Across the straits you'll see the lighthouse. It has been guiding ships to safety for over a hundred years."

"Looks isolated."

She nodded. "The island is uninhabited, but there are some great hiking trails. You can camp on the beach west of the point."

He placed his hand over his eyes to shade them from the sun as he peered at the view.

"The few boats anchored in the harbor belong to the people here on the island, mostly year-round residents."

"Doesn't look like very many. I only see about ten or twelve," he commented between gulps of air.

Skye paused at the far side of the runway to give him a chance to catch his breath. "Wait until summer. There'll be three times as many boats."

"You live here year-round?"

She nodded, glancing at the rocky shore where stupendous waves crashed during winter storms. She looked at the clear spring sky, usually cloudy and rainy this time of year.

Danny shifted his duffel to his other shoulder. "Must be tough to live in a place this far from the city."

"I suppose you've lived in the city your whole life."

He nodded.

A wave of pity washed through her. He said he worked for

Ted Randall, and Ted had moved his main offices to the metro-politan area. "Seattle?"

"For now."

"This'll be different." She smiled and turned to walk up a wooded trail. "Come along. It's not far."

Danny hefted his bag higher on his shoulder, wishing he'd traveled even lighter. He stumbled when his foot caught on an exposed root. Why hadn't he thought to wear boots? He envied the effortless way Skye walked through the forest, her long flowered skirt brushing against her hiking boots. Her thick blond braid bounced with each step. What woman wore hair that long these days? He shook his head. An unusual woman for sure. Like someone out of the seventies. Oddly reassuring in this primitive wilderness.

They passed a small cabin. "Why are the windows boarded up?"

"Protection against the winds." She gestured toward the Sound. "They can be harsh."

The trees thickened. The forest darkened. "You lived here long?" he asked, gasping for breath. When had he let himself get so out of shape? He plopped his duffel on the ground and grabbed his chest.

When she stopped walking and turned, Danny sighed with relief, glad for a break.

"On and off for the past thirteen years."

His pounding pulse quickened even more when she focused navy blue eyes on him. A scattering of freckles dusted her tanned cheeks; her smile showed even, white teeth. Images of sophisticated and fashion-conscious Virginia flashed, images he quickly buried.

She studied him and frowned. "You okay?"

He struggled to smile. "Just give me a minute. I've got to renew my membership at the gym." How long since he'd been there? He used to work out regularly, but since his breakup with Virginia, he'd let work take control.

Thankfully, she didn't stare. He breathed deeply and followed her gaze down toward the bay. "No wonder I'm puffing. We've climbed quite a ways up this hill."

"Nice view, isn't it?"

He nodded, taking in the contrast of blue sky and water against the dark green of the nearby islands across the channel. A few white clouds floated above the horizon. He studied the woman beside him, deciding she was as wild and beautiful as the land, standing straight and tall, breathing evenly. She had to be in great shape, probably from walking, although the island wasn't very big, only a couple of miles long.

She turned, and her gaze locked with his. Her lips curved into a warm smile. "Ready, Flyboy?"

For that smile, he'd pretend. He hefted the duffel on his shoulder. "You bet. Lead on, Pocahontas."

Her chuckle mingled with the sound of birds in the otherwise quiet forest. His feet sank into the thick carpet of fir needles. He took a deep breath, drawing in the scent of damp undergrowth. Maybe Randall had been right. His boss had noticed the burnout and insisted Danny needed this break. But two weeks? Should he be taking that much time off?

He followed as Skye wound up a wide trail. When they came to a clearing, she pointed to a small blue structure he could barely see through the trees. "That's my place. Just wanted you to know in case you need anything. None of your other neighbors are around this time of year."

He could see how people got lost in the thick forest. One

tree looked like another. He searched for visual markers. A large stump had two small cedars growing out of it. Ferns dotted the forest floor, and a blackberry patch lined the far side of the trail. "I think I'll remember how to get here."

"This is the only trail to your place, so you have to pass by to go anywhere else."

His shoulders sagged with incredulity. How far from the real world were they?

A dog barked. He looked up in time to see a huge black Lab lumbering toward him.

Skye stepped between him and the Lab. "This is Ace." She knelt while the dog ambled over to lick her cheek. "What a lazy-bones. Want to meet Danny?"

Danny lowered the duffel and extended his hand. Ace hesitated, sniffed his fingers, and turned back to Skye.

Skye gave Danny a penetrating stare. "You do get along with animals, don't you?"

He nodded. "Always wanted one as a kid."

"I take it you didn't have pets."

Like he could have had one in juvie. He shook his head.

She smiled. "Like most Labs, Ace is friendly. But he's too old to do more than lick your face." She patted the salt-and-pepper fur on the dog's head. "He was a pup when I moved to the island. Now he's almost thirteen."

"Not bad for a dog his size." Danny shifted the duffel back to his shoulder and peered beyond the woman and the dog, looking for signs of another house.

She stood up. "Anxious to get there? It's just around the bend." She started up the trail. The dog walked stiffly beside her.

Danny rounded the corner and gasped at the view. The trees had been cleared to the edge of a cliff where a natural cedar house sat, surrounded by a large wrap-around deck. Floor to ceiling windows looked out across the strait.

Skye's voice broke his reverie. "Nice, isn't it? The Randalls have one of the best sites on the island." She pointed to a wooden staircase at the edge of the cliff. "They aren't too far from the beach. Most of the view sites have a steep climb."

Danny ascended the two steps up to the deck and dropped his duffel on the bench that framed the outer edge. "Nice isn't the word for this." He gestured at the view, overwhelmed by the magnitude of so much uncivilized space.

She smiled, obviously pleased with his response. "That little shed over there has all the equipment for the boat. There's fishing gear also."

Danny gave the shed a cursory glance. He had no intention of going out in a boat. He eyed the deck and pictured himself sprawled out on a nice lounge chair with his laptop. His gaze drifted to the forest. No traffic noises, honking cars, or sirens. Almost too quiet.

He walked to the window and peered in at the rustic furniture. Rather primitive—and no phone. Well, at least no one would be demanding help. "This'll work."

She moved close to him and held out her hand. "Give me the keys, and we'll check out the cupboards to see if there's any food."

He dug in his pocket and pulled out the key. "I'll get it." He unlocked the door and swung it open. A damp, musty smell surged out.

Skye walked through the house to the back door and opened it to let in the salty sea air. "It won't take long to freshen up the place." She opened the windows in the kitchen and disappeared into a back room. "There's a bedroom back here, but you'll probably want to sleep in the loft." She reappeared and gestured up the wooden stairs. "That's where I'd sleep anyway. You'll wake up to a gorgeous view."

Danny looked out the window and agreed. The view was incredible. He walked into the open kitchen area. "Looks like all the conveniences of home." He turned a knob on the propane stove and watched it flame before shutting it off. Inside the ancient propane refrigerator, a few bottled condiments sat in a corner. Packages of frozen meat and vegetables filled the freezer.

Skye opened the cupboards. "Looks like you have most of what you'll need."

Not really caring about the kitchen, he walked back out onto the deck. Skye started down the steps where Ace waited for her. "I'll be on my way. Be sure and holler if you need anything."

Reluctant to see her go, yet anxious to settle in, he waved. "Thanks for walking me over here. I'll be fine." He walked to the edge of the deck. "Sorry about the close call earlier. Hope your day goes better."

Her eyes brightened. "Seems to be doing that already." She swung around and walked up the hill.

He watched her disappear into the forest, her dog traipsing beside her. An unusual woman, but he liked her. Thank God he hadn't run into her with the plane. He shuddered at the thought as he grabbed his gear.

After unpacking the few clothes he'd brought, Danny looked at the stack of books on the end table by the window. Several self-help books. No doubt Ted's. He picked one up and read the back cover. "How to commune with your inner self." How long had it been since he'd really done that? Too long. He put the book to the side. He should read it. But later.

Looking around, he pulled out his laptop and stepped outside. Protected from the wind, the side deck radiated the sun's heat. Sitting down, he snapped open the computer. With a couple hours of battery, he could sit outside and catch up on the email he downloaded before leaving.

He clicked onto Outlook Express and started reading. First message: a reminder of the staff meeting he would be missing. Next two messages were invitations to important charity functions, both held the same night, of course. Fourth message: the inner-city high school wanted him to talk to some students. Pain shot through his head as Danny read on.

The weight of the laptop pressed into his legs as he stretched out on the lounge chair, but the weight of his world pressed into his head. He couldn't keep up with the demands. As the senior counselor in his department, he couldn't provide for every teenage gang member's need.

The past week edged across his mind. He'd been so sure that Raul and Oscar were going to make it out of the neighborhood street gang. He'd counseled them for weeks, bolstered their courage. He'd even taken the two fifteen-year-olds to the local prison for a Scared Straight session with Carlos.

Danny rolled his head, easing some of the tension as he pictured the inmate. Carlos, doing time for dealing drugs, looked the part. Scars marked the few stretches of skin not covered with tattoos. The dangling cross earring pierced into his ear now replaced the skull and bones he'd worn before. Like Manuel.

Danny closed his eyes as Manuel's face sliced into his memory. The ex-con had come to the juvenile detention center housing Danny and his buddies. They'd made fun of Manuel at first, but the determined ex-con had broken through Danny's tough exterior and shown him what his heart had ached for all along. Someone who cared.

The tough love had worked for Danny back then. But not this week. Not for Raul and Oscar. Carlos had scared the boys; Danny was sure of it. So sure, that he'd let them return home. Alone. Where the drive-by shooting had killed them both.

Danny lowered his head into his hands. Ted had insisted he take a break, but how could someone reconcile the death of those young boys? He should have seen it coming. Should have done something to prevent it.

Weary of the burdens, he glanced around at the view and slammed shut the lid of the computer. He leaned back and closed his eyes. The warm sun began to soften knotted muscles, easing the tension. But his mind raced. Maybe Virginia was right. Maybe he should look for another line of work.

A noise startled him. A bald eagle flew out of a nearby tree, the white feathers on his head and tail shining in the sunlight. An ancient verse came to mind. Something about renewing strength like an eagle's. The image reminded him of the days after juvie when he volunteered at the local Y.

He'd been in shape in those days. He'd been idealistic, too. He honestly thought he could help the young teens. Now he wasn't sure.

Restless and uneasy with the trend of his thoughts, he jumped up and paced the deck.

A loud whack echoed from the house, followed by the sound of shattering glass.

Danny rushed inside.

CHAPTER 2

SKYE SAT ON A STUMP POLISHED SMOOTH by years of her hands and legs rubbing into the wood. Ace shifted onto his back, rolling across the mossy carpet at her feet. Legs crossed and palms up, she closed her eyes and tried again to clear her mind. She hummed but couldn't generate the sense of peace she craved. It had been like this for weeks. What was wrong with her?

She sighed. Something was out of order. Deep longings welled up inside her, longings she didn't understand. Danny's image crowded into her thoughts. Was it romance she missed? She straightened. No. She'd been fine all these years on her own. She didn't need anything—except for the "For Sale" sign posted at the edge of the lot to disappear.

She closed her eyes and breathed in the scent of sun-warmed pine needles mixed with a faint hint of floral essence from the nearby wildflowers. Restless, she looked out at the ocean and noted the shades of blue contrasting with the puffy white clouds floating across the horizon. The lighthouse on the distant outcropping of rock stood silhouetted against the sky, offering hope to the weary traveler. Not for her. Nothing. No calm. No peace.

Skye eased off the stump. "I'm not making much progress today. Let's go home, Ace. We'll fix dinner and then get to that letter."

Skye tore another sheet of paper from her notepad, wadded it up, and tossed it into the corner with the other ten crumpled-up pages sitting under the loom. She eyed the half-finished blanket with its simple design and then shifted her gaze to the pile of papers. She hated writing, but she had to appeal to Mr. Johnson's grandson.

But what did a person say to a complete stranger? How could she explain that she didn't want him to sell his land? Would he understand that she meditated every day on a large stump in the middle of the property? Would he care that she sat there and watched the change of seasons as she calmed her fears and drowned the painful memories of the past?

"I can't do this," she moaned and braced her head on top of her crossed arms. Visions of the "For Sale" sign flitted through her mind, and she straightened.

A loud knock startled her. Ace strained to get up from under the table, wagging his tail and barking. Skye clutched her fist to her chest and willed her heart to stop pounding. She swallowed hard. "Who's there?"

"Danny."

Sagging with relief, Skye smoothed back loose strands of hair and hurried to the door. She shoved Ace aside with her knee and unbolted the lock. "What's up? Do you need something?"

He stood, blowing hot air into his hands and shivering in the dark shadows cast by the setting sun. "A branch broke and crashed through a window. Even though I boarded it up, I'm freezing over there, and I can't find the heater," he growled, obviously annoyed as lines of frustration creased his brow. "There's no water, and the lights don't work. I looked for a power box in case the breaker needed to be set, but can't find that either. You don't know where they are, do you?"

She mentally rolled her eyes. City folk. They didn't have a clue how to function on the island without all the conveniences of home. "Didn't you realize how rustic this island is?"

"When Ted mentioned an island cabin in the woods, I was picturing a resort. You know—spa, health club, restaurants featuring seafood, charter fishing boats."

Her annoyance melted somewhat when she saw the irritated look in his eyes as he stood shivering in her doorway. "Come on in. I have a fire going." She gestured toward the wood stove, glowing in the corner. "The days are warm, but these spring nights can be chilly."

"You got that right. I tried being macho and toughing it out, but that sounded stupid, especially since you offered to help." He squeezed past her, patted the dog, and made his way to the stove, hands outstretched toward the heat.

The small room shrank when he stepped inside. The inherent male strength didn't fit with his expressed need for help. His tall frame filled the twelve-by-twelve-foot space and, for a second, claustrophobia flitted through her. Skye hurried to pick up the papers littering the corner and stuffed them into her pile of firewood stacked by the small hearth. She gestured toward her only chair, a recliner sitting in front of the fire. "Sit here and warm up while I go get my coat and a flashlight."

She hurried out the door. The wind had picked up. She wished she didn't have to go outside to get upstairs. What would Danny think of her odd house? It looked like a square box with another box sitting on top of it. Purely unconventional—as had been her father, who had built it. She climbed the ladder to the second story and ducked into the twelve-by-twelve bedroom that made up the whole second floor. She pulled out her parka and searched in the dresser for a flashlight.

She climbed back down and glanced at the darkening sky before she entered the main floor of the building. "I think a storm's brewing. Might be raining by morning."

Danny stood by the fire, rolling his eyes upward. "Great. That's all I need. I better get that heater cranked on for sure."

Skye paused and scratched Ace's ears. "Everyone shuts off their water valve when they leave. That won't be a problem to turn on; we just need to find where it is. But I don't remember the Randalls having a heater. You'll have to light the wood stove."

Shock hit his rugged face. "No heater? What do you mean?"

Skye bit back a smile, beginning to see humor in his plight. "No electricity either. No one has electricity unless you fire up a generator, which is frowned upon. They're too noisy. Ruins the ambiance of the island." Might as well make her viewpoint on that issue clear at the outset.

"You're kidding."

She shook her head.

He stared at the small room as if seeing it for the first time. A kerosene lamp on the table where she'd been writing lit the small space. He looked past the large loom to the cedar walls, probably searching for light fixtures, a frown of frustration growing. "How on earth can you survive like this? It's so primitive."

She shook her head. She'd been in enough therapy sessions to figure out what his real problem was. "It's not the simplicity that's bothering you. It's the fact you aren't in control."

He jerked back as if hit. His muscles flexed in his chiseled jaw. Then he suddenly relaxed and smiled. "I admit it goes against my grain to be asking for help."

Impressed with his honesty, Skye relented. "Some of the houses have propane lanterns. I'll go back with you and take a look."

His expression turned hopeful, yet remained irritated. "I'd appreciate it."

Ace waddled out the door when Skye opened it. Danny left the warm stove and followed.

"We'll get a fire started at your place. It won't take long to warm the house up," she assured him.

He walked out the door and shut it behind him. "I suppose you'll have to show me how to build a fire while you're at it?"

Skye heard the aggravation in his voice and rolled her eyes. "It's not that difficult. Come on. I want to get back before it gets dark."

She trooped up the trail. His uneven footsteps clomped behind her. She paused and let him catch up to her. He caught hold of her arm and tucked it under his elbow. "Thanks for being a good neighbor. I don't know what I'd do without you."

His touch unnerved her. It had been a long time since she'd had this much human contact, especially from a man. Not after her parents' murderers had entered the house. She shook off the thought, irritated that her past kept looming, as if ridiculing her attempts at normalcy. The last therapist had warned her, told her she needed to face what happened or the memories would pop up unexpectedly. Like now.

Danny interrupted her thoughts. "What do you do up here at night if you don't have electricity?"

She shrugged. When she tried to pull free, he tucked her in closer. "I…I…read, sometimes play my guitar," she stammered. "Or work on my weaving."

"I noticed the loom."

How could he not? "I weave blankets. Mount Baker Arts and Crafts sells them. The owner is a friend."

"You're self-sufficient. I guess you have to be, living out here in the middle of nowhere." He shook his head. "I'll figure something out. Maybe I'll get some sleep for a change."

She shook off the image of him asleep in the Randalls' loft and sighed with relief when they climbed down the hill to his cabin. She pointed to the stack of wood piled behind the house. "Grab some firewood. I'll see if I can find the water main."

It didn't take long to locate the main valve for the water. Skye made a mental note to come shut it off after he left the island. She turned the knob and hurried to the house, picking up more firewood on the way.

Danny met her at the door and took her bundle of split logs. "The wood stove is over there." He pointed to the far corner.

She tucked her long skirt behind her knees, knelt, and pulled close a stack of newspapers and a pile of kindling. "Watch me now. If you arrange these properly, the fire starts right up."

His breath fanned her cheek as he bent close, watching her wad up a piece of newspaper. She forced herself to ignore his nearness, the male scent of him. "Pile these on the paper like a tepee."

After he had placed each stick of kindling carefully on the paper, she handed him the box of matches.

He took out a match and paused before striking it, sending her a wry smirk that creased his rugged cheek. "You sure you trust me to do this? I never was a Boy Scout."

She laughed. "At least you aren't too proud to ask. Most men are."

"Most men aren't dying of thirst and freezing their tush."

He chuckled as he struck the match with long, steady fingers. But she could tell he was still annoyed with himself. "I should have offered you a drink at my house. Let me check and see if the water is running now."

She hurried over to the sink and turned on the faucet. Water sputtered and spit for several seconds, then flowed in an even stream. "I better let it run for a few minutes. It's been sitting in those pipes for a couple months."

"Where's the water supply?"

"We have a salt-water conversion plant." Thanks to the yuppies. She had to admit it was nice not to have to haul water anymore.

She returned to the stove and tried to remember the last time the Randalls had been out on the island. Flames flickered around the sheets of paper. "Nice job there. Now hand me a couple of those smaller pieces of wood."

Danny passed over two logs, and she showed him how to place them on the fire so as not to smother the flames. She closed the stove's glass-paned door, then stood and brushed off her hands. "That should do it."

"It's a miracle," he commented sarcastically. He walked into the kitchen area and brushed wood chips from his jeans. "Can I make you a cup of coffee?"

"I don't drink coffee." When a look of regret crossed his features, she gave in. "I'll have some tea though." There was a full moon tonight. She could make it home in the dim light if the clouds didn't thicken too much.

While he banged about in the cupboards, she glanced around the familiar house. The walls were cedar, made from trees off the lot—like her place. The Randalls had been one of the first on the island. Their house had many improvements, but still had the simplicity of a rustic cabin.

She sorted through the books on the end table beside the couch. A novel by Tom Clancy. Several books by Max Lucado looked like self-help books. She glanced over at Danny. "It appears you brought plenty of reading material."

Water sputtered into the kettle as he filled it. "Ted wants me to read his books." He shrugged. "Guess I'll have the time now." He set the kettle on the stove and lit the burner. The garlic scent of propane wafted in the air for a second before it blended with the smell of wood smoke from the fire.

She walked over to the propane fixture on the kitchen wall. "I better show you how to light this. It'll be dark soon. You'll need it to read by because kerosene lamps are hard on your eyes."

She showed him how to light the lantern. "You've got all the amenities here. Stove, refrigerator, and lamps—all fueled by propane."

He rolled his eyes and grunted. "No heater, though."

"That would use too much gas. The propane delivery truck only comes to the island twice a year. You have to make it last."

Danny studied her incredulously. "You stay through the winter without a heater?"

Skye nodded, chuckling at his expression.

He walked over and stretched his hands out to the wood stove. "At least there's plenty of firewood. Ted said it's delivered every fall."

Skye joined him, enjoying the snap and crackle of the fire. "Don't worry. You'll be a pro by the end of two weeks." Or would he be disgruntled and bored like most of his city contemporaries? For some strange reason, that thought bothered her. "I'll be happy to show you around the island tomorrow. You'll see what a special place this is."

He smiled. "I'd like that. Not too early though. I need to do some work on my computer."

She returned his smile. "Thought you were going to say you'd be sleeping in. My granny used to always say fresh air does wonders for a good night's sleep."

His brow creased. "Used to?"

Memories edged into her mind, some pleasant, some painful. "She passed away when I was in high school. Left me her place here on the island."

"Interesting house. Did your grandfather build it?"

The kettle whistled and Danny hurried over to shut off the flame. Skye followed and found the tea in the cupboard. She selected an herb blend and handed him the box. "My dad built it for my granny as a getaway cabin. It was never meant to be lived in year-round." Images flashed of her father's long hair blowing around his suntanned face, his tie-dyed T-shirts and faded jeans hugging his fit body.

Danny opened the cupboards and found two mugs. He handed one to Skye and filled them both with the boiling water. The aroma of herbs filled the air. "Why so small? And why is the staircase outside?"

Skye remembered the laughter in her father's deep blue eyes, eyes like her own. "He didn't want to go to the hassle of getting a building permit. You don't need one for a building that's less than twelve-by-twelve."

Danny gestured toward the couch and pulled over a side table so they could set down their mugs. Skye sat but held onto her cup, enjoying the warmth.

The couch sank in his direction when he sat down next to her, his masculine scent mingling with the smoke from the fire. "And the outside staircase?"

"Gave us more room inside."

Danny frowned in puzzlement, and Skye chuckled. "You'd have to know my dad to understand. He hated rules and went out of his way to defy them."

Danny blew on the hot tea before taking a sip. "Even to the point of living in a box?"

Skye laughed. "That was mild compared to some of his other idiosyncrasies."

He scrunched his nose at the tea and set it on the table. "Guess I'm more of a coffee man."

Did he know how to make coffee on a stove?

"What kind of idiosyncrasies?" he asked.

"The Volkswagen van where my sister and I grew up. The bong he carried everywhere. The places he would find to stay that didn't cost any money. Naming me Sunny Skye."

He choked, covering his grin with his hand.

Skye shifted on the couch. "You think that's bad, they

named my older sis Mary Jane."

He couldn't hide the laughter this time. "You've got to be kidding."

"Bona fide hippies. My parents were authentic flower children."

He studied her from head to toe. "That explains a lot. Must have been good for you. You look healthy and relaxed."

Uncomfortable with his attention, Skye jumped up and paced from the window to the wood stove and back. "That's my own doing. I'd be doped-out if I'd followed in my parents' footsteps. And dead. Like they are."

Silence echoed in the room, broken only by the occasional pop or hiss from the fire. She eyed Danny, sorry now for her blunt outburst. Her therapist always said she needed to refine her tact.

Danny stood up and placed his hands on her arms to stop her pacing. He stared. "I'm sorry about your parents."

Moved by his words, she stared back into his brown eyes. "It was a long time ago. I've dealt with it." But had she? Nightmares still haunted her. Loud noises rocked her with fear. The countless parade of therapists over the years had been a waste of time.

Danny studied the haunted look in her eyes and wanted to pull her close to his chest, wrap his arms around her. If only he could protect her from the fears he saw in her face. "You're a real trooper, and I'm glad you're here."

Her suntanned cheeks bloomed pink. "I...I...I better go."

He stepped back and lifted his hands. "Sorry. For a moment there, you looked like you needed a hug."

She backed away slowly. "No, that's sweet. I mean..." She spun around and hurried to the door. "I'll see you in the morning. Around ten."

Danny rubbed his cheek, amazed by his reaction to the woman. His heart raced, and his chest burned. But no, he couldn't afford another involvement. Hadn't he learned anything from Virginia? Besides, a relationship was impossible with the tight schedule he had at work.

Yet Skye was warm and caring. Maybe... He was here on vacation after all. Had been told to rest and relax. Skye would be an interesting diversion. He shook off the thought and picked up their cups, frowning at their contents. He'd better find a coffeepot soon.

The fire in the stove crackled as he inspected the cupboards, mentally cataloguing their contents. He pulled out an old-fashioned, blue-enameled coffeepot and scratched his head. "Must be from the antique store," he muttered to himself. He glanced around the cabin, feeling like a pioneer and wondering how he could relax in such primitive conditions. "This place is like stepping back in time."

A heavy weight settled inside him as he set up the coffee for the morning. His eyelids drooped, yet his back and neck ached with tension. He hadn't slept well in weeks. He looked around and wondered what he would do with himself during the night.

He eyed the books on the table and cringed. Did Ted honestly think he needed self-help books? His boss had told him to work on his mental health. And what good would that do? He peered up at the loft. Maybe he should lie down and try to sleep.

Danny crawled up the stairs, stripped off his clothes, and climbed into bed. Wide awake, yet tired, he fought off the images of the stacks of paperwork on his desk. He tried not to think about the three boys who had just joined their group, boys beaten near to death because they opted out of their gang.

Or the two who had been shot. Raul. Oscar. He forced himself to think of trees, forest glens, and a blond-haired nymph. It did no good. He finally got up and paced.

Loud knocking pounded in his brain. Danny woke with a start. The pounding continued—real, not a dream. He sat up and shook his head, amazed he had slept at all.

The door creaked open downstairs. "Danny? Are you all right?" Skye called out.

The yeasty smell of hot bread wafted into the room. Danny perked up, hunger jarring him awake. "You aren't torturing me, are you? Do I smell fresh bread?"

"Baked you a loaf this morning." Skye's voice carried into the loft. He heard her walking across the wood floor into the kitchen area. "You must have been tired. It's almost ten thirty."

What? He sat up. "You've got to be kidding!"

"Told you the fresh air would make you sleep well."

He flopped back onto the pillow. Pleas for help raced through his head. The boys. Oscar. Raul. His shoulders sagged with the weight of the daily demands. Demands he could only make a dent in, never resolve. He closed his eyes and rubbed the back of his neck.

Shaking off the heavy feelings, Danny forced himself to remember he was on vacation. He climbed out of bed, tugged on jeans and a sweatshirt, and went down the sun-warmed stairs in his bare feet.

He stopped when he saw Skye, her hair loose and shining in the sunlight that streamed through the windows. Her skirt flowed around her long legs and a bulky wool cardigan covered a knit halter-top.

She turned and smiled. "Welcome to the land of the living. I take it you slept well."

He combed his hair with his fingers. "You were right. The fresh air put me out." At around five a.m.

She cocked her head and studied him. "You look more rested, but you'll be doing even better in a couple days."

"I hope so." He stepped into the kitchen and turned the stove on under the coffeepot. "I'm having coffee. Can I get you some tea?"

She shook her head and walked to the door. "No, I'll give you a chance to wake up. I'm going down to the beach to check out what the tide brought in. I'll be back in about twenty minutes."

She strode across the deck. Ace greeted her at the edge. A breeze tossed a golden cloud of hair about her. Her skirt molded against her slender legs and the tails of her wool sweater flapped around her thin and trim hips. His blood pounded with male appreciation as he watched until she disappeared down the wooden staircase to the beach. He shook off the sense of loneliness that snuck in when she left.

The coffee started boiling. Good. A little caffeine ought to clear his brain. He strolled into the bathroom, whistling his favorite song and enjoying the smell of fresh coffee. Several minutes later, a loud sputtering noise came from the kitchen. Danny rushed out of the bathroom to find coffee boiling and bubbling out of the pot all over the stove and splattering on the loaf of bread.

"No. Not the bread!"

He reached to shut off the gas, but jumped back when a splash of hot coffee landed on his hand.

"Yeeeeowww!" Yelping, he gingerly turned off the burner.

The coffee settled in the pot. He reached for the handle to move the pot out of the mess. The hot metal burned his hand.

He sucked his fingers and looked around, glad Skye had left for the beach. He didn't want her to see what a disaster he'd created.

He grabbed a potholder and poured a cup of coffee. He took a sip and promptly spit it out, grounds and all. "Yuck. No wonder she drinks tea." He'd never again take his drip coffeemaker at home for granted. The bread was soaked. He hid it in the cupboard so Skye wouldn't see what he'd done to it. Too bad he hadn't had a piece before making the coffee.

Not sure what to fix for breakfast, he decided to go find Skye and see what she was up to. He grabbed his sunglasses and stepped outside.

The crisp breeze smelled of the sea. Sun filtered through the trees, throwing a kaleidoscope of color on the forest floor. He climbed down the wooden stairs and searched the rocky beach for Skye.

She stood on a spit of land that stretched into the sea, looking down at something in the rocks.

He started toward her. "Skye?"

She turned, her smile warming him down to his toes. She'd wound her hair into a pile on the top of her head. "Do you like oysters? We can pick some up for lunch."

His tennis shoes crunched on the barnacles covering the rocks. "I thought you said there were no stores around."

She bent to the ground and picked up a small stone. "They're here." She held out her hand and laughed. "See?"

Danny reached for the object in her hand and saw it wasn't a stone, but a rough-shelled oyster. She pointed down at the rocks. He looked around and suddenly realized there were hundreds of oysters strewn on the beach after the tide had gone out. "I don't believe it. You can just pick them up?" He stooped and selected a couple of large oysters.

"Go for the small ones. The big ones aren't as good to eat."

He gathered several small shells like the ones she had.

"This is amazing. How can there be so many?"

She lifted up the hem of her skirt to hold the oysters. "The whole Sound used to be covered with them, but the commercial people almost cleaned them out. Now no one is allowed to take any off the island."

Danny grabbed more oysters. In minutes, he'd filled her skirt.

She stepped away from him. "Whoa there. How hungry are you? We don't want to take more than we can eat."

He tossed the three in his hand onto the beach. "Guess I got carried away. It amazes me how you can walk out here and grab the food you need."

"There's plenty of seafood around. We get crabs out in the Sound." She pointed toward the channel. "We can dig for clams, and of course there's plenty of fish."

He looked around him. "I thought you were self-sufficient before, but now I'm sure of it. I have to admit, I'm dependent on fast food and the local restaurants in town."

She stared at him for long moments, looking as if she was about to respond to his comment. Then, holding her skirt hem below her knees, Skye moved around him. "Grab that bucket by the stairs." She pointed to a pile of plastic pails and metal pans tucked under the landing of the staircase. "Fill it with sea water, and we'll take these oysters up to the fire pit."

Danny felt like a native when he grabbed a good-sized bucket. He stepped onto a large rock and filled the pail, managing to keep from falling in the water. "How's this?" he asked, proud of his accomplishment.

Skye's smile did crazy things to his insides. "The water will keep them fresh until lunchtime."

His stomach growled. When would that be? He wondered, but he didn't ask. He didn't want her to think he was any more of a klutz than she already did.

She poured the oysters from her skirt into the pail, which Danny then carried up the wooden stairs. Skye pointed to a fire pit between the back door and the storage shed. What was next? He set the bucket in the shade and straightened.

She didn't disappoint him. "Ready to go explore the island, Flyboy?"

He rubbed his hands together in anticipation. "You bet."

Her smile brightened. "We're a small island, but we're packed with all kinds of surprises."

A movement in the forest captured his attention. He looked up in time to see the eagle soar through the trees. A surge of new energy swept through him. Danny glanced at Skye and saw she was watching the raptor.

She waited until the bird settled in a dead tree. "That's our resident bald eagle. He and his mate nest on the island. The forest around the nest is protected land. No one can build or cut lumber on it. I'll show you, if you like."

A protected species. Just like her. He smiled. "Lead on, Pocahontas. I'm ready for adventure."

A loud explosion rocketed through the forest. Birds erupted into flight. Danny's ears rang. He looked at Skye.

Her eyes darted in surprise, then filled with fear. He stepped close, his muscles tense, ready.

CHAPTER 3

SKYE FROZE, HEART POUNDING, breath catching in her throat. She clutched the lapels of her wool sweater, her knuckles turning white.

Danny turned toward the docks. "Sounded like something blew up." He pointed. "Look, there's a cloud of smoke."

Skye spun around and stared at a blue cloud drifting across the bay. "Jack!" she cried, running up the driveway to the trail. "Something's happened. He could be hurt."

Fear clutched at her heart, a fear she hadn't known since her parents were killed. A fear she never thought she'd have to face again as long as she stayed on this island. Here she was insulated, cocooned—safe from urban violence.

Danny ran behind her, his breath heavy. "Does he have explosives around the place?"

"Nothing that would blow like that. Unless it's a propane tank." She sprinted down the hill. If anything happened to Jack, she didn't know what she'd do. She couldn't bear to lose Jack. Or Lenny.

Dashing out of the woods and into the clearing above the airstrip, she scanned the buildings. Nothing looked amiss. Then she saw the fire. She halted in mid-stride. "I don't believe it."

Danny crashed into her, grabbing her shoulders and gasping for breath. "What is it?"

She pointed at the bay. "Davis's skiff. It's on fire."

"A local?"

"Yes. Hurry." She started running across the airstrip toward the dock. Relief poured through her at the sight of Jack and Lenny.

Her footsteps echoed across the wooden pier. Danny clumped along the wood, close behind. Skye hurried to Lenny's side. "What happened?"

Lenny braced against the rail. "We have no clue. We were in the house when it blew. Scared the peaches out of me."

"Me too," Skye admitted. "I thought something had happened to you or Jack."

Sympathy filled Lenny's brown eyes. She reached for Skye's hand and squeezed it. "We're all right, honey. Thank the Lord. Jack's going to get his boat and go see what happened."

Danny walked over to help Jack, who was busy tossing portable fire extinguishers into his boat. "What can I do to help?"

Jack pointed to the lines holding his boat to the dock. "Untie those and push us off before you jump in. We'll go over and see if there's anything left to salvage."

While the two men in the boat sprayed foam on the skiff's flames, Skye waited on the pier with Lenny. Other island residents joined them.

"How did it happen?" one asked.

Lenny shrugged. "Davis and his son rowed it out to their fishing boat this morning. I doubt there's anything on it to make it blow."

Ed Smith, another resident, stepped closer. "Don't suppose it was set, do you?"

Uneasiness sliced through Skye. "There's no one here on the island who would do something like that."

The man shrugged. "Can't think of any other reason."

Skye turned her back on him, not wanting any part of his negativity. There had to be another reason, and Jack would find it.

By the time he and Danny extinguished the fire, the skiff was charred beyond recognition. The back end started to sink.

Lenny shaded her eyes with her hand. "Looks like she's going down. Come on, Jack," she shouted. "Get back here."

Skye heard the worry in Lenny's voice and tightened her arms across her chest. Rubbing up and down on the sleeves of her sweater, she watched Jack and Danny try to unsnap the skiff from the buoy so the ball wouldn't be dragged under. Finally, the snap gave, and the buoy bobbed free. Jack turned his boat toward the dock.

Skye sighed with relief when Danny jumped ashore and secured Jack's boat.

Voices rumbled as the men on the dock crowded around Jack. Danny shouldered his way through the crowd and joined Skye on the upper dock. "Whew! That's more excitement than I need for the rest of the week."

"Could you tell what happened?" she asked.

He shook his head. Taking her elbow, he guided her off the dock and away from the people. "I didn't want to say anything back there. Jack should handle it."

Skye froze. "Handle what?"

Danny paused and rubbed the back of his neck. "Looked like an explosion had been set. Jack figured a homemade bomb."

Her heart thumped in her chest. "Why would someone do that? It's just an old skiff Davis uses to get from the dock to his fishing boat."

Danny shoved his sunglasses on top of his head. "Any kids around here who like to cause trouble?"

Tendrils of fear curled up and down her spine. "No. Never." That was why she'd moved to this isolated island. To get away from troublemakers.

Danny studied the men on the dock. "Any strangers hanging around?"

She looked into his dark brown eyes. "Only you."

He shifted his weight from one foot to the other. "It

doesn't make sense. Someone should talk to the owner and see if he has any enemies out to make trouble for him."

Lenny walked up and wrapped her arm around Skye's waist.

Skye leaned into the hug. "Danny says the blast was set. What's Jack say?"

Lenny sighed. "Pretty much the same thing. I wonder if it's the same clowns who have been messing with the crab pots."

"Seems like a stretch," Danny said. "Crab pots to bombs."

"Not if it's kids trying to make trouble."

Skye brushed back a loose tendril of hair. "Why our island? And why now?"

"Don't know, but some strange things have been going on lately. Come on up to the house." Skye and Danny fell in step beside Lenny. "Jack has been thinking of calling the sheriff. He'll have to now."

Danny held open the door for Lenny. "What kind of things?"

"Not anything we've thought too much about, but they're starting to add up." Lenny stepped inside and motioned for them to follow. "Tools have been missing out of the garage. Windows in houses up your way have been busted." She pointed toward the opposite end of the island. "Nothing taken, just malicious vandalism at most."

Danny closed the door behind him. "A branch broke off a tree and crashed through one of Ted's windows last night. Are you sure the other broken windows were done by vandals?"

"They weren't near any trees."

Skye sat down at the kitchen table in the same chair she'd used for the past twelve years. "You never mentioned it."

"We didn't want you to worry." Lenny set out a plate of homemade cookies and Danny dove into them.

Skye shook her head when he offered her one. She placed clenched fists on top of the table. "It can't be locals. None of us full-timers have kids."

"Jack thinks someone's anchoring in Arch Cove on the far side and coming ashore when the tide is in."

Images flashed through Skye's mind. Beads of perspiration began to form on her brow. The pictures on the wall blurred.

Danny set down his third cookie and leaned toward her. "Are you all right?"

Lenny brought a glass of water. "Don't get all panicky now, honey. Jack always keeps an eye on your place."

Lenny's voice penetrated the blur when she said to Danny, "Her parents were murdered by street thugs."

A chair scraped back as Danny sat down next to Skye. He curled his arm around her shoulder and pulled her against his chest. "It's okay. I'm right down the trail from you. You've got Ace. He'll warn you if anyone is near your place."

He was trying to comfort her, but nothing could chase away Skye's fears. She shuddered, wanting the clock to go back in time. Back before the blast today. Back before she'd turned seventeen.

Danny's heart ached for her. Her shivers shook him to the core. No wonder she'd turned pale as a ghost. How tragic to lose both parents. From his own experience, he knew the deaths had to have been violent. He tightened his arm around her and glanced up at Lenny. "Do you want me to fly to the mainland and talk to the sheriff?"

Lenny shook her head. "Jack has a CB radio. He'll fire up the generator and give his office a call."

Danny laid his cheek on the top of Skye's head and held her tight. How did a young girl handle that kind of violence? How had she found solace? Had she received counseling? He'd make a point of asking her later.

He lifted his head. "How about that tour of the island? You'll feel better if you get your mind off the explosion."

She straightened and stared at him as if surprised to be leaning against him. "You're right." She took a deep breath. "I'm overreacting. Let's go." Skye stood.

Lenny reached over and patted her hand. "You come by this evening if you want some company, honey."

Skye attempted a smile. "I'll be fine."

Danny stood and stepped beside Skye. "You can come by my place and help me build another fire," he teased.

Her smile was genuine this time. "I'm sure you can handle it on your own." Taking another deep breath, she walked toward the door. "But I will show you the sights."

"Good. I want to see every inch." And he'd take a look at the cove Lenny had mentioned and see if he could spot any signs of unusual activity.

Lenny waved from the porch as they left. Skye proceeded toward the opposite end of the island. From the Cessna, Danny had noticed the island was in the shape of a Y, with Ted's cabin near the foot of the longer stretch of land. The airstrip and dock were in the middle and, north of them, were the two jutting points. The nearest point stretched out into the Sound with buildings dotting the treeless shores. Dense rain forest covered the far point.

He walked beside Skye as she took the road down the center of the closer projecting stretch of land, listening closely as she told him who lived in each dwelling. "These are the newest houses. Mostly folks from the city." She gestured toward a hot tub, built onto the porch of one of the modern buildings. "You can see they don't like things as rustic as the rest of us."

He studied her face and noticed a faint frown creasing her forehead. "Do I detect a hint of prejudice against us city folk?"

She shrugged and cast him a sheepish smile. "I try not to be judgmental, but the newcomers have caused a lot of changes."

"Changes you don't approve of, I take it."

She walked into a grove of trees that stood at the end of the point. "Let's say that I prefer the old-fashioned quality of the island. I like simplicity and a sense of peace."

He pushed a low-hanging branch aside so she could continue on the trail. He sympathized with those from the city. Too much simplicity made life difficult. "It makes a nice getaway," he conceded.

She brushed past him, leaving a faint hint of her lilac scent. "That's true, but when you start bringing in all the elements of the city, then you aren't really getting away. Cell phones, radio, television news are all an invasion from the outside world."

He stepped to the edge of a rocky cliff and looked several hundred feet down at the bay. Past the bay he could see the island where the lighthouse stood on its rock promontory. He'd seen it from the dock, too. The quiet seeped into his soul. "It is peaceful and still. Is that what helped you overcome the tragedy of your parents' deaths?"

She nodded. "I have a special place where I can sit and commune with nature. It does help."

He could picture her sitting like a wood nymph in the forest. A yearning welled up in him, a long-lost connection. "Aren't you lonely?" Why in the world had he asked her that?

She turned away, color rising in her cheeks. "You sound like my sister. Janie is always bugging me to turn my life around and return to what she claims is civilization."

His heart sank. "I didn't mean to sound judgmental."

She sighed. "I can't imagine living in the city." She turned her blue eyes and looked deep into his. "Janie seems at peace, though."

He remained silent, sensing more of a question from her than an observation. He pushed his sunglasses to the top of his head and gestured around. "So what else is on this island, Pocahontas? I'm ready to see the beach."

She chuckled. Relief crossed her features. "We don't have a 'traditional' sandy beach. Ours are rocky. But we have a couple of places where we dig for clams. You have oysters for lunch; do you want clams for supper?"

Dig for her own clams? Was there anything this woman couldn't do? He lowered his glasses and led her toward the center of the island, down the path they had come. "Sounds like a plan. Oysters for lunch. Clams for supper. Let's go."

She laughed as she walked beside him. "Not until we finish the tour. The tide's too high right now. By the time I've shown you around, the tide should be out, and then we can start digging."

They walked the two-mile length of the island. Skye told him about the piece of land near the Randall place, protected because eagles nested there. They passed several houses and eventually reached the other projecting land formation of the Y where a large log house stood in a cleared area. "That's the Davis place. He's a retired Marine. Owns the plane parked next to yours."

Danny made a mental note to meet the man. He wanted to check and see if he had any ideas about the explosion. Had he seen any teens hanging around?

As if reading his mind, Skye said, "I'll introduce you tomorrow. He's out fishing with his son today. Fred owns the third plane. He flies over from the mainland about once a month to go fishing with his dad."

Danny wondered if Fred had any interest in Skye. "Does he bring his wife?"

Skye chuckled. "He's not married. He brought a date one time, definitely a city girl. Wouldn't step foot on the island unless all of her friends came along. No place to shop. No health spa. No Mocha Frappuccinos."

The woman sounded exactly like Virginia. The Seattle socialite hated the fact that Danny dealt with people she considered scum. She would also hate this primitive island. In spite of his history with Virginia, Danny kicked himself for caring whether Skye was involved with anyone or not. But he had to know. "Anyone come to visit you on the island?"

Holding onto her long skirt, she scrambled down the embankment to an isolated cove. "Just my sis now and then."

No men. He almost sighed in relief even though he had no right to be glad. They barely knew each other, and he had no interest in involvements right now. Still, it made him happy. He grabbed onto a limb to ease his way behind her. "She likes to take a break from the rat race, does she?"

Skye laughed, the sound echoing against the rock walls surrounding them. "No, Janie loves the rat race. The more going on, the better. She comes here to try and convert me. She thinks I need to be rescued."

Skye stopped in the middle of the forty-foot cove and pointed toward a rock formation. "See the archway? That's why this is called Arch Cove."

A small space carved by the crush of waves and wind separated a piece of gray granite from the rock wall jutting from the shore. So this was the cove Lenny was talking about. Danny studied the beach for signs of unusual activity and noticed Skye doing the same.

"Everything look normal?" he asked.

She shaded her eyes with one hand. "Looks like someone has built a fire against the rocks. But the locals could have done that."

Danny walked to the rocks and looked for a clue to who

had been there. In the ashes he found cigarette butts and several half-melted aluminum beer cans.

Skye stepped beside him. "Wouldn't be anyone from the island. Even the tourists are strict about not leaving garbage on the beach."

She walked farther along the rocky shore and pointed to several boulders that looked like they had been scraped. "Someone has landed here. Lots of boaters cruising the Sound moor off the island for the night. This is private land, so they aren't supposed to come ashore, but some do."

"It could very well be the vandals that Jack and Lenny are worried about." An uneasy feeling settled in his gut as he watched Skye search the deserted beach. She seemed so vulnerable, like an innocent lamb. He didn't want to think of her being afraid at night. Of anyone landing unnoticed on this beach—or anywhere on her island for that matter.

She whirled around, surprising him with her blue-eyed glance. Quivers crept up his spine. "Don't see anything else," she said. "Want to finish the tour, Flyboy?"

He braced himself against the luring pull of her gaze. "What about this rubbish? Shall we pick it up?"

"I'll bring a garbage bag back later. Once a place is trashed up, people get careless and don't feel guilty about making more of a mess. It always pays off to clean up litter."

He didn't want her to be on this beach alone. "I can help."

"How about those clams? Looks like the tide is down." She ignored his offer, took the path, and climbed back up the steep rocks with an ease he envied. He struggled over the rough boulders, praying he wouldn't fall and make a fool of himself.

She reached the top and waited for him. "There's only one last point to walk down, and then we'll be at your cabin."

Huffing for breath, Danny joined her at the top of the

cliff. If he didn't do anything else this week, he was at least going to exercise and get back in shape.

Skye led the way down a narrow path that ran parallel to the water's edge, pointing out a couple of houses that were empty. After they passed a wooded area, he nodded at a "For Sale" sign on a dirt road that led into the dense forest. "What's this?"

She hesitated before answering, her jaw clenching and unclenching. "It's the Johnson place." She shrugged and spun around. "Just an empty lot."

Danny studied her back as she led the way down the path. Something bothered her about the lot. Her response had been too casual and hadn't matched her body language. He shrugged away the thought. Maybe the mention of Johnson brought unpleasant memories. After all, his place was close to hers. He could see the blue walls of her cabin through the trees.

Skye stopped at the path to her house. "I'm going to get Ace. He loves to walk the beach when I go clam digging."

"You want me to wait here?"

She waved. "We'll clam from your beach. Go on ahead. I'll join you in a few minutes."

Danny walked down the path, the silence of the forest weighing down on him. As if she were a ray of sunshine, Skye's presence brightened his day. Sunny Skye. An appropriate name for a wood nymph. Whistling, he ambled toward Ted's cabin, hands in his pockets.

Maybe he did need a woman in his life. Skye's unconventional yet positive outlook was the lift he needed to keep from being bogged down beneath the weight of pressures in Seattle. If he had someone like Skye to come home to, someone who was so far removed from the world he dealt in, he could be refreshed instead of weary.

Then again, she could be just like Virginia, wanting him to

be a certain way. Virginia had wanted a fellow socialite. Skye probably wanted a mountain man. He was neither.

Skye hurried into the bathhouse and washed up, then splashed lilac scent on her wrists and neck. She stood at the mirror and laughed. "You're just going clamming. Who do you think you're going to impress with all this froufrou?"

Danny Fraser.

Nonsense. She shook out her hair and pulled her brush through its tangled strands, staring at the face reflected there. *You don't need to get all hot and bothered by this stranger. Just because he's an absolute dream to look at, has the kindest eyes you've ever seen, and is tender-hearted, doesn't mean you don't know he'll be gone in a few days. That's what happens with most island visitors, especially city dudes who can't hack the inconveniences of rustic living.*

The warmth of his arm around her shoulder crept into her mind. Too bad. It would be nice to finally find someone to relate to—share time with. But he'd be gone in two weeks. "Don't go getting your heart in a dither. Just show him how to dig for clams."

But he'd seemed to truly enjoy the island tour. He'd appreciated the beauty of the forest, the solitude and silence, the awesome grandeur of the Sound. She separated her hair and braided the heavy strands, unable to stop thinking about Danny.

He's from the city. Don't forget that unsettling news. He'll probably start hassling you to leave the island, just like Janie. Then again, he hadn't persisted with the subject earlier today. Maybe there was hope.

One of the strands slipped from her fingers. She stopped

and took a deep breath, wishing for the hundredth time since Danny had arrived that thoughts of him didn't fluster her. She reached for her hair and finished the braid.

She refused to do any more primping, so she called Ace, grabbed her shovel, and closed the door behind her. A brisk spring breeze tugged at her skirt. She swung the shovel over her shoulder and forced herself to walk—not run—to the Randalls' cabin. She found Danny lying on a lounge chair on the deck. At first, she thought he was asleep, but then noticed his lips were moving. She stood there for long minutes simply enjoying the sight of him.

It had been ages since she'd desired to be close to a man. Not since one of her parents' killers turned his attentions toward her. But something about Danny called to her. A wave of loneliness washed through her and made her wish for a love she knew she'd never have, maybe never deserve. No man would want someone as broken as her.

"Danny," she whispered, his name rolling like honey off her lips.

His eyes opened, and she found herself caught in his smiling gaze. "You're beautiful."

Heat flushed her cheeks. She lowered her eyes and looked down at her clumpy hiking boots. Her wrinkled skirt and bulky sweater sagged around her body. How could he think she was beautiful? Yet he sounded sincere.

She hefted the shovel off her shoulder and planted it in the ground. "Come on, Flyboy. We have work to do."

Danny stretched. He looked tired but less stressed. "Did anyone ever tell you that you're a slave driver?"

She smiled. "My daddy used to." She remembered sitting on his shoulders as a child whenever he hiked in the woods. The scent of pot in his clothes. Dancing when he played the guitar, singing Janis Joplin and Bob Dylan songs.

Danny stepped near and broke through the flashbacks. "Can't compete with a daddy." He grabbed the shovel. "I'm hungry for lunch. Let's go get at those clams."

Laughter bubbled up. "We can't eat the clams until later, after we get the sand out of them."

"We've got the oysters, don't we?"

"We'll build a fire when we finish clamming."

"I'm ready, Pocahontas."

Skye led the way to the wooden steps with Ace gimping at her heels. She reached the bottom and jumped onto the beach. Danny followed close behind.

Ace growled.

Something moved under the landing.

Skye clasped her throat to squelch a scream.

CHAPTER 4

A SEAL PUP HUDDLED under the wooden landing, shivering against the rocks. Skye grabbed Ace's scruff and pulled him away. "Stay back," she ordered the dog, then turned to Danny. "I bet he was near the skiff when it exploded."

Danny looked at the small animal. "What should we do?"

Skye bent to get a better look at the seal. He shifted, dazed, but apparently there was no external damage. "Not much. Hopefully when he settles down, he'll return to the sea."

Danny crouched beside Skye, his nearness a distraction she tried to ignore. "Do you think he's wounded?"

As if out of energy, the seal lowered its head. Skye's heart ached to see the little tyke suffering. Slowly she reached her hand under the landing, letting the pup sniff her fingers. When it didn't pull away, she stroked its fur, crooning to reassure the small animal. "Must be in shock, or he'd be stressing with us this close."

Danny held onto Ace's collar. "He's not minding your touch."

She glanced up at Danny. "Its heart is racing. My voice is a comfort."

To her surprise, Danny murmured, "It's okay, little one. You're safe with us. You'll be all right."

Her own eyes drooped at the soothing, rhythmic tones. She forced them open and stared at his profile, wondering what it would be like to have him whispering to her. He swung his head around, and their gazes locked. She gulped as she realized his touch would cause a lot more than soothing comfort.

"He doesn't look injured," she stammered.

Ace nudged closer. Skye started to hold him back, but before she could grab him, he bellied down and nudged close to the seal, licking its fur. The pup touched noses until satisfied that the dog meant no harm, then plopped its head back on the rocks.

Danny hunkered back on his heels. "Would you look at that? I would never have believed this if I hadn't seen it with my own eyes."

The note of awe in Danny's voice brought forth a smile. "For a city boy, you're learning a lot about nature appreciation."

Turning to her, he carefully tucked a loose strand of hair behind her ear. "You care. That's big."

Disturbed by his touch more than she wanted to be, she backed away. "When you live out in the wilds, you care about the animals. They're part of your life. Your existence."

"It takes an incident like this to remind me."

The seal shifted position. In spite of his stiff joints, Ace managed to stand and wag his tail. Skye crawled out from under the landing as Danny straightened beside her.

"The pup looks better," he said.

She surveyed the outgoing tide. "Hopefully he'll stay here and rest until the tide comes back in."

"Should we watch out for him?"

She shook her head and pulled her sweater close against the nip in the sea breeze. What was happening to her island? Her haven of peace? Vandalism, and now this explosion. "Let's go dig those clams. I'll check on him later. If he's okay, he'll return to the sea. If he's still around this evening, I'll bring him some food to strengthen him."

Skye stood, noticing the look of skepticism on Danny's face. Shaking away the chill of foreboding, she smiled. "Don't worry. I know what I'm doing. This little guy won't be the first creature I've rescued around here."

"Now why doesn't that surprise me?" He shook his head, keeping pace as she hiked down the beach.

Skye laughed, the sound carrying in the wind.

His footsteps crunched in the gravel alongside hers. She liked Danny walking beside her, sharing her day. What would it be like to have him near every day? Dangerous thinking. He wouldn't be here every day. He would return to the city, a place she abhorred. Dreaded even. *So don't go getting attached to his company*, she scolded herself.

Uncomfortable with her thoughts, she glanced across the water at the clouds darkening to the north. "Looks like that storm is going to hit after all. We better get those clams and go back up to the house before it rains."

"You mean we won't be able to cook the oysters?"

Skye paused and studied the clouds. "I'd say we have a couple of hours. Plenty of time to build a fire."

Danny hurried ahead of her. "Let's get cracking then. I'm starving."

Skye grabbed the tail of his shirt and tugged. "Whoa there. You're stepping on their air holes. We'll never find the clams."

Danny froze, and Skye showed him how to search for the tiny holes in the coarse sand that gave away the site of a butter clam. "When you see the hole, you can figure the clam is going to be about ten to fourteen inches down." She positioned the shovel and carefully sank it into the loose gravel. "Start a few inches away and go easy so you won't crush the shell."

She worked the shovel around and around, tossing the loose gravel and sand into a pile. "Do you see the small clams? Go ahead and pick those up. They're steamers."

Danny sifted through the sand and found five steamers measuring from one to two inches. He tossed them into the bucket she'd brought while she worked the shovel. When the metal hit the shell, she quickly worked it back and forth until the clam was exposed. "Found a good one."

"That's huge. About five inches across." Danny's look of amazement made her chuckle.

She found another hole and started digging again. Danny was so busy studying the clams they'd gathered, he forgot to collect the steamers coming up with each shovelful. "Hey, get busy here," she chided. "Do you expect me to do all the work?"

He cast a sheepish grin and quickly gathered the steamers. "Besides being smaller, these look different than the big one." He held up the butter clam in one hand and a steamer in the other.

Glad he was interested in her world, Skye explained the difference. "Look at the line markings on the shell. The butter clam's lines circle around the shell. The steamers have lines that radiate out."

While he studied the markings, Skye studied him. His brow creased with a look of intent, and his hair tossed in the breeze, reminding her for a few brief seconds of her father. He'd loved nature and imparted that love to Skye. She focused again on Danny's face, wanting to smooth her hands along his whisker-roughened skin.

Unwelcome spirals of desire twirled into her heart. Stepping back, she shook her head. She didn't want to desire him. Getting close to a man would only bring back unwanted memories of the past. Her life was fine as it was. Solitary. Solid. No complications. At least, not until recently.

Shaking off the doubts, she handed the shovel to Danny. "Here, you try." He took the shovel. His fingers brushed hers, sending shivers up her arm. Skye stepped back, almost tripping over Ace, who had stretched out behind her.

She glanced over to see if Danny had noticed her discomfort, but thankfully, he stood with his foot on the shovel, ready to dig. She smiled at the eager look on his face as he forced the shovel into the sand. He brought up a pile of gravel. Skye quickly sorted through it and found three steamers. Danny dug several more times until she heard a sickening crunch.

"You found your clam."

"I crushed it."

Her lips twitched at his look of disappointment. "Toss it over. We can still use it. We'll have to be careful to get rid of the sand, that's all."

He held the shovel out to her. "You better finish."

She stepped back, the crushed clam dripping from the palm of her hand. "No way. You aren't getting out of the hard work with that excuse."

A sheepish grin formed. "You're not going to let me, are you?"

Laughing, she shook her head. "You won't learn unless you practice."

He scowled, and then he sighed, his stress lines deepening. "You're as bad as my boss."

Sorry that she'd reminded him of work, she searched for another air hole. "Here's a good spot," she said and watched him dig more carefully. She had to admire him. He was a good sport. Her father would have tossed the shovel down and given up. Danny wasn't too proud to learn from his mistakes. In front of a woman at that.

Thinking of his remark about his boss, she pictured Ted Randall. Whenever he came to the island, he could always be found tinkering on one project or another. "Ted's a hard worker. He built his cabin and put in all the improvements himself. Not like the newcomers who hire strangers to come to the island and build their homes, strangers who don't care about the integrity of the land." She hoped Danny wouldn't turn out to be one of those types of visitors.

He hefted another shovelful of gravel and sand. "Ted's a

good man. He cares about others. A solid Christian."

She chewed on his words for a moment. "He has one of the biggest firms in the state. I'd think it would be difficult to maintain Christian values with that kind of power."

Pausing from his digging, Danny placed both hands on the end of the handle and leaned on it. "Difficult, true, but not impossible. I've seen the man work miracles."

"Miracles?" Memories of Ted's helpfulness came to mind. Times he'd chopped wood for Granny. He'd offered tools to her father. He never judged. Simply was the friendly neighbor.

Metal scraped on rock as Danny resumed his shoveling. "Ted has wealth, and he uses it for many worthy causes."

As she picked out a couple more steamers, Skye noticed the stress lines had reappeared on Danny's face. "Sounds like you know firsthand."

"I should. I work for one of his causes."

Hearing the strain in his voice, she studied the way his knuckles whitened on the handle of the shovel. "From the looks of you, the job involves a lot of stress."

He hefted the shovel midair and paused, salt water dripping from the metal edge. "I used to think it was the perfect job." He lowered the sand onto the pile, ignoring the exposed butter clam in the hole.

Before the mollusk dug in, Skye knelt on the wet sand and reached for it, grabbing the cold shell with her nimble fingers. She held the clam, surprised that Danny was so deep in thought he wasn't even aware he'd uncovered the creature without crushing it. "What do you mean? Do you feel like you owe him?"

He lowered the shovel and pushed his sunglasses on top of his head. "No. It's not that. We have a big budget, but it doesn't begin to meet all the needs."

She held out the clam, wondering if he was going to tell

her what this mysterious job was. "And you're feeling guilty because you can't do everything?"

Absently, he reached for the large shell and nodded, his eyes boring into hers. "Did Ted talk to you?"

Ace, seeing her on her knees, ambled over for a nuzzle. She patted his ruff and looked up at Danny, sensing there was more than his work that bothered him. "No. Was he supposed to?"

He squeezed the clam so tight it squirted water all over his hand. Jerking back, he stared at the shellfish. "Hey, I did it." His eyes lit up. The stress lines eased when he grinned. "This fellow is at least six inches." His shout excited Ace, who stiffly bounced a couple of times as he wagged his tail.

"And the shell's not squished." Standing and stretching her legs, Skye smiled, relieved Danny found pleasure in so simple a victory. "Go ahead, Flyboy. Get us another."

Instead of watching him work the shovel, she watched the play of emotions on his face. Of course he was burned out. He lived in the city. Who wouldn't be wound tighter than a tick with the hordes of people, traffic, noise, and pollution? She glanced around at the sea, feeling the cool breeze and smelling the salty seaweed piled on the beach, and knew that Danny needed this respite. She vowed to make it a time to remember. A time he could think back on when he returned to Seattle.

Danny paused from his digging to glance over at Skye. "I think I found another one."

Kneeling beside him, she peered into the hole. "Congratulations. I better stop sloughing off on the job and get these steamers picked up."

"Do you steam the butter clams too?"

She shook her head and stood. "No, we'll use these for chowder."

He groaned, the sound coming from deep in his throat. "Don't even mention clam chowder. That's my favorite."

"Manhattan or New England?"

He licked his lips. "New England is the best."

"You sound like you haven't eaten in days."

He set down the shovel and grabbed the butter clam. "As a matter of fact, the only food I had today was the cookies at Lenny's. I'm ready for some lunch."

Stepping back, she stared. "No wonder you were scarfing those down. Grab the bucket. We'd better get back and build a fire and get those oysters cooking."

"You sure we have enough?"

His eagerness made her chuckle. She looked into the bucket. "I thought so, but your hunger pangs are giving me doubts."

He took the bucket and counted the mollusks. "Looks good to me. These would put the best restaurant in Seattle to shame."

"Well, we aren't at a restaurant. There's still a lot of work to do." She smiled at his look of chagrin but liked that he didn't pout.

He headed for the stairway. "Come on, Pocahontas. You have much to teach this Pilgrim."

She hurried after him. Thinking the baby seal might still be under the landing, she called Ace to stay with her. Danny slowed as he approached the stairs. "The pup's gone." The relief on his face matched hers.

Danny started to climb the stairs when she called out. "Whoa there. We need to put those clams out to sea."

His brow furrowed in confusion. "I'm not throwing these back," he insisted.

Reaching under the landing, she pulled out a large gunny-sack. "Help me dump them in here. We'll put them in the water for a few hours to filter out the sand."

He looked around. "Where can you do that? There's no pier."

She pointed at a skiff beached a few yards away. "That's my skiff. We'll tie the bag onto the boat and let her float in the water."

Danny helped her drag the skiff across the rocks to the water. He tied the gunnysack onto an aft cleat while she grabbed the bowline. "Push when I tell you. The current will carry the boat into deeper water."

He shoved, and the boat floated out into the bay. She tied the fifty-foot line to a large rock and waited to make sure it would hold. "We'll come back and get them later. The tide will be coming in so there should be no problem dragging in the skiff."

Danny shook his head in wonder as Skye stared out to sea. Sun reflected in her hair, and the breeze molded her skirt to her long legs. Her strength and stamina amazed him. Her compassion and caring touched him. He'd better be careful or he'd be falling for this island woman. What an odd match that would be. As much of a mismatch as he and Virginia would have been. He chuckled to himself as he followed her up the wooden stairs.

She walked toward the fire pit, Ace following at her heels. "Okay, Flyboy. Let's see if you remember how to build a fire."

"I don't mind watching you do it," he teased, as he approached the woodpile.

"You need to practice. I don't want you knocking on my door tonight crying because you're cold."

"Ouch. You know how to hurt a guy."

Remorse crossed her features, which endeared her to him more. "I didn't mean that like it sounded. You're welcome to come over anytime you need something."

He dumped an armload of wood beside the pit. "No, you're right. I need to learn. I'm going to learn." He took the hatchet and started splitting cut logs into pieces of kindling. At least he knew how to do that. "I guess I don't need to tell you how humiliating it is to feel dependent for my survival."

She propped her hands on her hips. "And on a woman at that."

He whacked at the wood, feeling like a pioneer. "Well, I've never been accused of being chauvinistic, but it doesn't help matters."

"In that case, I'll volunteer to look inside for some veggies and pasta to go with our oysters. What do you think?"

His mouth watered. "I hate to beg, but would you?"

She laughed. "This might cost you."

He quirked his brow, more interested than he should be. "And how is that?"

Looking smug, she walked toward his house and called over her shoulder. "You'll have to help with my crab pots tomorrow."

Crab pots? He didn't have a clue what to do with a crab pot. "Does that mean we'll have crab to eat?"

Skye grasped the rail and hurried up the steps. "That's the idea."

Danny called back, "I'm game as long as you realize you're dealing with a novice."

"We made a good team this morning, didn't we?"

He watched her disappear into the house, Ace at her heels. Yes, they did make a good team. Too good of a team. Frowning, he waited to hear a voice of wisdom warning him to stay away from Skye. Only silence echoed in the woods. Danny swung the hatchet, the sound of splitting wood breaking the stillness.

Skye appeared in the doorway, Ace poking his head from behind her. "Do you prefer frozen broccoli or green beans?"

His stomach growled, deeper in his gut this time. "How about both?"

"You got it. I'm going to steam them, then stir up some pasta. I found garlic cloves in the fridge."

Thoughts of lunch quickened his hands. In seconds, he had the kindling ready and newspaper wadded into a pile. He stacked the small pieces of wood like she had shown him and then brought out the matches. Flames licked at the paper. Smoke curled upward as the cedar kindling caught, the scent wafting across his nostrils. He straightened, amazed that he could be so productive. He'd built a fire. Looking around at the thick forest and at the sea beyond, he felt as if he could conquer the world. He had Skye to thank. If she hadn't been so helpful, he'd still be freezing and trying to figure out how to make coffee.

Yeow! The coffee! He spun around and rushed toward the house, hoping Skye hadn't discovered his mess in the kitchen, but knowing she had. Hurrying up the steps onto the deck, the aroma of fresh coffee tickled his nostrils. He charged into the cabin and found Skye rummaging through the cupboards. Two pots of water were boiling on the stove. The blue-enameled coffee-pot perked politely between them, the aroma teasing his senses. The sad loaf of bread sat by the sink.

"I see you found my mess. I forgot all about it or I would have had you build the fire while I came in and cleaned."

"No problem." Skye pulled spice containers out of the cupboard, reading the labels before setting them on the counter. "I see now why you're so hungry though." She nodded toward the bread. He swore she was hiding a grin.

Heat crept up his cheeks. "I had a little fiasco this a.m."

Her grin broadened. "There's definitely a trick to a stove-top coffeepot. You bring it to a boil." She stacked the spices back into the cupboard. "Then, once it starts boiling, you turn the burner down and simmer it for five minutes."

The wind-up timer dinged. Danny watched as Skye closed the cupboard door and turned to shut off all three burners. Pleasure and anticipation had him moving closer. "Does that bell mean what I think it does?"

"Coffee's ready, Flyboy. Bet you could use some." Taking a potholder, she filled a mug and handed it to him.

He held the steaming brew under his nose, inhaling the delicious aroma. "I've died and gone to heaven." He sipped carefully, letting the hot liquid slide across his tongue, looking forward to the rush of caffeine.

Skye chuckled. "You're so easy to please. You enjoy that coffee while I run to my house and pick up some herbs. The Randalls didn't leave what I need in your cupboards."

Setting the cup on the counter, he reached for her hand as she passed and turned her to face him. "Seems like the tally sheet of what I owe you is mounting. Thanks for the coffee."

Her skin turned pink under her tanned cheeks. She pulled her hand away. "You don't owe me a thing. I'll bring back another loaf of bread."

He lifted his hand, wanting to brush his fingers along her cheek, but refrained. She always shied away from him. He wondered why. "I don't want you to be gone that long."

She fled to the door. "I baked two this morning. Good thing. We'll feed your loaf to the rabbits."

Reluctant to see her leave, he picked up his mug and followed her out the door. "What about the fire?"

She paused to inspect the flames. "Looks good. You'll want to put another log on it and then let the coals burn down for cooking."

Danny set the mug on an upended log and tossed another chunk of wood on the fire. Skye ordered Ace to stay before she walked into the forest and out of sight.

The fire crackled and hissed as the new log caught fire. Danny picked up his coffee and sat down, savoring the hearty flavor. "Well, fella, looks like the Good Lord knew I was going to be out of my element here and sent me your Sunny Skye to the rescue." Ace limped over and nuzzled his head against Danny's knee. He patted the dog before the mutt plopped down at his feet with a sigh.

Silence settled around Danny. He took another sip of coffee and closed his eyes. He hadn't expected to feel a sense of peace returning to his tired soul. Maybe Ted was right. Maybe this island retreat was exactly what he needed. To be close to nature. Close to God.

Wrapping his fingers around the warm mug, several forgotten verses of Scripture flitted through his mind. He shook his head. How long had it been since he'd taken the time to reflect on the Bible? To pray? Too long. And he was paying the price. Tense muscles. Poor sleep. His decision-making abilities all but gone.

Thinking of all his trials since coming to the island, he drained the last drop of coffee. No power, no heat, explosions and injured seals, learning to collect his own food. "And you have a sense of humor too, Lord. Sending a beautiful woman to remind me how much I need You." Danny's laugh echoed in the forest. A woman who was definitely the opposite of Virginia. He laughed again, thinking of how his former girlfriend would have fared in this primitive setting.

A gust of wind surrounded him with smoke. Jumping up, he stepped away from the blue haze and looked across the bay. Sheets of rain blocked his view of the distant islands and even the nearby lighthouse. "Uh-oh," he muttered to Ace, who had followed him out of the smoke. "Looks like we'll have to forgo those oysters."

A twig snapped behind him, and he turned around in time to see Skye approaching, arms laden with supplies. "Don't tell me you'd let a little rain stop you from feasting."

Happier than he should be to see her, he smiled. "You tell me, Pocahontas. Do we have time to get those oysters cooked before the storm hits?"

Sidestepping Ace, she peered at the coals. "Set the grill over the fire and put the oysters on top. By the time they're cooked, I'll have the veggies and pasta ready."

He stared at the bucket of oysters. Sounded easy enough, but his record of accomplishments hadn't been that great so far. "Nothing ventured, nothing gained," he muttered. He hefted the heavy metal grate to the stones obviously placed there for the grill. Dumping the water out of the bucket, he grabbed the sharp mollusks and placed them evenly above the coals.

Ace followed him as he went into the kitchen to pick up the tongs and back out again to the fire. It seemed like forever to cook the oysters, but in about fifteen minutes the delicious aromas wafting from the fire pit made his stomach growl.

Lightning crackled, raising the hair on the back of Danny's neck. Thunder boomed less than a second later. He looked up in time to see the wall of water coming right at him.

"Skye!" He grabbed the oysters with the tongs. With a steaming bucket full of hot oysters, he charged for the door.

Skye must have heard him, because just as he clumped across the deck, the door opened. "Perfect timing. The rain is going to hit any second."

She'd barely finished speaking when a downpour reached the deck with a deafening din. The room darkened as sheets of water obscured the light. The sulfur smell of lightning wafted into the room before Skye slammed the door.

"Where do you want the oysters?" Danny asked, aiming for the kitchen.

Skye hurried around him and cleared off the counter. He hefted the bucket and set it where she indicated. Rubbing his hands together, he glanced at the maple table by the window.

"I'll set the table. I see you found a bottle of Martinelli's Sparkling Cider. Let me open that." He set to work, careful to avoid disturbing Skye's cooking.

She pressed against the counter to let him by. "Now I'm impressed. You may not know how to do everything, but what you do know, you do well."

He chuckled. "Hunger is a strong motivator."

In a matter of minutes, Skye served the food. Danny held the maple chair for her that he had positioned in front of the view out the window—a view now blurred by sheets of afternoon rain.

Seating himself at the head of the table, he smiled at Skye. Just as he folded his hands to say the blessing, loud footsteps pounded on the porch. Someone banged on the door.

"Help! Let me in."

CHAPTER 5

SKYE AND DANNY JUMPED UP at the same time. Danny rushed to the door and yanked it open. Heart pounding, Skye waited behind him.

In a wet flurry of motion, blond hair plastered to her head, Skye's sister, Janie, stepped inside the cabin. "I thought I'd make it before the rain hit, but obviously I didn't. Oh, it smells yummy in here." She shook off her rain-soaked coat and pushed wet hair behind her ears.

Skye grabbed the coat and hung it in the corner. "Janie, I wasn't expecting you. How'd you get here? The ferry isn't until tomorrow."

Janie shrugged with her usual nonchalance. "A friend was sailing to Victoria, and he dropped me off." She held out her hand. "You must be Danny. Jack told me you were visiting." She shook his hand and turned to Skye. "I went to your place, and when I couldn't find you I walked down and had a talk with Jack and Lenny. They said you might be here." She turned back to Danny with an assessing stare. "I'm Janie Larsen by the way. Skye's sister."

Color crept up Skye's cheeks. Surely Janie didn't think anything was going on between them. "I've been showing him the island."

Janie stepped farther into the room, directing her gaze at Danny. "Aren't you blessed? Skye knows the island like the back of her hand." Janie spied the books on the table and rushed to pick them up. "Oh, you have Max Lucado. Isn't he the most? Have you read these yet?" Without waiting for an answer, she swung around to Skye. "You simply must read these, my darling sister."

Startled by her squeal as much as by her presence, Skye stood open-mouthed, not sure how to react.

Danny came to the rescue. "We were just about to sit down and eat. Won't you join us?"

Janie placed the books back and flounced to the table. "I'm famished. Smells like your cooking, Skye."

Danny seated her across from Skye and hurried behind the counter to the kitchen area for another place setting. Skye sat down and started serving the food that was still steaming. Janie reached across to stop her. "Let's wait until we say the blessing." She turned to Danny and held out her hand.

If she could have crawled under the table to hide, Skye would have. Her outspoken sister hadn't wasted a moment to persist with her faith-converting.

"I'll do the honors." Danny sat down, and with aplomb, took Janie's hand and held out his other for Skye. Trembling with embarrassment, Skye placed her hand in his. Warm fingers wrapped around her hand and gave a gentle squeeze. She looked up to see a smile on Danny's face as he bowed his head and blessed the food.

Her sister, as usual, talked nonstop, which was fine as long as she didn't talk about Skye.

Janie glanced around the room. "This place is nice and roomy inside."

"The Randalls did a great job," Skye agreed.

Janie handed Danny the bowl of oysters. "Are you finding it comfortable?"

He grimaced. "Comfortable, but primitive. A lot more work than I anticipated."

Janie turned to Skye. "See. I'm not the only one who thinks its aboriginal out here."

Defenses rising, Skye dabbed her lips with her napkin. "The island is natural. What's unnatural is massing human beings in a huge city. All that noise, pollution, and overcrowding. No wonder there's so much violence and so many people using drugs to escape."

"Not everyone in the city is violent or uses drugs." Janie gestured toward Danny. "Look at us."

She did look at them and saw the lines of tension in their faces, the hyperactive restlessness that came with high stress, the inability to sit still and enjoy the quiet solitude. She closed her mouth, knowing they would deny her observation, and hoped her sister would drop the subject.

Janie wasn't going to let her pet theme go, especially now that she had an audience and a possible ally. "Danny, don't you think it's weird that Skye lives out here all alone?"

Danny shifted uncomfortably, chewing his food longer than necessary. "Well... Um..."

Janie persisted. "And look at that cracker box you call a house. You've just got to come to Seattle and join the real world."

Skye placed her napkin in her lap with studied care. "We've been over this before. You know I will never leave this island. I'm happy here. There is no reason to move to the city."

Skye almost heard the wheels grinding in her sister's head. "I know." Janie shifted position on her chair with renewed excitement. "I'm going to participate in the Marvella Three-Day Walk for Breast Cancer next month." She waved her hand and pointed to Skye. "You simply must come and join us."

Keeping her eyes averted, Skye twirled pasta on her fork. "I'm not going to Seattle."

"But it's for a good cause. They're going to walk sixty miles, and you only need to raise $1,000 sponsor money."

Danny pulled apart another oyster and sucked the meat into

his mouth as he eyed Janie. He tossed the shells into the bowl in the middle of the table. "I've heard of the walk. It gets a lot of publicity."

"We raise thousands of dollars that we donate for research." Janie glanced back at Skye. "Make an exception this time and come over. You can stay at my place."

Knowing she didn't have the courage, Skye shook her head. Janie lived in a loft downtown, where she could be close to the shelters. Skye couldn't imagine staying in the small house where strangers came and went at will, taking advantage of her sister's generous heart and hospitality. Nor did she think she'd last a day with her bossy sister without them coming to blows.

Studying Skye, Danny helped himself to another piece of her homemade bread. "Let me know when you arrive in town, and I'll take you out to dinner. I owe you at least that much after this feast."

Janie shrieked, "Ooooh! How fun is that? Let's all get together."

Skye turned from the speculation in her sister's eye and looked at Danny. "You don't owe me a thing. I'm just being neighborly. That's all."

Janie dropped her fork onto her empty plate with a clatter. "Come on, Skye, don't be such a bore." She rolled her eyes at Danny. "The only time she steps foot off this island is for her annual checkup." She swung her blue-eyed gaze to Skye. "You're due for one anyway. Make your appointment the same week and kill two birds with one stone."

"My doctor's in Bellingham. Besides, where could I get a thousand dollars? Lenny and Jack might donate a hundred, maybe Davis, but who else could I ask?" There weren't many full-timers on the island who had big money to pledge for cancer walks. And she rarely associated with those who arrived for weekends and summer vacations. That should put a halt to her sister's persistence.

Janie frowned and then brightened. "What about Danny? You must make big bucks if you work for Ted. What do you do for a living anyway?"

Skye clenched her fists, wanting to throttle her sister. "Don't bother Danny with your causes, Janie."

Acting as if nothing were out of the ordinary, Danny smiled at Skye as he rose from the table and started stacking dishes.

Skye slid out of her chair. "Ted's his boss, and he's on a much-deserved vacation, so let him be." She tugged on Janie's arm and pulled her into the living room area. "Sit here while I help Danny clean up."

Much to Skye's surprise, Janie didn't protest, but sat down on the sofa, her forehead creased with a deep frown.

Danny dumped the dirty dishes into a plastic dishpan full of hot water. He squirted liquid soap, making a pile of suds. "I'll do these later. Go visit with your sister while I put away the leftovers."

Skye started to protest but changed her mind when she saw his look of determination. She shrugged. This was his place. For the next two weeks anyway.

Ace flopped at Skye's feet when she settled on the couch next to Janie. The fire crackled, the sound blending in with the steady pounding of rain on the roof and deck. Wishing she were home alone in front of her cozy fire, Skye closed her eyes, taking advantage of her sister's unusual silence. She felt more than saw Danny's presence when he entered the room. She peeked between her lashes as he put another log on the fire, noticing the confident air and ease with which he moved about the cabin now.

Throwing back his shoulders, he cast her a look of pride.

"Looks like I've got fire-making down pat."

She smiled and started to congratulate him, but Janie straightened and interrupted. "So what exactly do you do for Randall, Inc.? I've been wanting to talk to Ted about funding one of our projects."

About to sit in the maple chair by the wood stove, he paused and frowned at Janie. "I'm afraid I'm not in that division. I can give you the name of the director, though." He lowered himself into the chair.

"Sally's Place needs money to keep their safe house open for abused women and their children." She turned to Skye. "We've been trying to find sponsors."

Danny sighed. Bracing his elbows on his knees, he pressed his fingers into his forehead. "Hundreds of people petition Ted for charity. He has to make choices."

"Could you put in a good word for us?"

Skye grasped her sister's arm. "Janie, that's not fair."

Janie shook off Skye's hand. Tension crackled in the air. "No, it's not fair. There are six women staying there. Six women with no place to go if the place shuts down."

Skye winced at the pain reflected in Danny's eyes. "Look," he spoke through clenched teeth, "I don't have any say in what Ted does with his money."

Janie relented slightly. "I'm sorry. I worry too much."

He raked his fingers through his hair. "Believe me, I know the feeling. I'll talk to Ted when I get back."

Janie was up in a flash, screaming with delight. "Really? You're wonderful. We prayed and then I came hoping to find Ted here and look who I meet? It's like the angels led me to you. Isn't the Lord awesome? Oh thank you, Lord." She bounced over to Danny, pulled him out of the chair, and gave him a giant hug. "I knew God wouldn't let us down."

Skye wanted to find a hole and crawl in it. Did her sister

actually believe there were angels leading her around? Sure, it was an amazing coincidence that she happened to meet Danny here of all places, but wasn't that pure luck? Or fate?

Danny peered over Janie's shoulder, seeing Skye's look of dismay. He knew the feeling. The joy of meeting someone face to face who struggled with the same needs he did almost surpassed the horror of the nightmares that plagued him. Janie stepped back, still holding onto his arms, her eyes filled with trust. Danny cringed. "I can only talk to him. I don't have much pull, nor can I guarantee anything."

Janie waved her hand. "The Lord always provides."

His shoulders sagged with the weight of despair. He'd give her the money himself if he had it.

Skye stepped beside Janie and grasped her hands. "Come on, Janie. Let's head for home. Danny is here to rest."

Thankfully, he'd been released from the young woman's grip. Rest, yes, but he didn't want to be alone. Not where he could hear the voices in his mind. The rooms echoed with silence. His inner voice nagged for him to sit still and listen, but he didn't want to hear what God had to say. "It's still raining. You'll get soaked. Stay here. We can play games or talk some more."

Skye stared at him in surprise, her look saying, You've got to be kidding. "We won't melt."

Janie appeared like she could be talked into it. He captured Skye's hand and led her to the sofa. "Do you like to play Scrabble? I have to warn you though: I'm a killer player."

Clumping sounds of boots crossed the outside deck, followed by a loud knock on the door. Danny sighed with relief.

Saved by the bell—the knock, anyway. He swung open the door to be greeted by a giant of a man standing on the stoop.

"Howdy." With dark curly hair matted against his wet head, the man grinned through his beard and moustache.

Behind him, Janie shouted, "Fred. Is that you?"

Fred peered around him. "Hi, darlin'. Heard you were on the island."

Danny opened the door, wondering who else would show up—not that he minded since he didn't want to sit around the house alone. "Come on in. Appears you know everyone."

The man held out his hand. "Except you. Name's Fred. Fred Davis."

"His father owns the big house on the other end of the is-land," Janie piped up.

He glanced at Skye, trying to remember all the places she'd shown him.

"The retired Marine. The owner of the skiff," she filled in. "This is Danny Fraser, a friend of the Randalls."

He shook Fred's hand. Images of a large log cabin with so-lar panels flashed through Danny's mind. "Come on in. Under-stand you flew over here."

Fred stepped inside. "The red Cessna. You have the blue one, right?"

Nodding, Danny closed the door against the damp chill. "We heard the explosion."

Janie stepped forward. "What happened?"

Danny guided them into the room as Fred explained what little the sheriff had discovered.

"Why do you think someone blew up your dad's skiff?" Skye looked worried.

"Maybe kids, getting their kicks," Danny observed.

A look of annoyance crossed Fred's face. "Figures. Pop said there've been some incidents of vandalism."

Skye coughed, a worried frown creasing her brow. Danny resisted the urge to wrap his arms around her, wanting to keep her safe. Like she needed him for that. "I take it you don't usually have problems like this on the island?"

Skye shook her head. "Not since I've been here."

"Better start locking your doors," Fred advised.

Danny stepped forward. Time to change the subject. "We were about to play Scrabble. Want to join us?"

"Scrabble? How about some cards?" Fred asked as he shrugged off his coat and hung it on a hook in the corner next to Janie's.

Janie tucked her arm into the crook of Fred's. "You know I'm not going to gamble, Fred Davis. We're playing Scrabble."

Fred rolled his eyes at Skye, who chuckled and said, "You knew that was coming."

Danny watched the camaraderie, wondering if Fred and Janie were an item. It didn't fit with what he'd come to know of Skye's sister, but they sure cozied up to each other.

Danny rooted through the games he'd noticed earlier sitting on the shelf by the staircase and found the dark brown box. Heading for the table, he gestured for them to follow. "Who's good at keeping score?"

Janie slid into one of the chairs. "Skye always does that. She's the math whiz."

Interesting. So, she had a penchant for math as well as science. He wondered what she might have done with her life had she remained on the mainland. He could picture her as a research scientist or a teacher. The latter made him smile. Given how she liked her privacy, she'd probably scoff at the idea. Yet, she'd been patient and encouraging, teaching him how to build a fire and dig for clams.

They drew tiles and Fred's letter was closest to A, so he started the game. "Sure glad you're here. A game is perfect for a rainy afternoon."

Danny agreed but wondered about Fred's sincerity. He didn't seem the type to hang around playing games. Maybe he was as reluctant to be by himself as Danny was.

Skye spelled the next word. "Jack said you were out fishing with your dad? Have any luck?"

"Not much. The water got too rough. I was ready to call it quits a couple hours ago, but you know Pop."

Skye and Janie chuckled as they nodded. Skye glanced at Danny and must have noticed his confusion. "He's a retired Marine. Never gives in."

Fred snorted. "Made for some interesting incidents when I was growing up."

Skye drew more tiles. "Didn't you grow up in several different countries?"

Fred gave them a mini account of the places he'd lived, throwing in some funny anecdotes. The girls laughed, but Danny heard the underlying bitterness of a son whose father was more strict and demanding than nurturing. He'd seen enough of it in some of the boys he worked with.

Danny picked up his new tiles and sorted them into possible word combinations. He smiled. He had a winner.

"What are you grinning about, Flyboy?"

"Just enjoying the company." True, but not the real reason he was smiling.

Fred eyeballed him. "Must have good letters. Watch what you put out there," he warned the women.

Danny held his hands up in protest. "Don't get all paranoid. Do you really think I can get by any of you? You watch those words like hawks."

"You bet we do." Skye studied the board. "But I've noticed how much you like to win."

Danny shrugged. "Can't help it." He thought of the gang

he'd hung out with as a kid. "Competition is in my genes."

Skye placed a couple of letters. "Where'd you grow up?"

"San Francisco. Lived there until I graduated from college." He didn't mention the time in juvie before school.

Skye frowned at her letters. Danny held his breath, hoping she didn't have any to mess up his big move. "Did you play sports in college?" she asked.

Trying to keep a straight face, Danny watched Skye put out a five-letter word—worth double points, no less.

"Naw."

"Too much competition?" Fred asked.

They weren't about to sign an ex-gang member from the inner city, but he wouldn't tell them that. "Got involved in church. Was thinking of divinity school."

Janie froze, her hand in midair. "You were going to be a man of the cloth?"

Fred thumped the table impatiently. "You heard him. Let the man play already."

With exaggerated slowness, Janie lowered her hand and winked at Danny. "Fred hates to lose, too."

"I haven't lost yet."

Danny chuckled as he quietly put out all seven letters, making a fifty-point word. "Sorry, man, but you lose this time." He ignored their groans.

Fred placed his next word while Skye gave points to each player. Janie stared at Danny as if boring into his soul. "So what happened? Why didn't you become a pastor?"

Danny shifted, wishing he'd never mentioned it. He'd been so wrapped up in the game, he'd let that tidbit of past history slip out.

Skye thumped her pencil down. "Janie. Enough already."

Danny studied the strained look on Fred's face as he sorted his letters. "What line of business are you in, Fred?"

"Nothing high-class."

Janie took her turn and made a three-letter word. "Any job that serves the community is worthwhile. Don't be putting yourself down, Fred Davis."

Fred seemed to brighten under Janie's praise. "I work for the city of Bellingham. A meter reader."

"Are they going to start rationing water soon?" Janie asked. "The drought has been really bad these past couple of years."

"They're thinking about it. I've had enough games. It's stopped raining. Want to go for a walk, Janie?"

Janie laughed as she pushed back her chair. "You're behind in points, Fred. No wonder you want to quit."

Danny stood and stretched. "Sounds like a good idea." He pulled the chair out for Skye. "What do you think? Does a walk appeal to you?"

It surprised him to see pink tingeing her cheeks. She acted like he was asking her out for a date. Well, it did appear as if they were pairing up, but he realized he didn't mind.

Skye peered out of the floor-to-ceiling window. "I think I'd better take advantage of the lull in the storm to get those clams. If we're going to make chowder this evening, we'll have to clean them."

He'd rather go for a walk. But he wanted to be with Skye. "I'll help you then."

She shook her head. "You go on ahead and walk with Fred and Janie. I can take care of it."

Fred held Janie's coat for her. "Clam chowder sounds great. Are we invited?"

Janie shrugged into her coat, brushing at the drops of rain still clinging to the slick fabric. "Sure we are. Skye makes the best."

Skye chuckled, obviously not upset with the fact that they had invited themselves to dinner. Ace followed Fred and Janie out the door.

Danny handed Skye her sweater and grabbed his jacket. "You promised to show me the process, and I'm not reneging on the deal."

Skye looked like she was about to protest but agreed with an uncertain smile. "Grab a pot to put the clams in and come along then. Next lesson coming up."

Carrying a large kettle, Danny shut the door and hurried after Skye. "Right on, Pocahontas. Island survival—who would have thought this city boy would choose clams with a pretty woman over a walk?"

Skye tossed back her head and laughed. "You might wish you'd gone for the walk after you see what a job it is to clean them."

He followed her down the steps. His feet crunched in the gravel as they aimed for the rope. As promised, the boat was easier to maneuver now that the tide was up. He tugged and pulled with Skye, the rope burning his hands. Skye grabbed the bow and swung the boat around so she could untie the gunnysack from the cleat. With a heave, she tugged the bag ashore.

Danny helped her haul it to the steps. "These clams weigh a ton. I'll carry them up the stairs for you."

She pulled a knife from her pocket. "No need. We'll clean them here and toss the shells into the sea." She reached into the bag and grabbed a large butter clam. He swallowed hard as he watched her pry it open and cut out the meat. "The seagulls will love this." She tossed the guts into the water.

Danny looked down the beach, almost wishing now he'd decided to walk with Fred and Janie. "I think I prefer ordering chowder in the restaurant—New England style, of course."

She handed him the knife. "Try the next one. Be quick about getting the knife in before the clam closes its shell. Otherwise you'll never get to the meat."

Too late. The clam closed tight.

Frustrated and disgusted, he reached for another clam. This time he got the knife in, but getting the meat was a lot harder than it looked when Skye had done it. "I'm obviously not cut out for this." He tossed the mangled piece of clam into the pot.

Skye's mouth twitched. "You're doing fine."

"You're working hard not to laugh. Admit it."

A chuckle escaped.

Danny smiled at her crumbling composure. "You think this is funny."

Laughter bubbled forth. Danny shook his head and reached for another clam. "Okay. I'll show you. I'll get these clams cleaned if it takes a month of Sundays."

"Go to it, Flyboy. I'll get the steamers." She bent down, her shoulders shaking, and separated the butter clams, placing the smaller mollusks in a scarf she'd pulled from around her neck.

With each clam, the process became easier. Feeling rather proud of himself, Danny grabbed another clam. "So what's the deal with Fred and Janie? Are they an item?"

Skye finished sorting the steamers and straightened, looking far down the beach at her sister. "Fred's been after Janie for years. She likes him as a friend, but that's all."

Poor sucker. There was nothing worse than hankering after a woman who had another agenda. Virginia came to mind. He'd cared about her, but she couldn't deal with the fact he worked in the inner city. With gangs, no less. "He seems like a nice enough guy."

"He is, but he has issues, mainly with his father. Fred always wants something he can't have." She turned back and leveled her blue-eyed gaze at him. "His father is very strict. Very basic."

Danny thought of his childhood. At least Fred had a parent who cared. His father had cut out when Danny was ten. If he'd stayed around, Danny wouldn't have gotten in trouble, spent time in juvie, met Manuel. Memories of the youth pastor raced through his mind. "Strict boundaries build character."

Skye frowned. "If they're tempered with love."

There was never any doubt that Manuel loved him. Cared. Danny shook his head, sorry for young men who didn't get that reinforcement.

Danny finished the last clam and walked to the water to clean the knife and his hands. Cleanse his mind of the memories. "What's next? I can almost taste that chowder."

A gunshot exploded in the forest.

An eagle flew out of the trees, its cry harsh and shrill.

Danny gripped the knife. "What was that?"

Skye screamed. "Someone's shooting near the eagles."

Another shot boomed.

CHAPTER 6

DROPPING THE STEAMERS she'd gathered, Skye tore up the steps. Danny followed close with Ace limping at his heels. Before she reached the top, she noticed Fred and Janie running toward them. Waving for them to hurry and catch up, Skye reached the top of the stairs and ran up the hill.

Another shot rang through the thick forest.

Skye screamed. "Stop shooting."

Danny puffed behind her. "Skye, come back. You don't know which direction they're aiming."

More concerned for the eagles than her own safety, Skye cut through the forest. Bushes scraped her legs and arms. She jumped over a fallen log, almost tripping in the thick underbrush. She yelled once more.

Another shot echoed, louder and closer. Adrenaline burst through her system, and she ran faster toward the sound. A shadow of a figure moved. "You there," she gasped between each word. "What do you think you're doing? The eagles are protected."

A man spun around, pulled his hat low, and ran toward the cliff. Brush snapped in his path. Skye pumped her legs harder. "Stop. Talk to me."

The man picked up speed when he reached the clearing by the cliff. Skye noted blue jeans and a brown flannel shirt. He didn't look familiar.

Danny crashed through the brush behind her. "Stay back, Skye! He has a gun."

Ignoring him, she ran into the clearing. Her heart pounded against her ribs. Her lungs burst with pain as she struggled for breath. Muscles screamed in agony as she pressed on.

The man disappeared down the cliff, pine needles and forest debris tumbling behind him.

Skye clenched her fists against her body's demand to slow down. "Come back here," she yelled.

The roar from a motor echoed from below.

"Oh no, he's getting away in a boat." Dismay tore through her. Reaching the edge of the cliff, she peered down to see a small aluminum fishing boat skim the water. The man in the brown flannel shirt sat at the bow. Another man steered the outboard away from the island.

Danny grabbed her by the shoulders. "He could shoot you." Gasping for breath, he shoved her behind him. "Do you know them?"

"I can't tell from this distance. I don't recognize the boat." Clutching at the pain in her chest, she brushed away his hands and started picking twigs from her sweater. "What on earth were they thinking?"

Underbrush snapped in the forest. Fred and Janie emerged from the trees into the clearing. Ace followed.

Fred called out, "Did you see who they were?"

Skye shook her head. "They were too far away."

Janie ran over to Skye. "What did you think you were going to do, Skye?" She held her side. "You're crazy to run after anyone with a gun."

Danny raked his fingers through his hair, then turned and again grasped Skye by the shoulders. This time he shook her. "Don't ever do that again."

Her teeth rattled until she clamped them shut. She stared at the worry in his eyes and shuddered. "But they were shooting at the eagles."

Danny released her, regret showing in his eyes. "Sorry, I..."

"You were concerned." She rubbed her arms, more from the chill coursing through her than from his touch.

Danny stepped forward. "Look. If you hear shooting, yell, but don't run after the shooter. You have no idea what they're up to."

"Of course. You're right." She turned toward the forest. "But… I've got to go check and see if they hit one." Without waiting to see if they followed, she hurried to the dead tree with the nest perched near the top. Pushing aside ferns, she searched around the trunk. Neither eagle was on the ground or up in the sky.

Danny remained close beside her, muttering to himself words like "stubborn" and "reckless." She pretended not to hear. Fred and Janie followed several feet back. Her dog, stiff and limping, nudged past Danny to sniff the ground. "Find the eagles, Ace." Wagging his tail, the black Labrador plowed through the underbrush. Looking for things was a game they often played. Only they'd never had to look for eagles before.

Skye straightened and yelled at the others. "Fan out and search. If he shot one of them, we might be able to save it."

Fred slapped at his pants, brushing away loose debris. "Give it up, Skye. You aren't going to find a dead bird in this brush."

Janie shrugged and walked along the side of the cliff. "You're wasting your breath, Fred. She'll search every inch of this place. We might as well help her."

Danny edged his way through the thick brush to Skye's left. "The sooner you start, the sooner we'll be finished."

Nodding her thanks to Danny, Skye moved deeper into the forest. She breathed easier when she heard Fred stomping his way through another section of the lot.

She motioned to Danny and directed him south. "Come on. Ace headed that way. I'm going out on the point."

Danny waved her on. "I'm right beside you. Be careful."

Skye followed the trail she'd packed down over the years to her special spot. The log glistened from the earlier storm. An eagle's feather lay on top of the polished stump. Her heart raced with dread as she edged around the stump, looking for the bird. Nothing. Just grass and stones. A sigh of relief escaped her.

Danny approached with the Lab close behind. "Find anything?"

She shook her head as she bent to give the gray-muzzled mutt a pat on the head. Knowing she was upset, Ace whined and sat at her feet, pressing against her legs.

Tears threatened. Danny curled his arm around her shoulders, pulling her close. Coming down off the adrenaline rush, she leaned her head against his chest, feeling the solid strength of his support.

"I imagine those birds have quick enough reflexes to escape a gun." His breath warmed her cheek. "Besides, we don't know the shooters were aiming at the eagles."

A flicker of hope edged the horror in Skye's mind. "What else could they have been firing at?"

"Target shooting, maybe." Danny rubbed his hand up and down her arm.

She realized the action was for comfort, but uncomfortable shivers formed. Not now. But she didn't have the strength or inclination to be sensible and draw away.

She searched the sky. An eagle flew into sight. "Look, there's the female." She shaded her eyes with her hand and stepped away, looking for the male.

Janie emerged from the thick foliage. "Did you find anything?"

Danny pointed up at the eagle. "At least one of them is safe."

"Thank the Lord." She hurried over to Skye. "You poor dear, you must be worried sick. I'm sure the birds are fine.

Probably some idiotic kids fooling around."

If only that were the case. But Skye had seen enough of the shooter to know he wasn't a kid.

A rustling to their left startled her. Ace straightened. Then she realized Fred was plowing toward them. "Did you find anything?" she asked.

He shook his head. Stomping debris off his boots, he stopped beside Janie. "What's going on? First an explosion, and now this. Sounds like someone is up to no good around here."

"Vandalism is one thing, but they're biting off more than they can chew if they mess with the eagles." Janie took a step away from Fred. "They'll have all the environmentalists up in arms, not to mention Greenpeace and the Forest Service crawling all over the island."

Fred frowned as he tugged on his jacket. "Who cares? No one's even heard of this place."

Skye shuddered. "If something happens to the eagles, that piece of land will no longer be protected." It would go up for sale like the property next door.

Janie jutted out her chin. "See, Skye? Things aren't much different here than in the city. I don't like the idea of you being alone on the island with this kind of stuff going on."

"She's right, you know," Fred said. "You're isolated out here. If you did run into trouble, who would you call?"

"Your dad for one," Skye snapped, stepping away from the others. "Or Jack and Lenny. I'm not alone, and I'm not isolated. We look out for each other." She glared at Janie. "Unlike in the city, where most people don't know about their neighbors. Or care."

Danny stepped between her and Janie. "Shouldn't we leave so the eagles can return to their nest? I don't know about you, but I'm ready to go back to the house. Looks like another storm is coming our way."

Skye glanced up at the sky. A shiver coursed down her back as if the black clouds darkening the horizon were an omen of events to come.

Danny held out his hand. "Come on, Pocahontas. Let's get that clam chowder started."

Janie stepped over and tucked her hand through Skye's other arm. "We can play another game while we wait for the soup to cook."

Looking disgruntled—possibly at Janie's lack of attention to him—Fred led the way down the path. "What is this place anyway? Why is there a trail here?"

Skye frowned. Bad enough to have other people wandering around her private sanctuary, but she didn't want them to know about it. She could picture Janie protesting against what she called "Skye's heathen practices." She shuddered.

Danny tucked Skye close to his side. "Are you cold?"

Thinking it better to have him believe that rather than the truth, she nodded.

Janie squeezed her arm. "Of course you are, darling. All that running probably put you in a sweat. Add this freezing wind to it and voilà, you'll catch a cold." She waved a hand at Danny. "Let's go sit her down by that warm fire of yours."

Heat flushed Skye's cheeks, but she remained silent. She hadn't had a cold in years, but she knew it would do no good to point that out. Once Janie set her mind on something, there was no changing it.

Danny started for his house. "You're joining us, aren't you?" he asked Fred.

When Fred paused at the end of the path, the "For Sale" sign hanging a few feet above him, he looked toward his father's place and shrugged. "Sure, why not? The ol' man's probably napping."

Skye pulled her hand out of Danny's. "I'll go down and get

the clams. You can put a pot of water on to boil."

To her relief, the others trooped into the Randalls' house, leaving her some much-needed time alone. The last two days had been alarming. First, the "For Sale" sign, then Danny practically running her over with the plane, the explosion, and now shooting.

Danny. She shivered. Thoughts of his arm around her sent electricity charging through her body. He had been so tender. So caring. Moreover, she had let him treat her that way. What was the matter with her? She had no business allowing a man to get this close, especially a man from the mainland.

She took a deep breath and eyed her dog. "Come along, Ace. We have work to do."

Later that evening, Skye sat in her rocking chair in front of her fire. The events of the day paraded through her mind. The explosion, the tour of the beach, lunch with Janie, and then Fred's arrival. A smile creased her face as she thought of Danny learning to dig for clams, only to disappear when the shooters came to mind. Why would anyone set off an explosion? Shoot at the eagles? Were the two incidents related?

Her head ached with the thought. Rubbing her temples, she forced out the unpleasant memories. At least the rest of the day had been uneventful. After the incident with the shooters, the afternoon had passed swiftly. Scrabble and visiting. Janie, of course, kept the conversation lively. Everyone loved Skye's clam chowder. Lenny's recipe had served her well over the years. The steamed clams were also a hit.

Beside her, Janie stretched out on the floor, sound asleep with Ace. Her soft, snuffling snores were a soothing rhythm that blended well with the snap and crackle of the fire. The potpourri on top of the wood stove filled the room with the aroma of cinnamon.

Skye closed her eyes, unable to get the sight and scent of Danny out of her mind. All male, he invaded her senses unexpectedly. His touch. His smile. His deep voice. All had plucked chords that she wasn't aware she had. She glanced around her room at the candles and wood carvings on the wall. She had found peace here. Contentment. Now slivers of loneliness crept into her heart.

Danny paced in front of the window, glancing out at the dreary gray light of dusk. Silence echoed in the large house now that Skye and the others had left. Outside, the clouds hung low and heavy, about to burst with more rain. Soon it would be dark. He glanced at the books on the table. Picking up the Tom Clancy book, he scanned the back cover and sighed. He'd already read it.

He turned away and grabbed another log. Opening the metal and glass door, he threw a piece of wood into the stove and clamped it shut. Standing back, he watched the flames lick at the dry bark, hissing then finally catching fire.

Flopping onto the lumpy couch, he rubbed at his temples. What was happening at his office? Paperwork piling up by the minute. New boys checking into the program. How would he handle them after being gone so long? Would his staff make the right decisions in his absence? He stood and paced again as images of Raul and Oscar flashed through his mind. Surely he could have done something to prevent the shootings that killed them.

He shouldn't be here. Playing games and visiting as if he didn't have a care in the world. What had Ted been thinking to send him out to the boonies? He glanced again at the Bible but turned away. It wasn't going to work. He couldn't sit quietly and contemplate godly matters when there was a pressing need for help. Real help. Real needs.

Heading for the kitchen and a glass of water, he shuddered at the sight of dishes piled high along the counter. Skye had offered to do them. He'd insisted he should take care of the mess since she'd worked so hard to cook the meal. Echoes of her laughter, traces of her smile crossed his mind. He should have taken her up on the offer. Then she would still be here.

Strange how that thought interested him. He'd been so busy lately, he hadn't had time to search out another relationship since his breakup with Virginia. Oh, sure, a date here and there, more business than pleasure. Was his interest in Skye herself, or was it simply the fact that this was the first time in ages that he'd had time to notice a woman?

No. He shook his head. The attraction was definitely to the woman. The loneliness he caught in her expression when she didn't think he was looking called to him. Didn't he have an answering need? They were strangers, yet so much alike. Both so wrapped up in themselves, they didn't have the time or inclination to become involved.

Looking out the window, he saw a dark spot circling below the clouds. An eagle. Was it the one they had seen earlier or its mate? Grabbing his jacket, he hurried out the door. Maybe he would see them both. Wouldn't Skye be glad to hear the news? Rushing up the hill while keeping the eagle in sight, he stumbled into the thick underbrush. Where was that path they had been on earlier?

Searching in the dim light, he found the trail just past the "For Sale" sign. If he remembered correctly, it led to a clearing close to the nest. Droplets of water dripped off the hemlock trees, splashing his nose and cheeks. He brushed back his hair and pressed on to the end of the trail. Heading for the polished wood, he looked up. The solitary bird of prey circled, a lone figure in the gray sky.

Danny studied the flat top of the stump. It had been smoothed to a glossy sheen. He wondered why. Perhaps Skye came here often. He brushed away the drops of water and sat on the smooth surface. A majestic view of the Sound spread out in front of him. He could see the light from the lighthouse glowing in the darkened sky. His breath caught in his throat. She did come here. He knew it, deep in his soul. A sense of peace enveloped him.

How long had it been since he'd sat quietly and communed with God? He raked his fingers through his damp hair. Too long. Not since his college days when he'd been idealistic and full of excitement. He'd volunteered for service programs at the university. Then he'd hired on at the local gym in the nearby inner city, convinced he was attending to his God. What had happened to him since then? Too busy with daily demands, he supposed.

A high-pitched cry broke into his reverie. He looked up in time to see the second eagle join the first before flying past, heading for the trees and its nest. "Skye's going to be ecstatic," he murmured, thinking of her smile and the light dancing in her eyes.

Again, he glanced out at the view, taking in the contrast of the calm silvery waters beneath the dark, roiling clouds. The land and sea, majestic and endless. His problems were insignificant compared to the immensity of nature. Maybe he had needed to get away from the city and capture a measure of peace.

How long had it been since he'd heard God's voice? Paid heed? He lowered his head in shame. Unable to sit still, he stood. After another quick glance across the waters, he hurried down the path back to the lonely house and another night of pacing.

The next morning, Danny backed the gas golf cart he'd found out of the shed. It chugged up the hill toward the path to the dock. Why hadn't Jack or Skye told him about this cart? Why hadn't Ted, for that matter? He rubbed at his back where it still ached from carrying his duffel up the hill. He turned toward the airstrip, eyeing the clouds. They looked high and puffy, not the kind that would dump rain on him before he returned to the cabin.

When he reached Skye's place, he stopped the vehicle and peered through the trees, hoping to see a sign of her. Nothing moved. No smoke curled from the chimney. Skye and Janie must still be asleep. Pressing on the gas pedal, he continued down the hill.

Charging around a bend, he almost ran into Skye, trudging up the path, carrying an overloaded backpack. He slammed on the brakes, set the parking brake, then leaned forward. "I have good news for you."

She stared as if nothing else mattered in the world but him. "I love good news."

He jumped out of the cart. "I saw both eagles last night."

She grasped his arm, her fingers pressing in as pleasure danced in her eyes. "Both of them? You're sure?"

He nodded, wanting to bend down and plant a light kiss on her smiling lips. Instead, he pointed to her pack. "What have you got there? Want some help?"

Sliding the pack onto the ground, she smiled a killer smile that sent his heart racing. "Supplies. The ferry came in this morning."

He glanced down at the bay and saw a small ferry scudding across the channel toward the next island. He grabbed the pack. Grunting from the weight, he hoisted it onto the back of the cart. How in the world did she manage to carry this much? "How often does the ferry come?" he asked instead.

She frowned at the sight of the pack in the cart. "Once a week. It brings in supplies." She started to lift the pack out again. "I can carry that."

Danny placed his hand on hers, liking the feel of her soft skin. "I won't hear of it. After all the help you've given me, the least I can do is carry your supplies."

She started to protest. He gave her that *don't argue with me* look that always sent his staff scurrying. She backed up and chuckled. "Guess you aren't giving me a choice."

"Clever girl." He placed his hand under her elbow and seated her in the cart. "Are there more supplies at the dock?"

Laughing, she nodded. "Don't let Jack see you carting my supplies."

He studied her face, liking the easy smile. "Why not? What's wrong with some help?"

"That's the point. He always insists on driving the supplies in the truck, but I always insist on carrying them myself. He'll be hurt if I let you haul them and won't let him."

He pulled the cart to a stop in front of her house. "Ahhh, I get it. You don't want to succumb to the luxuries of us yuppies."

She stepped off the cart and reached for her bag. "You're clever yourself. If he sees you helping me, there'll be no stopping him from hauling my supplies in the future."

Danny took the pack from her and hefted it over his shoulder. "Your secret is safe with me. But should you carry this much weight? What if you injured your back? There're no medical facilities close by."

"I'm careful." She opened the door. "And strong, I might

add." Ace walked out on stiff legs, wagging his tail. She side-stepped and took the pack from Danny.

Danny patted Ace's head. "It doesn't make you less of a person to accept help once in a while."

She pulled out two cartons of milk and put them in the refrigerator. "Keeps me fit." She lifted eggs and cheese out of the sack.

He reached inside and brought up a bag of apples. "You're always helping others. You need to learn to receive as well as give. It makes us men feel good to help out a beautiful woman."

Her cheeks turned pink, but she kept smiling. "My mother would roll over in her grave, hearing a comment like that."

He handed her the apples and reached for the oranges. "Aha. I bet she was one of the original women's libbers."

Skye placed the fruit in a three-tiered hanging basket. "She insisted Janie and I hold our own."

He looked around the small room. "Speaking of Janie, where is she? Still asleep?"

Skye bent over to reach into the bottom of the bag, her loose hair spilling around her shoulders and over her face. Straightening, she held up a bag of potatoes. "She left on the ferry."

"Short stay, wasn't it?" He brushed a tendril of hair back from Skye's face and saw the pulse at the base of her neck pick up speed.

Her eyelids fluttered; her cheeks pinkened at his touch. "She never stays long. Knows better," she said, her voice low and husky. "We'd be at each other's throats, trying to make the other do what we want."

He chuckled. "She's persistent."

Skye took the potatoes outside and dropped them into a bin. "That's a nice way of saying she's domineering."

He followed her out the door. "I'm not as concerned about

you as I was at first. You hold your own. Kind of sneaky-like."

She peered over her shoulder, her brow quirked in question.

He hurried to explain as he walked her back to the golf cart. "You let her tell you what to do and then you quietly, but firmly, do things your own way."

She cast an innocent blue-eyed gaze at him and winked. "Being an older sis, she can't help herself. I'm just being me."

In some ways, more stubborn than her sister, Danny thought. At least she wasn't arguing any more about the cart. He slid into the driver's seat and rotated the key. "Are we off to the dock, Pocahontas?"

She smiled. "You're more determined than Janie. Something tells me I don't have much choice about carrying the rest of my supplies."

He shifted into reverse, chortling to himself. "Not only beautiful, but bright, too."

She pulled away from him with a bounce of excitement. "Let's go see the eagles."

"Now?"

"After we finish unloading." She grabbed the bar overhead as he shifted into drive. "Now I'm glad you're hauling my supplies. We can get out there much sooner."

He shook his head, amazed at what simple things gave this woman so much pleasure. He rounded the corner and pointed toward the airstrip.

Skye paused, a look of concern crossing her face. He studied her. "What's the matter?"

She pointed to the dock. "See that boat? That's the sheriff."

CHAPTER 7

SKYE ALMOST JUMPED OUT of the golf cart to run across the airstrip. Surely she could run faster than this vehicle could go. Danny floored the pedal, sending them chugging across the grassy field. Bouncing with each bump, she clutched the bar.

Danny drove past Jack's house and swung into the lane by the garage. The engine died when he braked at the end of the dock. Skye jumped out and ran down the pier, her boots echoing on the weathered wood. She edged beside Fred. "What's up?"

He cupped his hand over his mouth so as not to interrupt the sheriff and whispered, "Jack called the sheriff to report the explosion." He turned his back to Jack and the sheriff when Danny walked up. "More windows have been broken."

Alarm raced through Skye. "Whose house?" she asked.

"Merve's cabin."

Danny stepped closer at her sharp intake of breath. "Is that near yours?"

Skye clutched at her throat, watching the sheriff write in his notebook. "It's one of those we passed when we walked out on the point."

The sheriff closed the pad, put his pen in his shirt pocket, and turned to the crowd gathered near Skye. "Anyone notice any unusual activity these last few days?"

Skye turned to Fred. "Did you tell him about the eagles?"

Fred shifted uncomfortably. "Naw. We don't have any proof that anyone was actually shooting at the birds."

Skye frowned, wondering why Fred wouldn't think that important. "They had guns," she called out.

Danny walked beside her down the dock to the sheriff. Skye edged toward Jack. "Yesterday, late afternoon, two men were on the point. One of the men shot a couple of rounds with a shotgun."

Jack clasped his hand around Skye's arm. "They weren't bothering you, were they?"

Skye shook her head. "Not me, but they scared the eagles."

Fred elbowed his way between Skye and Jack. "They were more than likely target shooting. We would have heard them if they were breaking windows."

The sheriff opened his notepad and thumbed the end of a ballpoint, in and out, *click, click*. "Why don't you tell me everything and I'll look into it."

Skye filled in the details, interrupted several times by Fred. "That's about it," she finished. "We didn't recognize the men or the boat."

Fred shuffled his feet. "Bet they were kids messin' around."

Danny straightened. "No, Fred, the man I saw was definitely an adult." He turned to the sheriff. "I'd guess he was around thirty."

The sheriff scratched his chin with the top end of his pen. "Odd behavior for a thirty-year-old."

Fred thrust out his chest. "My sentiments exactly. You were upset, Skye. And running. You couldn't have gotten much of a look at him." He glanced at Danny. "And you were behind her."

Skye remained resolute. She knew what she had seen. A man. But they were right about one thing. Why would a grown man be shooting on an inhabited island? It didn't make sense.

Danny bent forward, his arm brushing her shoulder. "Have there been problems on the other islands?"

The sheriff shook his head. "Not that we know of. We haven't had any trouble in these parts in a long time."

Great. Skye's shoulders sagged. Of all the hundreds of islands in the Sound, hers had to be the one developing problems.

Jack plopped his baseball cap onto his head. "What do you want us to do, Sheriff?"

The sheriff tucked his pen and notebook in his shirt pocket. "Keep your eye out for unusual behavior—strangers hanging around who don't belong. If you see anything, call me." He eyed Jack closely. "And don't go trying to handle it yourself. We don't want to add bodily harm to the list of grievances."

Jack turned toward Skye and Fred. "That goes for you, too. No more chasing men with guns. You come to my place, and we'll call the sheriff."

Her cheeks colored at the reproof. She looked from beneath her lashes at Fred. His jaw was clamped shut and his fists tight, the only indication that he was annoyed. He spun around and stomped back to the shore. Anger radiated with each step.

Skye reached over to grasp Jack's hand. She knew Fred enough to know how much he hated taking orders from his own father. She doubted he'd take kindly to orders from Jack. "He'll stay out of trouble."

Jack patted her arm. "I know. He doesn't like being told what to do. Can't blame him."

Skye nodded, thinking of the times she'd seen Fred's father coming close to physical abuse with his demands for military perfection from his son. If it hadn't been for his tender-hearted mother, she doubted Fred would ever come back to the island.

"I for one am glad someone is telling you two to keep your distance." Danny rubbed his neck and turned to Skye. "You added a few more lines of stress to my face when you went chasing after those yahoos."

She tossed her braid behind her shoulder. "If the animals are threatened, you better believe I'm going to act."

The sheriff snorted a sigh of resignation. "Just be careful."

He closed the briefcase sitting on the dock and returned to his boat. "I'll come by more often to check on you."

Skye stood out of the way while Danny helped Jack cast off the sheriff's lines. She waved. "Let us know when you're coming. We'll fix some supper."

The sheriff laughed. "You know I'll be back if it means some of your clam cakes." He added to Jack, "Tell Lenny thanks for the cinnamon buns."

Jack laughed as he tossed the last line. "You sure you aren't the one behind this trouble in order to have an excuse to come over here?"

"Now that's a thought," the sheriff shouted as he started his engine. "Something to keep in mind." He waved as the boat roared to life and powered into the channel.

Jack pointed to a stack of supplies. "Want me to haul those up in the truck?" he asked Skye.

Danny turned and walked back to the shore. "I've got Ted's cart. I can help her."

Jack glanced questioningly at Skye. She shrugged, watching Danny jog to the cart. "Don't you say a word." She fisted her hands on her hips. "I'm perfectly capable of carrying my own things, but Danny and I have a project we want to get to."

"Glad to see you socializing. Lord knows, you don't get enough of that around here." Jack smiled a knowing smile, making Skye cringe. She would get the third degree from Lenny later this week. Guaranteed.

"But be careful. We don't know him," Jack added.

"He's a friend of Ted's," Skye protested. "And I'm just helping him out. Nothing to worry about." She grabbed a box and braced it against the rail until Danny drove up in the cart.

Jack's brow furrowed skeptically as he lifted another box and waited beside her. "You're like a daughter, Skye. You know Lenny and I are concerned about you."

She sighed. Yes, she knew. And wasn't that the part of this island and its inhabitants that she loved? Not like the city, where people locked their doors if someone was in trouble. Like they'd done when her parents were attacked. "I care about you too, Jack. And I can handle things by myself."

Jack nodded. "I'm not worried about that. I just don't want to see you moping around with a broken heart."

"Whoa!" She raised her hands. "I'm just having some fun here. Nothing as drastic or deep as the heart."

He eyed her, then grinned and shook his head. "Heaven help anyone who crosses you, child."

Danny parked the cart beside the pile of goods. Skye set her box on the back, while Jack hefted his on the seat facing backward. Danny jumped out and grabbed more boxes. She looked at the two men, both eager to help. Warmth crept through her.

It didn't take long to haul the goods to her house. Before she started helping Danny unload, she gave Ace a pat on the head. "No need to get up, lazybones." Ace flopped back down on his giant pillow, wagging his tail. Remembering with nostalgia the days when he was constantly underfoot, she sighed and turned to help Danny.

She stacked the boxes he brought in beside the door, thinking maybe a cart would be nice to have. Sure saved a lot of wear and tear on her back.

Traitorous thought.

Kicking the door shut, she walked toward Danny. "Thanks for the help."

"Piece of cake." He nudged her onto the cart. "Let's go have a look at those eagles. Make sure they're all right."

Delighted that he was eager to see the birds, Skye held onto the bar and leaned forward, searching the sky. No eagles were in sight, but that wasn't unusual. After an early morning feeding, they generally roosted in the tall hemlocks on the point.

The cart bounced, hitting a rut in the deep track, and Skye nearly flew out the open side. Danny reached an arm around her shoulder and pulled her closer. "Hang on there. Don't want to lose you."

She liked the protectiveness, but his touch caught her off guard. Was this man too forward? Too friendly? Jack's words of warning came to mind. Alarm bells zinged through her as she inched away. "Maybe we should walk."

He didn't let go. "No you don't. I'm enjoying this."

She looked at his hand on her shoulder and then up into his dark chocolate eyes. "You *are* talking about the cart, aren't you?"

"But of course." He winked, and her heart turned to mush. He gave her a light squeeze. "You're good for me, Pocahontas."

"Exercise is good for stress," she reminded him as her stress level rose with the pressure of his arm around her.

He nodded, his dark brown hair lifting in the breeze. "We'll be walking soon enough. I don't want to scare the eagles with this contraption."

She liked that he was interested in the wildlife. She liked that he was open to learning about the natural life of the island. She liked that he was interested in her.

She held her breath. A man in her life? No. She shouldn't want his arm across her shoulder. Her heart shouldn't race every time he smiled at her. She sighed, relieved when they arrived at the trailhead into the preserve.

Danny parked the vehicle and set the brake. Skye slid out, trying not to notice the "For Sale" sign posted on the tree. What would happen if she took it down and burned it in her wood stove?

As if reading her thoughts, Danny pointed to the sign. "Wonder what they're asking for this place."

Her heart thudded to a stop, then thumped wildly. "Too much."

Danny frowned.

"At least that's what Jack said."

His frown eased, and he nodded. "I'll talk to Jack and ask him. Do you know the boundaries of the lot?"

"They wouldn't be hard to figure out." She hurried down the path, hoping to change the subject. If no one knew about the lot, no one would buy it. "The eagle's nest is farther south. The authorities prohibited building on the lots near the nest."

Danny followed close behind. "Does the preserve border this property?"

Skye clenched her fists. *Please don't ask about this property.* She turned and put her finger to her lips. "Shhh. We're almost there." Actually, they weren't really that close, but keeping quiet and off the topic of the lot for sale would be best. All the way around.

Wondering why she was acting so removed all of a sudden, Danny closed the distance between them. "I'm interested in the property. Maybe I'll buy it."

She stopped so suddenly that he ran into her. "You can't buy it," she hissed, stepping out of his way.

He straightened. "I'm not that bad a neighbor, am I?"

She held onto her stomach as if it were hurting. "It's not that." She shifted, restless and edgy as she gestured at the forest around them. "This property should be a park or wildlife preserve."

"You mean for the eagles?"

"No... I mean yes."

"Well, which is it?" He studied the worried look on her face. Was she afraid to have someone living so close?

Spinning around, she walked deeper into the forest. Puzzled, Danny hurried after her. He caught up to her and reached out for her arm. A flapping noise overhead stopped him in his tracks.

Skye peered up. "There's the male," she whispered, pointing to the huge raptor perched on a high branch of a hemlock tree, its white head blending into the cloudy sky.

Awed by the sight, Danny caught his breath. "So regal. King of the area."

"The eagle is on the property that's for sale," she pointed out. "He doesn't recognize human property lines."

"He comes here often then?"

She nodded, the breeze wisping a blond tress from her braid around her face. He reached out to brush the strand behind her ear, but dropped his hand before he touched her, not wanting her to shy away. She was as wild as the eagle. And just as leery of human touch.

"That's why this land should be part of the preserve." Skye motioned for him to follow her down the trail. "Let's see if we can find the female. She might be on their nest, although it's still early in the year for her to have laid an egg."

Danny searched the terrain for signs of property markers or a fence. The more he thought about it, buying the lot appealed. Even if he didn't have time to get over to the island much, it would be a good investment.

He watched Skye's skirt sway around her legs. Forget the investment part; he should get to the island more to spend time with Skye. She had a soothing affect on him. To be honest, more than soothing. Much, much more.

Skye halted a few yards from a dead tree and placed her finger to her mouth before lifting it upward. He wanted to see where she pointed but couldn't take his eyes off her lips. Full and begging for a light kiss.

"Do you see her?" Skye asked.

Shaking himself, he cleared his throat. "What did you say?"

She placed her hands on her hips, scowling at him. "Danny Fraser, you aren't paying a bit of attention to me."

"Actually I'm paying too much attention to you, but not to your words."

He loved the color creeping up her neck and into her face. Her lip quivered when he traced a finger down her cheek. Bending his head forward, he brushed his mouth against hers. Hints of lilac floated around him. He wanted to bury his face in her hair and take in the full effect of the fragrance. And of her. Instead, he lifted his head and stared at her closed eyes, her sweet smile.

When her eyes flew open, he stilled her protest by placing his finger lightly on her mouth. "I know. I had no right to do that."

She pulled his hand away from her mouth but didn't let go, her grip strong. "No, it was nice…"

"But?" He could hear the word in her voice.

"I'm not experienced in these things. I've lived alone too long."

Danny's heart melted. "I know. I promise not to hurt you, Skye."

She stared deep into his eyes, hers huge and trusting. "You will hurt me, Flyboy. In two weeks you'll take off and head back to the big city."

"My job…" He closed his eyes, knowing she was right. He would leave and dive back into the work piled on his desk. There wouldn't be much time to think about this wood nymph.

She caressed the palm of his hand with her thumb. Electricity charged up his arm. "It's okay," she said, sighing. "I'm honored to know you. We'll spend this time together." Her gaze lifted to his, the look in her eyes pensive and sad. "However, when you leave, it will be over."

"It doesn't have to be."

"No." She smiled. "There'll always be an empty spot in my heart."

He pulled his hand away, sagging under the responsibility she placed on his shoulders. "I don't want to create an empty spot in your heart."

"Too late." She smiled wistfully. "The damage is done. You've made me realize how lonely my life is right now. But I know where you're coming from. I know you have to return to your work—your life."

He studied her, liking her calm acceptance. "Then we'll enjoy these two weeks for what they are. A respite from the rat race for me, as well as an inspiring friendship. And for you?"

"A pleasant companion, giving me a nice change of pace from my solitary existence."

He held out his hand. "Deal."

She placed her hand in his to shake. Instead, he pulled her close. "Sealed with a kiss." He brushed his lips lightly against hers.

When he pulled away, she blinked, her lip quivering. "I'll treasure your friendship. But the kisses and…" Her cheeks fired up with color. "I can't go there. Let's keep this a friendship only."

Again Danny's heart melted. He brushed her cheek with his knuckle, feeling the heat from her blush. "Saving yourself for marriage?" Respect mingled with the desire.

Skye nodded, but lines crept across her brow. She turned and faced the sea. He had the feeling there was more behind her response. He sighed, wishing he could pull her into his arms and erase any doubts or misgivings. But he couldn't do that.

Not without commitment on his part. It wouldn't be fair to her.

"We've found the eagles, Pocahontas. What's next?"

She turned to him, and his breath caught at the sight of the tear ready to spill down her cheek. He clenched his fists against the urge to wipe the moisture away.

She dashed the back of her wrist over her eyes. "You promised to help with my crab pots. Are you game to venture onto the seas?"

He peered at the lighthouse standing steady and sure. He studied the high gray puffs of clouds and the calm channel waters. So much like Skye. Outwardly calm, but shades of gray hiding internal storms. "Looks like a good time to do that. Do I need to bring anything?"

"Just some muscle. Those pots are heavy."

He held up his arm and flexed his biceps. "These are building up. By next week I'll be in fine shape. Thanks to you and your island."

Her laughter bounced against the large trees, making him smile. She tilted her head and looked him up and down. "When you return to the city, you'll need to get into an exercise program. Is there a gym nearby?"

"Actually, there's a well-equipped gym on the third floor of our building. I used to exercise regularly." Exercise wasn't the only thing he needed to attend to. He realized that now.

"Don't tell me." She raised her hands as she continued back down the path. "You're too busy to work out."

Thinking about the job, Danny shook his head as he trailed behind her. Ted was so right. He did need this break to get his head back together. He needed some time to build his spiritual strength as well. "Guilty as charged. But things are going to change."

"I'm glad to hear that." She turned to study his face. He

shifted, uncomfortable with her discerning stare. "Life's too short to be wasting it with all that stress."

He frowned, remembering the demands that caused the tension. The faces of the young people needing his help. "You're right, but I want to help everyone who steps foot in my office. I can't. I know that, but it kills me. And I feel like I've failed."

Skye reached the cart and climbed in on the passenger side. "It never hurts to seek assistance. Or so Jack is always telling me. I'm afraid I'm just as lacking in that department as you are."

He slid into the driver's seat and turned the key. "Do you ever pray?"

"I guess not in the traditional sense of the word. I do sit in my special spot and commune with nature. Meditate."

He thought about the stump in the woods and wondered if that was where she went. It would explain the smooth, polished condition of the old wood. "What about God? You do believe, don't you?"

She turned her head and stared into the distance. "I don't know much about God. We never went to church." She shrugged. "I've lived here off and on since my parents died. Besides, there's no church on the island."

"Jack and Lenny are believers. Where do they go to church?"

"Bellingham. They sail to the mainland every two weeks." As if reading his thoughts, she continued "They've invited me, but I didn't see much point."

"God can take away your fear. Your pain."

She turned to stare at him with rebellious eyes as deep and blue as the ocean depths. "I'm not afraid."

He thought of the times he'd seen her tremble. He'd seen hints of fear during the moments when she didn't think he was looking. But who was he to advise Skye when, until this trip, he'd been avoiding God himself?

"Well it's something to think about." He pressed the gas pedal. "Where to? The beach or the dock?"

Her brow smoothed and she sighed, obviously relieved about the change of subject. "Neither. We'll stop at my place to get some bait. Then we'll head for the beach and take the skiff to my boat."

"Does Ace go along?" he asked.

"He used to, but he's getting so old. Nowadays he prefers to sleep next to the fire."

Danny parked the cart in front of her small shack. "Well, let's wake the lazybones up."

Chuckling, she slid out of the cart. "Good luck trying. He's set in his ways and, to be honest, I let him do what he wants. Any pooch that has put up with me and can hang on as long as he has deserves to be spoiled."

Memories of his childhood flashed in Danny's mind. He'd always wanted a dog. Now, he had no time or space for a pet, so it wouldn't be fair to keep an animal.

"Ace, we're home."

He waited for Skye to open the door. He looked around and saw her dog on the floor. "Ace?"

Skye froze. "Oh no."

CHAPTER 8

SKYE ROLLED HER HEAD, trying to relieve the strain in her neck. She'd been sitting on the stump for hours, attempting to meditate. She couldn't focus. Her attention drifted again to the mound on the point where Danny had helped her bury Ace. She thought she had been prepared for his death.

Ace had lived way past the years allotted to a dog his size. He had been healthy until the end and died peacefully in his sleep in front of the fire. Wasn't that how she had wanted it? A tear slipped down her cheek. She brushed it aside and took a deep breath. Yes, that was what she had wanted for Ace, but how was she going to live without him?

More tears wouldn't come. Instead, memories of the Lab raced across her mind. Ace running through the forest, swimming in the water, snuggled next to her in front of the fire.

The drone of a plane interrupted her thoughts. She peered into the sky, wondering who was coming in, but not really caring. Danny had wanted to stay with her. She'd let him, for a little while, but then realized she needed to be alone to sort out her feelings.

She looked out across the Sound at the expanse of water dotted with islands. Clouds hung heavy, brushing the tips of peaks, drifting down the valleys like puffs of cotton. The solitude washed over her. Her heart ached with loneliness and longing. Longings for Ace, yes, but other yearnings as well. For what, though? Love? Companionship? If so, she would have to leave her beloved island. Her sanctuary. Did she really want to do that?

Maybe Janie was right. Maybe she longed for God. But

how could someone she couldn't even see help the ache in her heart? Skye closed her eyes, trying to envision a holy presence. She sighed. It was no use.

Her hair lifted in the slight breeze. She slid off the stump and raked her fingers through the loose strands. Danny had invited her to his place for dinner. She had thought about declining, but she couldn't face being alone in her cabin. Not this evening.

Leaning against the stump, she closed her eyes. A light mist dampened her cheeks. Silence echoed in the forest. Even the animals seemed to be mourning. There were no twitters of birds. No hum of insects. Only silence. And memories.

Skye straightened. The memories were torture right now. Danny would help her through this. He had offered earlier in the day. She pictured him, smiling, eyes filled with caring, sympathy. Yes, she should go to him.

But was it a good idea? So what if she filled her days with Danny? He was leaving too. Then the loneliness would be that much more poignant. More painful. Maybe she should go visit Jack and Lenny instead.

Images of Danny filled her mind. His laughter. His eyes. The wonderful thrill of his simple touch. She longed for more. She wanted to be held and cared for. Was that possible?

Dark memories crowded out those of Danny. The punks who had killed her parents. The flash of a knife, a knee in her back, arms holding her, hurting her. She groaned, the sound halting the images. Silence echoed in the forest.

She shuddered. They'd scarred her. Hadn't she tried to live again in the city? Work there? Many times. But whenever she saw a group of boys hanging together, memories and fear swamped her. Every time a kid would enter the store or restaurant or office where she'd taken a job, she'd freeze. And run.

Therapy sessions hadn't helped. Living with Janie had been miserable for both of them. She'd even tried church, but she always retreated to her place on the island. But the island was changing. How much longer would it offer a retreat? She shivered. Images of the explosion, the shooting, and the eagles' frightened flight out of the trees pelted her.

Maybe she should try therapy again. Maybe this time, with all the other changes, she would be more motivated to work out her problems. Certainly Danny was a motivation, but would it be fair to offer more than friendship when she was such a fearful and broken woman?

Loneliness welled, her heart breaking into shards of unfulfilled love. Filled with the trembling thought, she tromped through the woods to the Randalls' place. Danny sat on the front deck looking out to sea. A book lay open in his lap, but he wasn't reading it. She paused, warning bells clanging. She didn't want to lead him into believing they could have more than a friendship. They couldn't, could they?

She took a tentative step toward him. A twig snapped underfoot. He turned, spotting her. A smile crept across his face, into his eyes. "I was worried you wouldn't come."

She climbed the two steps up and sat on the bench framing the deck. "I debated."

"So you trust me?"

She hesitated. "I'm vulnerable right now. Teary. I don't want to burden you with my emotional turmoil."

He got up and sat next to her. Wrapping his arm around her shoulder, he pulled her close. She hadn't realized how chilled she'd become until heat from his body seeped into hers. "That's what friends are for, don't you know?" He tucked a finger under her chin and lifted her face. He smiled, his gaze warming the chill. "I know how fragile you are right now. Don't you think I'll be taking extra care?"

Her heart raced. Reason fled. "I...I...I know that," she stammered. "That's why I came."

"Good, because we have a lot of things to celebrate." He stood and, taking her hand in his, gently tugged and pulled her up. "I've been sitting quiet this afternoon. Something I haven't done in far too long. Doing so reminded me that in death there is always newness of life. We can mourn the loss of a loved one, but we must celebrate too."

Skye tried to pull her hand free. Danny held on and coaxed her into the house. She swallowed hard, trying not to cry. "I'm sure Ace has crossed over the rainbow, as they say, and is romping in dog heaven, but I'm going to miss him."

Danny opened the sliding glass door. A ball of yellow fur tumbled toward them.

Taking a deep breath, Skye dropped to her knees. A puppy launched into her lap and licked her face. Laughing, she pushed his nose aside and looked him over. "A yellow Lab! How adorable you are," she crooned, hugging the pup close.

Danny hunkered down beside her. "He's a Lab mix, and he's in need of a home."

Her heart picked up speed, pounding in her chest. "Where did you get him?"

The puppy squirmed against her tightening hold. Wiggling onto the floor, he rolled over. Danny rubbed his tummy and chuckled. "Had him flown in. I know the director of the animal shelter in Seattle. He's been trying for months to talk me into taking a pup."

"I heard a plane land." Her shoulders sagged. "He's perfect for you," she said, trying to sound happy for him.

His face sobered. "I don't have a place for him, and I'm at work all day. It wouldn't be fair for me to keep him. He's yours."

"I can't take him, not so soon after Ace…" She barely got the words past the lump in her throat.

"He was scheduled to be put down this evening."

"No!" Skye picked up the pup and held him close to her chest in spite of his twisting and turning.

"If you don't want him—"

"I'll keep him."

Danny's lips twitched in a pleased smile. "Ace will always have his place in your heart. This dog isn't meant to replace him. He'll find his own spot."

Sadness crept inside at the mention of Ace. Yet when the puppy squirmed again, joy pushed at the sorrow. She hugged the puppy close. "I'll take good care of him."

Danny petted the pup's head, his hand brushing against her arm, sending shivers of anticipation across her skin. Sensations that didn't alarm her so much anymore.

"What shall we name him?" The puppy wriggled out of her lap and bounced around the floor. "It's a male, isn't it?"

Danny nodded. "What about Bo?" He batted a knotted sock in front of the dog. "Ace. Bo. You can go down the alphabet."

Skye laughed at the absurdity. "Sure. Why not? Only I'll be too old to chase a puppy starting with Z."

For several minutes, she and Danny played with the exuberant ball of fur. Skye rocked on her heels, puffing for air. "Where does he get all that energy?"

Danny sat back. "He'll keep you on your toes."

"I'll say. I'm used to Ace sleeping most of the day. This little guy is going to demand a lot of attention." Skye eyed Danny. "You've given me a special gift. You're pretty special yourself."

Shrugging, he stood. "Speaking of all that energy, I better feed you so you can keep up with the mutt."

Curious, she rose and saw for the first time that the table was set with white linen. A bottle of Martinelli's apple cider sat chilling in a silver ice bucket. "Come to think of it, I do notice enticing aromas coming from your kitchen. What have you managed to concoct?"

He sent her a mysterious grin. "I have all kinds of surprises for you."

"I had the impression you weren't much into cooking."

Chuckling, he walked into the kitchen area. "As much as I hate to disillusion you about my talents, I'll confess I didn't fix this meal myself." He waved a hand at the insulated containers on the counter. "I had this flown in from Anthony's. It arrived with the pup."

Eyes wide in wonder, she looked at all of the food he was taking out of the restaurant's containers. "I'm overwhelmed."

He brought the food to the table. "I had imagined a romantic dinner by candlelight, but I forgot how energetic a puppy can be. I'm afraid elegance is out of the question."

Laughing, she hauled the ball of fur rolling at her feet up into her arms. "Well I'm not into elegance anyway. This'll be much more fun."

Danny moved close in front of her, nuzzling the puppy. "That's what I like about you, Skye. You're a trooper. The simplest things bring you joy."

Her heart racing with new excitement, she shifted the puppy and stepped closer to Danny's warmth. "You've brought me more joy than you can imagine." She leaned forward and brushed her lips against his cheek. "In more ways than one. I love the puppy." And you.

Shocked by the internal admission, Skye jerked away, hoping Danny hadn't read her feelings in her face. Afraid he'd pursue the subject and she'd spill too much, she lowered the puppy to the floor and hurried to the table. "Go ahead, Flyboy, and bring on the feast. I'm ready to celebrate."

Danny stared at her, disappointed she'd fled from him. He'd seen the glow of love in her eyes. Sure, she loved the puppy.

Who wouldn't? But there'd been a spark for him, too.

Whoa boy. He rubbed his jaw and headed for the kitchen. *You don't want to move too fast here. And move toward what, anyway?*

He knew better than to be involved with someone who didn't share his faith. Besides, Skye was like a rare and fragile flower who flourished in her own special environment. He couldn't ask her to leave the island. He wouldn't. Involving her in anything other than grateful friendship wouldn't be fair.

But he could be a friend.

Carrying a platter of seafood and rice, he returned to her side. "Treats for the island princess."

Her eyes widened as she breathed in the aromas. "I've graduated from Pocahontas to a princess, have I?"

He brought another platter of steamed vegetables. "Pocahontas was a princess. One who helped with the survival of the early explorers. Just like you helped me."

She gestured at the spread. "Looks like you do quite well on your own."

Chuckling, he opened the bottle of Martinelli's. "I'm great at ordering out. Give me a keyboard and a phone and I'm all set."

She shook her head. "But I'll have to admit this is really a treat."

"Like I said, we're celebrating." He poured the drink, in spite of the fact that the puppy was chewing on his pant leg. He shook his foot. "Bo, get back, you crazy mutt. You're ruining the ambiance."

Skye's cheeks reddened. She looked up at him with earnest blue eyes. "I've never had this much attention before."

He sat across from her at the table and held up his glass in a toast. "We'll see that you have more."

Delighted that the order from the restaurant had come

through successfully, Danny relaxed and enjoyed her laughter when the puppy pestered them. Whenever her expression sobered, he'd tell her some absurd story that chased away the hints of sadness. Light danced in her eyes when he teased her.

After the meal, Skye offered to help clean, but Danny wouldn't hear of it. "You go play with the mutt while I put the food away. Keeping Bo out of the way will be a help in itself."

She sat on the floor and grabbed the sock Danny had knotted. "He sure is a frisky one."

Danny put leftovers in the refrigerator, pleased at how surprised she'd been by Bo's appearance and the happy light in her eyes. He'd have to think of more ways to make her eyes dance with such excitement. Watching her play with the pup, he chuckled. "You two have taken to each other."

"He's adorable. What gave you the idea to bring him to me?" She tossed the sock to Bo and a smile to Danny that quickened his pulse.

"I've heard that the best thing to do when you lose a pet is to get another. The sooner the better." And it had been some trick getting this one today. But he wouldn't tell her that.

Sadness flickered in her eyes. But when Bo tumbled onto his back, legs kicking in the air, the smile returned. "He does take my mind off of my problems, that's for sure."

Danny left the kitchen and stood beside her.

Patting the spot on the floor next to her in invitation, she smiled up at him and studied his face. "You look more relaxed than when you arrived."

"I'm getting there." He grabbed the sock from Bo and tossed it across the room. "Speaking of exercise, how about a walk? This little guy probably needs to go outside."

She got up off the floor, laughing. "Good idea. Don't want to mess up the Randalls' house. Come along, Bo. Let's show you around your new home."

Following her out the door, Danny shrugged into his jacket. "The walk will be good for us, too." He patted his stomach. "After that big meal."

The crisp spring air chased away the sluggishness from the dinner. He held Skye's hand and laughed with her as they watched Bo scramble around trying to sniff everywhere at once. At the landing for the stairs that dropped from Ted's lot to the beach, Danny paused with Skye and viewed the Sound. Deep indigo-blue water reflected the lighter shade in the sky. Islands dotted the horizon like dark emeralds. Sailboats tracked across the bay, their white sails billowing in the breeze. The lighthouse stood like a sentinel on its rock, guarding the surrounding waters. "The clouds have lifted. Do you think we'll have a clear day tomorrow?"

"Could be, although the weather at this time of year can change like"—she snapped her fingers—"that." She grabbed Bo in time to keep him from running down the steps. "It's not too late to take the crab pots out. Let's swing by my place and pick up some bait."

"What about Bo? You going to trust him alone in your house?"

She laughed. "No way. He can come along with us."

"Whoa. Brave woman."

"He's been in a plane today. What's a boat? Besides, if he's going to be an island dog, he might as well learn the ropes now."

Danny had to hand it to Skye. She was a patient teacher, with both him and the dog. In spite of his inexperience and Bo's antics, they managed to get aboard the small skiff without getting drenched. He pushed off the rocks, then sat in the bow, holding Bo, while she steered the outboard motor into the calm waters of the Sound. Keeping Bo corralled in the bow with his knee, he helped her lower the heavy crab pots into the channel. "What do we do now? Wait for them to fill up?"

"We leave them here and come back in the morning. They'll be full by then."

Smiling, he tugged on Bo. "Good. That means we're guaranteed some time together again tomorrow."

She blushed, grabbing Bo before he jumped up and licked her face.

Danny grinned. "We make a good team."

She turned from him and stared out to sea, a sad expression crossing her face. What part of his statement bothered her? The concept of "team"?

"Too bad it can't last." The slight bitterness in her tone gave him a measure of hope.

With one finger under her chin, he gently turned her face around so he could look deep into her eyes. "There are obstacles, but nothing is impossible. I care about you."

"You shouldn't. I come with a lot of baggage."

Painful baggage—he could see it in her eyes. He thought of his years in the gang, in juvie. "Don't we all?" The skiff rocked when he leaned back. "We can work through it. Sort it out." He gestured toward the island. "You've found peace here." He studied her features, her smooth skin tanned from living outdoors, her blond hair lifting in the breeze. He reached over and brushed his thumb along her cheek. "You're a rare treasure. I thank God that I met you. You've been like a breath of life."

She smiled. "I'm glad you think so." She started the small outboard and pointed the skiff toward the beach.

He blushed, pleased that he still had most of his vacation left. "I can't believe that two days ago, I could hardly wait to get back to the mainland."

"And you're content to stay now?"

He held her gaze. "I still feel like I should be at work, but there is a part of me that's content to be here. I'm thinking you're pretty special, Skye. I'm thinking I'd be a fool to let our friendship slip away."

Her hold on the throttle eased, letting the boat drift on the swells. She smiled, her eyes crinkling at the corners. "We'll always be friends. I just don't see how anything more than that could work."

Neither did he, but he had almost two weeks to figure it out. "Come visit me in Seattle? Lots to see and do."

Her eyes widened. "I'm a country girl. I can't handle the crowds, the noise, even the smells. I know because I've tried. Many times."

"You have to face changes." He shook his head as he bent to pet Bo. The pup wiggled around, decidedly restless. "Keep an open mind. That's all I ask."

An eyebrow curved upward. "I've sought help. Been to one therapist after another."

"Therapy?"

"My parents' death. But it's not just that. I mean, it was traumatic, but I have other issues."

He quirked his brow. Waiting.

"I don't do well in crowds." She shrugged. "Tried different jobs."

He fiddled with a piece of rope. "You've helped me here." He gestured around the island. "I'll help you in the city."

"What makes you think you can?"

"It's my job."

She quirked her brow and studied his face.

"I'm a counselor. I—" Her groan stopped him cold. "What?"

"Don't tell me you're a counselor."

"Why? Is that worse than being a yuppie?"

"Decidedly."

He sighed. "Another hurdle." He wondered if his work

with GANG would bother her. Virginia had hated it, but then she was after societal prestige. Skye had her problems, but she definitely wasn't into high society. He shrugged. "No one said friendships were easy."

She rolled her eyes before facing forward. "Don't get your hopes up. Every therapist failed."

He studied the stiff set of her back. "Did any of them talk about God?"

"No. Never."

"Some issues can never be solved. But with God's help, the impossible happens."

She turned. Skepticism showed in her eyes.

"I'm serious. Why don't you try adding His love to the mix? I bet you'll see results." Good advice, he realized, and he should listen to it himself. He used to discuss God with the kids. When had he stopped? Conviction ripped through him.

"I tried Janie's church." She sighed.

He studied the wistful expression on her face. "Janie's more than enthusiastic. Maybe try another church."

"Yours?"

He shrugged. He couldn't see her sitting among the kids he'd convinced to come in off the street. Dirty, smelly, most of them there for the free meal after the service. "Maybe something more traditional."

"Yours isn't?"

Before he could answer, Bo jumped up, placing his paws on Danny's shoulders. He jerked back, rocking the boat.

Skye laughed. "And what would this guy do in the city? I wouldn't dare leave him alone here on the island. He'd have all the residents in an uproar."

Laughing, Danny pushed Bo down into the bottom of the boat. "Don't make me regret getting him for you." But he'd never be sorry he had flown the pup in. The smile on her face had been reward enough.

Obviously glad to change the subject, Skye kicked up the throttle and sent the skiff across the water. "You might be sorrier than you know before your two weeks are up. Wait until he visits your place and chews up your shoes or gets a hold of the novel you're reading."

Danny groaned aloud but laughed inside. He had plenty of shoes at home, and he wasn't all that interested in reading when he could spend the day with Skye. The hassles at work receded into the background whenever he was with her. He'd enjoy it while he could.

And he did.

The two weeks flew. Skye showed Danny how to bring up the crabs, then cook and clean them. Gruesome process, but the result was worth it, especially when she acted so pleased to show him everything about her lifestyle.

Several times, she took him out in her sailboat, teaching him how to sail. Sometimes they fished, other times they cruised around the San Juans, through the Sound. The scenery took his breath away. The fishing bored him, but being with Skye more than made up for the languid activity. Besides, if he wasn't talking to Skye, he was playing with the pup.

Bo demanded attention and exercise, not only on the boat, but on the land as well. Danny looked forward to their daily walks around the island. At first, the pup stayed close, but by the second week, he romped happily at will, tail wagging as he explored each nook and cranny of the forest.

Often it rained, forcing them to find activities inside. Once, she invited him to her place, but the room shrunk in size. How she lived in so small a house on a permanent basis amazed Danny. Fortunately, she had no problem spending time at Ted's house as they were doing this rainy day, reading in front of the fire. Bo was sound asleep for a change. Skye sat on the couch, her feet curled underneath her, concentrating on the magazine she'd found on the shelf.

Danny glanced at the Bible in his lap. He read the verse again, the words convicting him. How long had it been since he had sat quiet and attentive? The peace that now settled over him testified that it had been much too long. He stretched, drawing Skye's attention. He pointed to the Bible. "If I'd been reading this, I wouldn't have gotten so stressed out at work."

Her brow furrowed as she considered his words. "And reading that has helped you to relax?"

He nodded, the truth of that realization hitting home.

She straightened her legs and sat up, interested and alert. "Janie left me a Bible. I tried reading it, but I found it very confusing."

Danny frowned. How did one explain? "I guess I've read these words for so long—since high school—that I take them for granted." He shrugged. "I suppose they did seem strange when I first read them."

Skye leaned forward, her eyes bright with curiosity. Her movement awakened Bo. Danny patted his knee, drawing the puppy's attention.

Silence echoed in the room, broken only by the snap and crackle of the fire.

Skye studied him, her blue eyes intent. "I'll take a look at it again, but I find my peace in the forest, sitting quietly and listening to the birds. Smelling the salt air, seeing the way the trees and plants grow in harmony."

"Creation—an amazing phenomenon."

She considered his comment. "The time spent here on the

island has been good for you. You're much more relaxed than when you arrived."

"But I can't stay here, hiding in isolation." Her shoulders stiffened, but he pressed on. "My work is important. Sure, I can't change things for everyone, but I do accomplish a lot. I realize that now."

She remained silent, staring at her stocking-clad feet.

"It's not natural to be so isolated and alone, Skye. You may have needed time away to recover from the trauma you went through, but that was years ago. It's time for you to move on. You need to be involved with other people." He pushed the puppy aside and sat next to her.

She looked up, tears brimming. "I want to be with you, Danny," she whispered. "I'm dreading tomorrow when you leave."

"Then come with me. Come to Seattle and stay."

"I can't do that."

He took a deep breath, knowing he had to be patient. "We'll go slow. I'll come and visit whenever I have a free weekend."

"I'd love that."

"I'll have a lot of catching up to do after this vacation. I won't be able to come for a while." Danny frowned. Would all of his work capture his full attention? Would his time here get pushed so far into the background that he would forget the peace he'd found here with Skye? Would his feelings for her stay as vibrant as they felt at this moment?

CHAPTER 9

DANNY WAS GONE.

Skye pulled the blankets over her head. She didn't want to face the day. She especially didn't want to deal with the shafts of sunlight peeking through the windows into her quiet bedroom. Traitorous sun. There should be rain today. Rain to blend with her tears.

How could she have let herself fall in love with the man? A yuppie and a counselor at that. She'd known he had to leave. But she'd left her heart unguarded, exposed. And he'd flown off with it yesterday afternoon.

Hyperventilating, she fought the waves of loneliness. Why had Danny shown up here on the island? Her life had order before his arrival. Now everything was in disarray. Ace was gone, her favorite piece of land was still for sale, and all the strange happenings on the island of late haunted her. But none of those compared to the fact that Danny had awakened her senses. If only she could sleep the days away and not have to think.

Whimpering sounded from below. Groaning, she rolled out of bed and tugged on her skirt. Bo required attention, and that was a good thing. Otherwise, she would spend the entire day in bed. "I'm coming," she yelled out the upstairs window.

The whimpers slid up a notch, and scratching sounded on the downstairs door. Skye pulled her sweater over her head, tugging at the tangles in her hair. Tossing covers left and right, she made the bed and climbed down the ladder.

Opening the door, she braced herself for the ball of fur leaping at her. "Down, Bo. You have to learn not to jump."

Chuckling at his antics and shaking her head at the same time, she pushed him down on all fours. "You're such a bundle of energy. I don't think Danny did me any favors by bringing you here."

Tail wagging, ears laid back, and a grin across his snout, Bo ran for a stick and dropped it on her toe. Laughing, she kicked the piece of wood out the door and shooed the mutt along with it. "Go do your business and let me see what mischief you were up to last night."

Staggering into the downstairs room of her cabin, she looked around and groaned. Shreds of a magazine littered the floor. A pillow lay limp with its stuffing hanging out where Bo had torn it with his sharp puppy teeth. At least he'd found the logs and chewed off their bark instead of chewing on her furniture like he'd done the night before.

"Whatever happened to my calm and peaceful existence?" she moaned. "Vandalism and shooting on my island. Danny comes into my life and turns it upside down, and now you're turning my house into a mess."

Would she have it any other way? In spite of the events on the island, weren't two weeks with Danny better than never knowing him, never hearing his laughter, seeing his caring eyes, feeling his gentle touch?

But a counselor? Didn't she mistrust all counselors?

No. She trusted Danny. He'd never put pressure on her or bugged her to talk of her past. He'd been a friend, not a counselor. More than a friend. And she missed him.

Stacking the wood back onto the hearth, she shook her head. And what about Bo? If he weren't here, the pain of Ace's death would be unbearable. No, she wouldn't trade a minute of those two weeks.

Stopping in the middle of the room, the torn pillow hanging limp in her hand, she closed her eyes. What was she going to do?

How was she going to live without Danny? Images of Seattle floated into her consciousness, but she shoved them out of her mind as quickly as they came. She wouldn't go to the city. Couldn't.

But she'd been thinking of it more and more.

Bo charged into the room with the leather chew stick Danny had given him clamped between his teeth. "What would I do with you in Seattle?" Skye asked. "Janie doesn't have a yard. You'd hate it there in her small apartment." Bo wagged his tail. "You're agreeing with me, aren't you? We have no business going."

With that decision reaffirmed, she cooked a quick batch of scrambled eggs for herself and fed Bo his portion of dog chow.

The day seemed empty. As did the following four weeks. Skye tried to keep busy, but everything she did reminded her of Danny. When she sailed her boat, she pictured his long fingers holding the boom. Digging clams brought strained smiles as she remembered the look of dismay on his face when he'd accidentally crushed a shell. The crab pots seemed heavier without his help.

But the most difficult times were the walks on the island. She missed holding his hand, feeling the warmth and strength. Bo searched every bush, wagging his tail, as if he would find Danny jumping out, teasing and laughing. Wearing the scarf he'd borrowed, she'd bury her nose in the wool and smell the spicy scent of his aftershave.

Hints of summer touched the island. Rainstorms weren't as cold or fierce. Between storms, the sun shone brighter. The berry bushes were in full bloom, and wildflowers dotted the airfield. Skye constantly watched, hoping Danny's plane would land, bringing a promised visit.

Planes came in and out, but none of them were Danny's Cessna. Skye hated how her heart picked up speed whenever she heard the roar of an engine coming in for a landing. He was a busy man. Why would she expect him to come all this way just to see her? Besides, there were plenty of women in Seattle.

He didn't need to fly this far to find companionship.

At least the incidents of vandalism had slowed. Windows in a couple of houses had been broken a couple of weekends ago, but that could have been boaters landing on the island. Jack thought they might have been unsupervised kids. Skye stashed the incidents in the back of her mind where she tried to stuff memories of Danny.

A plane roared overhead. Skye's heart raced as she hurried to the spot she'd cleared, giving her an unobstructed view of the landing strip. It was midweek, so it probably wasn't Danny. Unless he'd decided to surprise her.

A red plane flew into view. Not Danny's. Her shoulders sagged.

Forget Danny.

Impossible.

Wiping at the threatening tears, Skye called Bo and meandered down the trail to her favorite stump. She climbed on top and crossed her legs. Bo sniffed around for a few minutes and then stretched out at the base of the worn wood. Thank goodness, the pup was learning the routine and knew to be still while she meditated.

She closed her eyes. Would she connect today? She hadn't been able to focus since Danny's visit. An hour later, she gave up. She dreaded meditation now. Instead of peace, heart-tearing yearnings filled the time. Whenever she sat still, the only things swimming around in her head were images of his face creased with laughter, his arms loaded with firewood, or his eyes serious in concentration. And today Bo was a puppy pest, running around chasing bugs, clawing at the stump, yipping his demands for attention.

Sighing, she rubbed at her temples. Maybe she should try praying. Janie insisted it worked for her. She'd seen the changes in Danny after he'd told her he'd started praying again. He'd been more relaxed, settled, and at peace. She straightened and looked up at the blue sky. No, she couldn't pray. Even if she were sure He existed, she had no idea how to start.

About to push off the log, she paused when she heard footsteps in the forest. Bo stopped chewing and cocked his head from side to side, trying to raise his floppy ears.

The shooters. Were they back?

Skye scrambled off the stump and grabbed Bo by the ruff of his neck, holding the pup close and out of harm's way. To her relief, Jack emerged from the forest, followed by two strangers, out of place in their business suits. They gingerly stepped around the late-spring mud.

Jack raised his hand and waved. "There you are. We were looking for you."

Curious, Skye tightened her hold on Bo.

The dog wriggled out of control and ran toward Jack. "Hey, fella. You keeping out of mischief?"

Skye hurried to catch the dog before he jumped on the strangers. "Not hardly. I'll sure be glad when he's out of this puppy stage." She reached and missed. Bo greeted the first man. He stepped back, but not in time to avoid the muddy paw print on his trousers.

"I'm so sorry." She grabbed Bo's ruff and pulled him into her arms. "You can see he hasn't learned his manners yet."

"No problem." The man brushed at the mud, then straightened and forced a smile. "I'm James Sawyer from Sawyer Realtors." He waved to the other man. "My brother Jed. We came to look at the property that's for sale."

Skye dropped Bo. Her breath lodged somewhere deep in her throat. She coughed to clear it. "Not much out here to see that isn't undeveloped and primitive." She turned to Jack with pleading eyes. "Tell him about the water and power situation." That would surely put the kibosh on their interest in the land.

Jack's voice droned on as he explained the complicated utilities and building restrictions on the island. Fortunately, Bo wandered off toward the beach and out of the way. James followed him to the edge of the cliff and looked down the beach.

Jack raised his voice so the realtor could hear. "As you can see, there are tricks to building out here."

"Not much to do for entertainment either," Skye intervened, but the men weren't paying much attention to either her or Jack. With calculating glances, they surveyed the site.

Jed Sawyer stepped toward her. "Jack pointed out the piece of land you own. Interested in selling it?"

Speechless, she stared, her mouth open, her heart pounding.

"We'd offer you a fair price."

With a jolt, she straightened to her full height. "I couldn't. That's my home."

James Sawyer returned from viewing the beach and rejoined them. "You probably want to stay on the island. Would you be interested in Johnson's house? It's bigger, has a sea view, and is ready for you to move in."

The cottage was situated on one of the best sites along the beach, with three bedrooms, a large kitchen, and a living room that overlooked the sea. "Sure, who wouldn't want that house? But there's no way I could afford it."

"We'd make an even trade," Jed offered.

Floored, Skye turned to Jack. Surely these men were joking. Jack stood rubbing his jaw, his expression one of deep thought. He glanced up and caught her pleading look. "Why would you want her place? Johnson's piece of land has a much better view and is larger. Have you seen her house?" He turned to Skye. "No offense, but the place isn't very practical."

"Miss Larsen's property borders this lot. Combined, we would have a larger lot. More room."

Memories of her grandmother fed through Skye's mind.

The times she and Janie visited, baking cookies, sitting by the fire telling stories. Riding on her father's shoulders so she could reach to paint the bathhouse he'd built for Granny. Helping her mother plant vegetables and flowers whenever they visited. How could she let that go? Skye jerked to attention. "Your offer is more than fair, but my house means too much to me to sell it."

The men looked at each other. James set a determined expression on his face and started to speak, but Jed shook his head and turned to her. "You'll need time to think this over. It's a big step." Reaching into his breast pocket, he pulled out a wallet. "Here's my number," he said, handing her a business card. "If you change your mind, get in touch."

Skye hesitated, then took the card from his outstretched hand and tucked it into her pocket.

Jack started for the trail and called for the men to follow. "Let me show you Johnson's house. Maybe you'd prefer to buy it instead of building from scratch."

Much to Skye's relief, the men followed Jack down the trail. "Is Johnson's house and lot the only property for sale?" James asked.

"Actually there are a couple of lots inland from Skye's place. They don't have good beach access or a view, so no one has been much interested in them. I could show you…" Jack's voice trailed away the deeper he walked into the forest.

Skye debated whether to follow them. No, they might bring up selling her place again, and she didn't want to discuss it. Heading for the beach, she called Bo. He charged up the steep bank, sending rocks tumbling down in his wake. "You went in the water, didn't you?" She backed out of his path, trying to avoid the cold droplets spraying everywhere. "Let's go talk to Lenny. Maybe she knows what's going on."

Skye walked down the path and onto the road. Jack and the two men were nowhere in sight as she approached the Harris house. "Lenny, you home?"

"In the kitchen. Come on in," Lenny called through the open door.

Skye let Bo into the fenced pen where Jack and Lenny put their dog when they wanted him contained and out of the way. Mutt welcomed Bo with a wagging tail. Skye went inside and found Lenny sitting at her kitchen table with Fred. "What's going on with the two men?"

Fred set down his cup of coffee. "You mean the two suits?"

Skye nodded and accepted the cup of tea Lenny offered her, as she had done so many times in the past. She breathed in the mint aroma, wishing she could step back in time. Back to when her life was peaceful. "They want to buy my house."

Lenny sat down opposite Skye. "I thought they were interested in Johnson's lot. What would they want with your house?" She lifted her hand. "Not that it isn't charming, don't get me wrong, but it is a bit…unique."

"He offered to trade my house for Johnson's."

Lenny stared in disbelief.

"I couldn't believe it either."

"Some businessmen they must be." Fred plunked his cup on the table, sloshing coffee on the tablecloth. "I'd take the trade and run. No one in their right mind is going to want to buy that house of yours."

Skye stared at Fred in surprise. She was disappointed in his attitude. "It doesn't matter. I'm never selling. My house holds too many memories."

"And memories are going to help you climb that outside ladder on a cold, frosty night when you're an old lady?"

The warmth from the cup seeped into Skye's hands, warding off the chill of Fred's words. Old age was a long time off, but thoughts of a lonely life stretching ahead of her—a life without Danny—brought tears to her eyes.

"I'd hate to see you leave," Lenny said as she patted Skye's shoulder, "but you are so isolated out here. You need to be around young people."

Fred eyed her over the steaming cup. "What about Danny? You seemed hot on him. Wouldn't you want to move to Seattle? Get married? Do something meaningful?"

His words cut, but her tears dried up. Maybe she should do something worthwhile—like talk to Johnson's grandson before it was too late and get him to donate the land as a preserve. And see Danny. "When are you leaving for Seattle?" she asked Fred.

"This afternoon. Want a ride?"

She turned to Lenny. "Can you watch Bo?"

Lenny rubbed her forehead. "Gee, kiddo, Jack and I are going to Vendovi Island for a few days. I don't think we could handle the puppy on board the boat."

Disappointed, Skye sighed. "He is a handful."

Fred set his cup down. "Bring Bo along. Danny left the carrier, didn't he?"

Her spirits rose. "I have it at the house. I don't think he's outgrown it yet."

"I have plenty of room to strap the crate in the back of the plane. When we get to Seattle, I'll drive you to Janie's."

"When should I meet you at the airstrip?"

"I plan to leave at three. I'll come by in my cart and pick you up."

Skye stood and gave Lenny a hug. "Have a great time on your trip. I'll see you in a week or so."

Danny shifted the grocery bag from his right arm to his left and searched his pants pocket for the keys. Rain dripped off the brim of his hat into the bag. At last. He opened the door and stepped inside the large and empty foyer.

His footsteps echoed on the hardwood floor as he walked down the hall to the kitchen. Pushing the pile of mail out of the way, he set the bag on the island counter. He shook out his hat, dripping water onto the tile floor, reminding him of the downpour outside the picture windows over the sink. A curtain of rain blocked his view of the yard.

He glanced around the kitchen and family dining area. The large space dwarfed the lone table and pair of chairs he'd brought from his apartment. Several prints sat against the wall waiting to be hung. Shaking his head, he tossed his wet coat over a chair. Whatever possessed him to move into this house?

Yes, he was helping out a friend. George. He'd lost his job when Boeing downsized and had fortunately found another position in Los Angeles. But the house wouldn't sell quickly, and George couldn't afford to let the house sit empty. Danny had jumped at the chance to rent. And why? The real reason he'd moved into the large house?

Skye. Leeza Island. The peace he'd found in the silence of the forest. He'd hoped to find a measure of it here in the suburbs of Seattle. But all he'd found was a long commute and a larger space in which to be lonely.

Walking into the living room, he picked up the remote and turned the television to The Weather Channel. Sunshine predicted for the weekend. Good. He had finally managed time to fly to the island and see Skye. He'd pack tomorrow and take off after work on Friday.

Thinking of Skye lightened his spirits. Whistling and loosening his tie, he climbed the stairs to the large master bedroom.

The phone rang. Untying his shoes, he tucked the receiver under his chin. "Fraser here."

"Hi, Boss, sorry to bother you at home, but this woman has been calling. She sounds upset and insists you'll talk to her.

A Miss Larsen."

He jumped up, almost dropping the phone. "Skye. Skye Larsen?"

"Yes, she wants to—"

"Where is she? Is she on the other line?"

"That's what I'm trying to tell you." He could hear the exasperation in Joyce's voice but couldn't deal with it now. Not with Skye on the line. "Patch her to me."

"Hold on."

The seconds ticked endlessly as Danny stood motionless in the middle of his room, anticipating the sound of her voice.

"Danny?"

Instead of joy, his blood curdled at the tone in her voice. "What's wrong, Skye?"

Her words muffled into a sob, making it difficult to understand.

"Are you alone?"

"Y…yes."

His heart wrenched. "Calm down. Where are you?"

"I'm… I'm…in Seattle. At Janie's."

His pulse raced. Down by the docks. He could picture the homeless drifters that hung around the inner-city district. "Tell me exactly where she lives. I'll be there in half an hour."

He jotted down the address. Good grief, the Rainier district. "Stay where you are. Lock the doors. Turn on all the lights. Keep the phone in your hand. And Skye?"

"Yes?" Her voice shook, tearing at his heart.

"Don't panic."

He wanted to stay on the line and reassure her, but he had to hurry. He donned his shoes, tore down the stairs, and shrugged into his wet coat.

His windshield wipers swished like a ticking clock as he drove through the rush-hour traffic. Fortunately, most of the cars were heading away from the city in the opposite direction. Why had Skye been crying? Had some punks tried to scare her? Had memories of her past assaulted her? A number of reasons flitted through his head.

Gripping the steering wheel, he prayed—something he hadn't done since his return from the island.

Guilt tore through him. Why had he let his prayer life slip again? Hadn't he learned anything during his vacation on the island? Was he only going to pray when he needed something, instead of doing so on a regular basis? He slammed his fist on the steering wheel, apologizing and begging for mercy at the same time.

After the longest half-hour of his life, he found a spot near Janie's house to park. Running into the hallway of the apartment building, he searched for Janie's room number. He tried the knob while he banged on the worn wood. "Skye. It's Danny. Let me in."

The door flew open and Skye threw herself into his arms. He hugged her close, alarmed by her trembling and chilled skin. He set her away from him and looked into her eyes, eyes that were huge with fear. "You're freezing," he exclaimed. "What's going on?"

Tears spilled down her cheeks. "I tried to be brave, but I can't do this."

He opened his coat and tucked her in against his chest, feeling her heart beat next to his. "Can't do what, sweetheart?"

"S…stay here."

He glanced around the room with its eclectic arrangement of used furniture—clean and orderly, but cold and lonesome. "Where's Janie?"

"She's in Portland on a mission with her church. She won't be back for a week."

"She left you here alone?"

"She doesn't know I'm here." She shuddered.

He tightened his arms around her. "When did you arrive? How did you get in?" He shivered too as she curled her chilled body against him.

She slid her arms under the coat and wrapped them around him. "F...Fred brought me today. J...Janie gave me a key a long time ago. I don't know what I would have done if I hadn't brought it."

A low whine sounded. Danny looked down. Bo lay huddled on his belly at Skye's feet. "You brought the pup. He doesn't look too happy either."

Pulling away and leaving a cold spot, she bent and picked Bo up. Cradling the puppy in her arms, she looked at Danny. "I made a big mistake coming here," she sniffed, her eyes red from crying. "There's no yard for Bo, the neighborhood is dreadful to walk around in, and there's nothing in the fridge to eat."

His heart broke into a thousand pieces. He wrapped his arms around both her and Bo. "I'm taking you to my place."

She leaned back. "I can't impose on you like that." She said no, but her eyes pleaded.

He tucked his finger under her chin and lifted her face up until her dark blue eyes locked with his. He smiled. "I recall you went to a lot of trouble to help me out on the island. The least I can do is reciprocate."

She blinked, then gave a wobbly smile. "Do they allow dogs in your apartment?"

He shook his head. "No, but I moved out of the apartment. I have a big house and yard. Plenty of room for you and Bo." Which was exactly why he'd rented the place with an option to buy. But if he told her that, he'd scare her off. Plenty of time for talking after she was settled in.

Her shoulders sagged, and she took a deep breath. "I'm so

relieved. Fred's not flying back to Leeza Island until next week. I didn't know what I was going to do."

"Where's your bag? I want to get home before dark."

She set Bo down and walked toward the back of the apartment. "I don't have much. Bo's carrier is on the balcony."

Bo wiggled and squirmed, begging for a pat. Danny bent down and rubbed behind his ears, the soft puppy fur slipping through his fingers. "Well, fella. You're going to like your new home. But don't tell Skye."

Bo mouthed his hand, and Danny chuckled as he coaxed the pup into the carrier.

Skye returned with a backpack in her hand. "I'm ready."

Danny lifted the carrier onto the back seat of his car and tossed her pack beside it. After helping Skye in the passenger side, he slid behind the wheel. "I'm going to stop by work. Maybe I can talk Nina into staying with us at the house."

Skye frowned. "Who's Nina? I mean, if you're involved with someone, I don't—"

"Nina works with me." Danny grasped her hand and tugged. "She counsels the girls. I think it's a good idea to have her around."

He squeezed Skye's trembling fingers and noticed the pink tinge in her cheeks, the relieved sag in her shoulders. She took a deep breath. "You're right. I didn't think things through. I thought Janie would be home."

He smiled. "I'm glad you called."

She swung her head around. Her gaze bore into his. "Really?"

He nodded and lightly squeezed her fingers, liking the softness of her hands. "I'd stop at a restaurant and get some food inside you, but it wouldn't be a good idea to leave Bo in the car."

She nodded as she fastened her seat belt. "He'd be in the carrier, but still, he's been cooped up all day. He could use a romp in your yard."

"Consider it done." Danny turned the key, and the classic Thunderbird roared to life. "I just bought some groceries. We can fix something at home. After the pup has been there awhile and feels comfortable, we'll leave him and go out to dinner. I promise."

She turned to look at him. "I can't stay. I only came here to talk to the realtor and hopefully Johnson's grandson. Maybe I can talk them into changing their minds about selling the land. Then I'll call around and see if I can find a way back to Leeza Island tomorrow."

The light turned red. He glanced her way. The muscles of her jaw worked as she clenched her teeth. Her eyes darted nervously as she looked around the neighborhood.

"So you didn't come to see me?" Disappointment curled in his gut. "I was hoping you had."

CHAPTER 10

SKYE TURNED AND STARED at Danny. The look of hurt in his eyes tore at her heart. She reached over and placed her hand on his. "I did want to see you, Danny. I don't think I could've made the trip at all if I hadn't thought we would get together."

He turned his hand and clasped her fingers. "I'm glad, Skye. I've missed you."

Her heart skipped a beat. She opened her mouth to tell him how much she had missed him—how the nights had dragged as she lay awake dreaming of his touch, how everything on the island brought back memories of him—but she clamped her lips tight. She didn't dare let him know how much she needed him, not when she knew she couldn't stay in Seattle. Instead, she asked, "Do you think you can help me find Johnson's grandson? I received a memo from the realtor saying he would give my letter to the man, but I haven't heard back."

"I have a full schedule at work tomorrow. But I've cleared the weekend. I'm all yours. We can take care of business, and then I'll fly you home."

She studied his rugged features in the gray, cloud-dimmed light—features that tugged at her senses. She had to know. "Would you have used your weekend to come to Leeza Island if I hadn't come to Seattle?"

His eyes lit up. "I was planning to fly over after work on Friday. I can't tell you how frustrating it's been these past weeks. My calendar has been filled to the brim. But I finally managed to clear it, and I was going to surprise you."

"I'm sorry to ruin the surprise. But I didn't know."

He gently squeezed her fingers. "This is a better surprise.

You came all the way to Seattle. More importantly, you called me when you needed help. That's a big step, Skye." He cast her a quick smile. "Besides, I want to show you my house."

A horn honked. Danny let go of her hand and slammed on the brakes—barely missing the car ahead of them. She clasped the hem of his coat as if it were a lifeline. Then she realized that the congestion in the streets, the cacophony of noises, and the bright lights everywhere weren't penetrating the cocoon of safety she felt sitting beside Danny, and she relaxed. She gestured out the window with her free hand. "I can see why you were so tense when you arrived on the island. This is a madhouse."

He nodded as he swerved into a parking lot and slipped his car into an empty space. "Want to come in or wait here in the car?"

She glanced back at Bo, who was asleep in the carrier. "I'd like to see where you work."

While Danny walked around the car to open the door for her, she surveyed the walls of an old two-story building, moss covering the aged bricks. She peered around, wishing she had paid more attention to the neighborhood. As near as she could tell, they were still downtown. Danny guided her to a back door.

She followed him into a long corridor with nondescript walls and a linoleum floor. Stale air assaulted her senses, a combination of body odors and food, maybe chips or popcorn. Danny made a sharp turn and entered an open area. A scarred and pocked counter separated four desks from a waiting area with wooden chairs. A young woman sat at one of the desks. Several teens slouched in the chairs. The boys wore oversize pants and backward ball caps. The girls with short tops and bare waistlines sported tattoos. Skye stared, her heart racing.

Danny stopped in front of the woman's desk. "Hey, Nina, want to come stay at my place?"

Nina looked up from the file she studied and frowned at Danny. "Come on, Fraser. You know…" Her voice trailed off when she spotted Skye. She straightened and smiled. "Hello. Don't tell me you're with him?"

Heat crept up her cheeks. Danny hurried to explain. "She's a friend. Needs a place to stay." He shrugged. "I've got plenty of room. But—"

"Gotcha." Nina winked at Skye. "I'd want some protection too." She pointed to one of the girls sitting by herself. "I was wondering what I was going to do with Natasha. She needs a place too, and you know how small my apartment is."

Danny didn't hesitate. "Bring her along. The more, the better." He bent to draw her a map.

Skye stared at Natasha. Arms crossed, lips drawn, defiance radiated out of her eyes. Skye cut loose from the glare and studied the others in the room. Teens. From the looks of them, gang-bangers. Heart racing, she clenched her fists at her sides. Except for their age, they could have passed for the same thugs who had killed her parents.

She swung her attention to Danny, noticing for the first time the earring dangling out of his ear, his hair—longer now—brushing his shoulders. *No!* She wanted to scream. To run.

Danny waved goodbye to Nina and stopped in front of Skye. He frowned. "What's the matter?"

"You didn't tell me you counseled teens. Gang members."

He straightened his shoulders and smiled. "GANG it is. An acronym—God And Not Gangs."

She heard the pride in his voice. Saw it in his eyes.

He worked with gangs! Waves of horror washed through her. Of all the men in the world to fall in love with. A scream lodged in her throat.

"You okay?" He brushed her cheek. "Better get you home and get some food in you." He swung around to Nina. "I've got plenty. We'll keep it hot for you."

Nina waved. "We'll be out there in an hour or so. You go ahead without us."

Danny nodded and tucked his hand under Skye's elbow, guiding her back down the corridor. The walls closed in on her. She stumbled.

"Hang in there. We'll be home in a jiffy."

Barely conscious, Skye slid into the car. Danny smiled as he rounded the front of the vehicle. Revulsion washing through her, she closed her eyes. What now? Words of previous therapists echoed—a sick joke. *Take it moment by moment. Deep breaths.* She inhaled slowly, whispering, "*Take care of your business. See Johnson's grandson. And fly home next Friday. You can do this.*"

Danny folded into the seat. "Do what?"

She studied his face, the rugged features etched so dearly in her mind. "Handle the city," she choked. "At least for the next two days."

"Sure you can." He patted her arm before switching on the ignition. The Thunderbird roared to life. He shook his head as he accelerated out of the parking lot and up the on-ramp of the Interstate. "I miss the peace and quiet of the island, that's for sure. Didn't take long for me to get back into the rat race," Danny admitted and proceeded to tell her about his past weeks since she'd last seen him.

Skye concentrated on his words, amazed that she hadn't known. Hadn't guessed. No wonder he was so stressed. He worked with the toughest lot. Those rejected by family and society. The very beings who terrified her the most.

Skye's mind raced, and she barely noticed the rush-hour traffic through the swishing of the windshield wipers. After what seemed like hours, they left the Interstate and wound through a residential area with large homes set back in thick stands of trees.

Danny drove up a curved drive. Surprised, Skye stared at the huge house set far back from the road. Picture windows looked out at the tall cedar and hemlock trees that lined the yard. Gardens—bright with colored flowers—rushed up to hug brick walls. Wrought-iron balconies protected the French doors of the rooms on the second floor.

She was unworldly, uneducated, frightened of life, and unable to live in the city. Why had she thought she could relate to this man? She studied Danny's face, his joy at showing her his home apparent in his smile. He pulled up to a two-car garage, reached for the visor, and pushed a button. One of the doors opened automatically. Once inside, he took Skye's hands, helped her out of the car, and then released Bo from the carrier.

In spite of her inner turmoil—or maybe because of it— Skye giggled as the pup wiggled and squirmed, undecided whether to stay for rubdowns or to sniff the new surroundings. "We'd better get him outside quick or he'll mess up your nice garage."

She couldn't help but admire the ultra-clean linoleum floor. The carports of the few houses she remembered living in as a child had been caked with grease and oil. She could picture her mother squawking at her father when he came inside with grime-caked clothes and hands. Wouldn't her mother have loved this clean room?

Danny opened a side door and called Bo. Skye followed the pup to the opening and stopped when a blast of wet wind blew over them. "I hope you have some towels handy. He's going to be a muddy mess."

Hugging her against his side, Danny chuckled. "It's all grass. No mud. He'll be wet, but we won't melt."

"I'm thankful you have a yard. He hasn't really been out since we arrived."

"Good thing you called, Skye. I wouldn't want you staying alone in Janie's neighborhood. I don't see why she stays there."

And he could talk? After she had seen where he worked? "She likes to be close to her charity projects." Skye peered through the door, trying to see the yard through the rain. "You say you just moved into this place?"

He nodded. "I figured you'd want to see some green if you came to visit."

Skye pulled away, staring at him. "Don't tell me you moved here because of me?"

He shook his head, but she saw chagrin hiding in his eyes. "My apartment was close to work. But being on the island with you made me realize how much I needed to have a place to come home to and unwind. The forest and sea relaxed me. Since I can't get away to the island that often, I was hoping this place would be a haven, as well."

She understood now why he needed one. "And is it?"

He looked deep into her eyes. Desire and longing filled his dark brown depths. "Not yet."

Bo charged through the door, splashing water all over them. Skye sighed, glad for the break in the tension. "You'd better find those towels quick or we'll all be drenched."

Danny dried off Bo and then carried Skye's pack into the house. Their footsteps echoed on the hardwood floor. Skye looked around at the bare walls and empty rooms. No wonder he hadn't found a peaceful haven. The house exuded loneliness. It cried out for attention from its workaholic owner.

"My apartment was small, so I don't have much furniture yet. Maybe you can help me decorate and furnish the place."

She glanced into the living room and studied the pictures leaning against the wall. A leather couch stretched across the room. Beside it, a recliner beckoned one to sit in front of the fireplace. However, judging from the pristine bricks under the grate, the recliner had been used to watch television instead. "I doubt I'd be much help. I don't know the city, so I wouldn't be able to shop for you."

Danny took her coat and hung it in a hall closet in a huge foyer. The two large oak doors with etched glass had to be the front doors. With her pack in hand, he led her down another empty hall. She followed him into a kitchen so big that the entire downstairs of her cabin would easily fit into it.

"Wow!" She spun around, admiring the ash-blond cupboards, the roomy granite counters lining the large room, and the windows that brought the outdoors inside. "This is lovely."

Seemingly pleased, Danny set her pack on the floor and showed her a refrigerator hidden behind the façade that matched the cupboards, a dishwasher she had no idea how to use, and an alcove that swallowed his small table and two chairs. "I'm glad you like the place. You can see I need to hang the pictures. And I want a larger table in case I ever have a family." A crooked smile creased his cheek.

Her heart lurched. A family. With Danny. She could picture the children, stairstep in ages, with dark hair like their father's, sitting at the table. Laughter rang in her mind, the giggles of family stability and a home she'd never had herself. How she yearned for that. But here? In Seattle? She couldn't possibly live in the city. Not with her fears and hang-ups. Not with Danny, especially when he worked with dangerous and unpredictable teenagers.

As if he didn't notice her hesitation, he pointed to a sack of groceries on the butcher block island. "I was putting these away when you called. I didn't buy much because I figured I was leaving Friday for Leeza Island, but there's a roasted chicken in here that we can heat up in the microwave. I have some veggies in the freezer. There'll be enough for the four of us." He glanced down at Bo, who was wagging his tail, and frowned. "But I don't have dog food."

Skye reached for her pack. "I brought that, but I'll need a bowl." Still intimidated by the grand scale of Danny's house, she cringed at the thought of Bo messing up the beautiful tile floor. "We can put him out in the garage."

"No way. He's part of the family and belongs inside." Danny opened a cupboard and brought out two matching bowls. "These will have to do for now. We'll go to the store tomorrow and shop for what we need."

Skye stood frozen to the spot, unable to reach for the bowls Danny offered.

Danny set down the glassware and stood in front of her. He traced a finger down her cheek. "What is it, sweetheart? What's wrong?"

She clasped his hand, stopping the sensation of his touch down her cheek. Her heart thumped wildly in her chest. She looked deep into his eyes. "Twice now you've mentioned family. Twice you've implied that we are a family…"

He brought her fingers up to his lips. "That's how I think of us, Skye. I've thought about marriage." He shrugged. "The idea of spending my life with you has its appeal."

Her legs weakened. Her heart melted. She wanted those things too, but not here. "I don't know how we can do that, Danny. I don't think I can ever be the wife you need."

He wrapped his arms around her and pulled her to his chest. She leaned against him, feeling the beat of his heart, hearing his sigh. "Don't think about it," he whispered. "Let my love fill your heart for now. We are not going to rush into this." Chuckling, he tightened his arms and gave her a light squeeze. "We have to think this through, make several adjustments. I'm asking a lot of you, I know, but I think you care for me too."

He lifted her chin with his finger. "Don't you?"

She locked her gaze on the warmth and caring in his eyes. "I don't know much about relationships, Danny. I've never been seriously involved with anyone. I don't know if I—"

He interrupted her words with a kiss that sent her mind reeling, her pulse racing. After he took a deep breath, he lifted his head. "We'll work through it. Trust me."

Trust him? Could she? How she yearned to. But ever since the attack, she hadn't let any man close. She'd thought Danny could be the one.

But now?

The man worked with gangs.

Danny pulled away, leaving a cold, empty spot across her body. In her heart. He smiled. "We'd better fix that supper. Get some food in you. Then I'll show you the rest of the house."

How she managed to do anything after Danny's embrace was beyond her. But she did. She cut up the chicken and put the pieces on a platter while he fixed the vegetables.

She ate food she didn't taste, while conducting polite small talk. All the while, her mind raced with what-ifs. What if she could manage to live in Seattle? What if they did develop a relationship? What if she couldn't follow through?

The tour of the house left her breathless. Huge rooms with high ceilings admittedly gave her a sense of freedom she wouldn't have expected in a city home. The master bedroom with heavy oak furniture was the only bedroom completely furnished and was exactly what she'd picture for Danny.

The upstairs rooms were empty but sported large French doors looking out over the yard. "Pick out the room you and Bo want to use, and tomorrow I'll see if I can round up a bedroom set. Tonight, you can sleep in my bed."

His bed? Shocked, she started to protest, but he raised his

hand. "No argument. I can sleep on the couch."

She reached for his hand and shook her head. With a determined set of her jaw, she insisted. "You have to work tomorrow. I saw that couch. It's not big enough for you. I'll sleep just fine on it, and Bo can sleep on the floor next to me."

Much to her relief, he gave in. She wouldn't get a wink of sleep in his bed, surrounded by his personal things, his scent, his maleness. No, she would be fine on the couch.

"What about Nina? Natasha?"

"I have air mattresses in the storage room. After you pick out your room, I'll set them up in one of the empty bedrooms." He gestured toward the rooms in the front of the house. "I told Nina to bring sleeping bags and towels."

She looked out across the balcony and saw a car approaching the drive. "Looks like they're here now."

Stepping to the French door, he peered down. "Yep. That's Nina's car." He returned to her side and grasped her elbow, leading her into the larger room at the back of the house. "I thought you'd probably want this one. It's quiet."

She looked past the double French door into the backyard, a yard filled with trees and a large lawn. Closing her eyes, she tried to imagine living in this room. This house. Images of her island sanctuary superimposed. She shuddered. "It'll do," she murmured.

His heart sinking, Danny watched the play of emotions crossing Skye's face. She didn't like it. She had the panicked look of a deer caught in the headlights of an oncoming car. Taking a deep breath, he willed himself to be patient. As a counselor, he knew better than to rush her. He'd hit her with a lot, and as much as he wanted everything now, he had to wait.

She had many issues to deal with—the city, his work, the sale of the land near her house. Until she had solid resolutions, neither of them would be ready for a serious relationship. Still, he could dream. Set a goal.

Voices mingled with barking carried up the stairs. "Man, Fraser. You didn't tell us you rented a castle."

Skye glanced at him, and he shrugged. "So much for peace and quiet. Let's get them fed and settled."

She smiled. "Safe haven for all the waifs in Seattle."

"Sounds good to me." He chuckled, glad that she was going to be a good sport about the situation.

"I'll put out the food while you set up the air mattresses," she offered.

"What about Bo?" He clomped down the stairs, worried about the squeals and growls echoing in the hall.

Close at his heels, Skye laughed. "Sounds like they've already met."

Danny rounded the bend and found Natasha sitting on the floor of the kitchen, tugging at the towel Bo had between his teeth. Nina entered, two sleeping bags and pillows tucked under her arms. "Nice digs." She tossed the bedding into an empty corner.

"More room than the apartment." He gestured to the space around them.

"Don't let the word out, or you'll have everyone at the office begging to come stay."

Not displeased with the idea, Danny laughed. "Beats being out here all alone."

Nina glanced at Skye and back at Danny. "You looking to remedy that?"

Dinnerware clattered onto the floor. Danny hurried to help Skye pick up the forks and spoons she'd dropped. "There's no big rush. So come on out any time you have some girls to put up. If Skye's not here, I'll stay at the Y."

"Or you could stay at my place." Nina moved over to where Skye was taking the platter of food out of the oven. "I'm starved. Looks and smells divine."

Skye took the plate to the small table and set it on a trivet. "Come eat. Danny'll set up your air mattresses, and then you can make yourselves at home. You know, shower, read." She glanced at Danny. "Do you have reception on the television?"

Nodding, he backed toward the hall. "Out in the living room. Not much furniture, but we'll manage." He turned and hurried down the corridor and into the garage. For the first time since he'd moved into the house, he was happy to be there. The place needed people. A woman. His woman.

Liking the sound of that, Danny smiled as he rummaged through the storage closet. But did Skye? He frowned, his hand frozen on one of the bags holding a mattress. Had he scared her off? He shook his head and pulled the bag out from under the pile of winter jackets he'd stashed in the closet. She'd try. He'd seen the yearning in her eyes, sensed the longing to be with him.

He grabbed the other mattress and returned to the kitchen, where he found Nina and Natasha, a sullen expression on her face, sitting at the table digging into the food Skye had set before them. Skye sat across from Nina with her hands wrapped around a steaming cup of coffee. Bo curled against her legs under the table. Things looked normal. Relief poured through him.

"Good. You found the coffeepot. I could use a cup of that myself."

Skye started to rise, but he waved her down. "Let me put these upstairs, and I'll get mine when I come back."

She settled back in the chair, her smile tremulous.

"So you two met on the island?" Nina waved her empty fork in the air. "Must have been some vacation."

"Skye can tell you all about it." He shifted the bags under his arms and sidestepped out of the room. Bo arose and followed him up the stairs. It didn't take long to set up the mattresses. He gave the room a cursory glance, picturing it filled with furniture and children. His children. He shook his head, amazed at the way his thoughts kept drifting to family life. Before his trip to the island, the concept had been the furthest thing from his mind. Now the idea of a wife and family seemed to pop up constantly. Warmth crept through him as he turned off the lights and patted his thigh for Bo to follow.

Muted voices sounded from the kitchen. Nina turned when he entered. Bo charged in front of him. "Skye was telling me that you learned how to dig for clams, catch crabs, and collect oysters." She rolled her eyes, amazement etched in her features. "Will wonders never cease?"

Danny pulled a coffee cup out of the cupboard and poured himself some of the aromatic brew. "Not much she can't do." He smiled at the pink tinge in her cheeks. "Turned this ol' city dude into a native."

Skye straightened. "You enjoyed every minute of it."

"That I did." He slid into the empty chair beside Natasha. "You two getting enough to eat?"

Natasha nodded, and Nina grinned. "You did look rested. Guess I should try out some country life myself."

"You're welcome to come out on the island anytime." Skye sipped her coffee.

Natasha finished her food and stood. "Mind if I take the dog outside?"

Danny waved her off. "Go ahead. He'll be your friend for life."

The girl giggled as she led the pup out the back door.

When she had shut the door, Danny turned to Nina. "So what's the scoop?"

Nina shrugged. "The usual. She started mixing with the wrong crowd. Got friendly with one of the boys. One thing led to another."

Danny's gut tightened. "Don't tell me."

"Yep, gang rape."

He heard Skye's gasp before he saw her coffee sloshing on the table. Jumping up, he grabbed a towel and dabbed at her hands. "Did you burn yourself?"

Her hands trembled in his. "It's all right."

Danny glanced at Nina and ignored her raised eyebrow. Maybe he shouldn't have allowed her to bring Natasha. He pushed aside the towel and looked into Skye's eyes.

She smiled. "Tables have turned, haven't they?"

"What do you mean?"

"I'm the helpless one now."

He chuckled, relieved that her sense of humor was still intact. "Makes a man feel good."

"That's a relief." Sarcasm rang in her tone.

Nina cleared her throat, reminding Danny of her presence. She looked straight at Skye. "I have a court date at nine in the morning. Can I leave Natasha here with you?"

His gut tightening, Danny started to protest. "That's not going to—"

"Fine." Skye interrupted him. "I'll be here all day waiting for Danny. Does she need to go to school?"

Nina shook her head. "She's on probation right now. She'll probably want to sleep in. Watch TV."

Danny followed Skye's gaze out the window and saw the young girl running across the yard, Bo at her heels. "Looks like she'll have plenty of entertainment."

Nina stacked her plates and stood to take them to the counter. "When I get out of court, I'll give you a call and come pick her up."

Skye nodded, then swung her gaze to Danny. "When will you be home?"

He smiled, liking the sound of that. "Around five. Then we'll go do those errands we discussed earlier."

He ignored Nina's smirk.

CHAPTER 11

SKYE AWOKE THE NEXT MORNING to bright sunlight streaming through the windows. Bo sat on the window seat in the alcove, peering out at several birds foraging on the lawn. "Bo, get down." Fortunately, Danny had not put on seat cushions yet.

At the sound of her voice, Bo romped over and jumped up to lick her face. She pushed him away. "You're all wet, you goofy hound. Did Danny let you out already?"

She slid out from under the comforter, her blue sweats rumpled and her hair hanging in wild disarray. Good grief. One look at her like this and Danny would have second thoughts about wanting her to be around permanently.

She needn't worry. A quick tour revealed he had already left for work. A note taped alongside his work phone number on the island counter caught her attention.

Nina and I are off to work. I'll have my assistant try and track down Johnson's grandson. Make yourself at home, but if you get nervous or uneasy, call me. I'll phone during the day to see if everything is okay. Should be home around five. Love, Danny

Her hand trembled as she fingered the note.

Love, Danny.

Love?

The word swirled in her brain, first heating then chilling her. She wanted his love. Yet she didn't.

Yes, she did. If only he were here, he would chase away her doubts with one easy smile. But he wasn't. She was on her own.

For several long seconds, she fought the fear of being alone in a strange place—in the city. But she wasn't alone. Natasha was here. What on earth was she going to say to the teen? What did one say after that kind of trauma? Memories traipsed across her mind. Nothing. There was nothing she could say.

After checking to see if Natasha was still asleep, Skye wandered through the house, touching Danny's furniture, his paintings stacked on the floor. His male scent in the cushions and the silence calmed her nerves. She looked out the windows at the expanse of lush green lawn.

He would be home at five. That thought echoed over and over to reassure her. But what would she do to fill the time until then? She glanced again at the pictures and the bare walls. Maybe she could be of help to Danny after all.

Walking barefoot so as not to awaken Natasha, Skye held the paintings against the walls in several locations, deciding where they would best be placed. She left each one on the floor where she wanted to hang it and searched Danny's garage for a hammer and nails. The tools were easy to find on his organized shelves, and she brought them into the kitchen to wait until Natasha awoke before pounding on the walls.

Bo skidded across the hardwood floor, chasing the knotted sock toy she'd made for him. She poured a cup of coffee and took the pup outside to run off some of his energy. A low brick wall framing a patio made a perfect place to sit and sip from her mug.

Water droplets sparkled on the leaves of the nearby bushes. Flowers tilted their heads toward the early morning sun, drinking in the warmth. Skye closed her eyes and breathed in the crisp, clean air, washed by yesterday's rain. Peaceful. Surprisingly so for the city. If only Natasha would sleep all day and leave her alone to enjoy the quiet.

A frown creased her brow at thoughts of Natasha. All she could think of to say were common platitudes. "I'm so sorry about what happened." *Yeah, right.* Natasha wouldn't believe that in a heartbeat. Who was she to care? A stranger that showed up on Danny's doorstep. Bo romped across the lawn, spraying water with each step. Skye smiled. A stranger with a dog. At least that was some common ground they could start with.

As if thoughts of the teen had conjured her up, Natasha ambled out the door holding a steaming cup of coffee and looking half-awake. Her long black hair tumbled around the oversized sweatshirt. She'd slipped on her tennies, but hadn't bothered to tie the laces.

Skye smiled. "I see you found the coffee?"

Natasha nodded before taking a sip.

"Sleep well?" Skye struggled with conversation.

The girl straightened and glared. "I won't be here long, so you don't have to patronize me."

Skye sucked in her breath. "I don't mean anything to you. I know that. But civility never hurts. A friendly 'good morning'. A smile. Especially after what you've been through."

"And what would you know about that?"

"I know that you're hurting."

Natasha's breath hissed out between her teeth. Defiance radiated from her stance. "Did Miss Nina tell you why? Did she tell you what happened?"

Unsure whether she was supposed to know or not, Skye decided on honesty. "She told me about the rape."

The girl flinched, sloshing coffee on her fingers, which she ignored.

Skye paused, remembering as if it were yesterday the attack on her parents—on her. How she hated the way everyone had avoided the subject as if it hadn't happened. "Do you want to talk about it?"

Hatred and pain spilled in the form of tears from Natasha's eyes. "You can't help me."

"No. Probably not." Skye patted the wall next to her. "Come sit, and I'll tell you my story." She perused the girl. "I'd guess I was about your age."

At first, Natasha refused to sit, but soon after Skye started, she inched her way to the wall and sat down, sipping on her coffee and staring at the bricks at Skye's feet.

The sun had crept onto the patio by the time Skye had finished her story. The rays warmed her back, soothed her frayed nerves.

"So you weren't actually raped?"

Skye shuddered. "I might as well have been. I can still feel those strong hands forcing me down, the smell of sweat mingled with fear, drugs, filth. But no, the neighbors called the police."

"And they arrived in time?"

"For me. But not for my parents."

Natasha reached over and placed her hand on Skye's knee. Startled by the touch, she pulled back from the memories. "It happened so fast. Parts of it seem like a blur. Parts are so clear I could reach out and touch the place where my mom had straightened my blouse, braided my hair."

Natasha took a deep breath. "I know. That's what I feel, too. One minute I was laughing and having fun, and the next..."

Her face scrunched up as she struggled not to cry. The temptation to reach out and hug Natasha tugged at Skye, but she refrained, knowing the girl could easily retreat into her defiance and fear. "Just remember that you're not at fault. It's easy to think that. To blame yourself." She thought of all the recriminations that still tortured and ate at her. "But you are not responsible for another's behavior. Their choices."

Her throat tightened after the words left her mouth. How could she sit here and repeat the same platitudes issued to her by the parade of therapists and counselors she'd seen over the years? If only she could take the words back. "I didn't mean—"

Natasha stood, rubbing her hand up and down her tight jeans. "I know. Miss Nina explained how important it is to forgive. To move on. Put my life in God's hands."

Skye stared. Natasha actually appeared comforted by those words. Skye had heard them enough from Janie, but she hadn't taken them seriously. "How are you doing with that?"

Natasha shrugged, brushing her hair back over her shoulder. "They make the forgiving part sound easy, and sometimes, like now, I feel it's true. But most of the time, it's hard. I want to kill Rodrigo."

The intensity of Natasha's emotion threatened to suck Skye in. She held her breath. How many times had revenge played over and over in her head?

Natasha stared. "Did you ever feel that way? Like you wanted to get back at them?"

She looked the girl straight in the eye. "Yes. They were caught. Years later. But when I saw them sentenced to life in prison, it didn't satisfy me. Seeing them suffer didn't bring my parents back."

"So what did you do?"

"Returned to my island. To my retreat."

"And do you find peace there?"

"Sometimes." Lately, she'd found only turmoil. Her refuge had always been the island, but now her home seemed lonely, isolated. An unrealistic retreat that would soon disappear. She traced her finger around her cup. "But it's elusive. I don't know if the past will ever leave me completely."

"Miss Nina says I should stay with her program. Help others. She said that's one way to deal with the memories."

Skye recoiled, then eased her shoulders. Maybe she should try Janie's way. Her sister didn't have regrets, flashbacks, the haunting memories. Janie was genuinely happy and content with the direction of her life. Is that what accepting God in your life did to a person? "Sounds like you're making wise decisions already."

Natasha blushed. Before she could say more, Bo appeared. The minute he saw the girl, he jumped up, plopping two wet paws in her lap, sloshing the small amount of coffee she had left in her cup. "Whoa dog." Natasha stood. Laughing, she handed Skye her mug and bent to rub the pup's ears. "You're full of energy this morning. What is it? You want to play?"

The wagging tail and prancing steps spoke volumes. Natasha found a stick and proceeded into the yard with Bo. Skye watched the transformation in the girl's demeanor. She looked young and innocent. Why did life have to be so hard?

The phone rang, interrupting her thoughts. Skye hurried inside and answered.

"How's it going?" Danny's voice smoothed over her jagged nerves, melting the sharp edges.

She smiled. "Fine. Natasha and Bo are outside playing."

"No problems?"

"We had a nice chat."

He paused. She could hear tapping on the desk and pictured him with a pen, drumming out the rhythm. "Sorry I couldn't be there."

"We're managing fine." At least that was the truth. She curled the cord around her finger. "Shall I tell you how peaceful and quiet it is out here and make you jealous?"

His groan echoed across the wire. "I'm aiming for early."

"Then get off the phone and get cracking, Flyboy."

She heard his laughter before the click and dial tone. She hung up the phone and glanced out the window. Natasha and Bo were running across the lawn. She smiled, wondering if she'd ever see her children—Danny's children—out in that yard. The teen's image blurred, and a deep yearning welled.

Skye turned away from the sight and grabbed the fry pan she'd set on the counter. She'd cook up some eggs. Anything to keep her mind from wandering down dangerous paths.

After breakfast, Nina returned from her court date. "How're you doing?" She studied Skye. "I don't see any signs of abuse. You must have managed okay."

Skye pointed outside before she poured Nina coffee. "She's found a new best friend. I almost hate to split them up."

Nina watched the pair before reaching for the mug. "You've been a real blessing, Skye. This is so much better for her than sitting around in court with me."

Skye nodded, surprised that she hadn't felt put out by the unexpected responsibility. A teen, no less. "She's welcome to spend the day."

Nina sighed and set down the mug on the granite counter. "I'd like nothing better for her, but we have appointments to talk to the police, her attorney, and the social worker."

"Sounds daunting." Skye glanced outside, her heart aching for what was to come for the young girl. "Will she be okay?"

"Is anyone, after an experience like this?"

"No," Skye whispered.

"If she had family to lean on…" Nina slammed her fist onto the counter, then shook it, pain crossing her features.

Skye reached over and placed her hands around Nina's sore one. "There's no give in that granite."

Nina pulled her hand back, rubbing her wrist. "No give, huh? There's no give anywhere in life for these kids. At least we have our program." Nina eyed Skye. "You interested in working with us? We can always use more help."

Skye backed up, shaking her head. "I'll be heading back to the island tomorrow."

Nina studied her. "Too bad. Danny could use someone like you."

"Have you known him for long?" She wanted to ask the woman more, like if Danny had ever been serious with anyone.

"Do you mean, have we dated?"

Blood flushed color into her cheeks. "I wasn't going to ask, but since you brought it up, have you?"

"I wish. Danny's great, but he's been too wrapped up in these kids." She nodded toward the window. "He was involved with a woman once. Society chick. Couldn't stand Danny's line of work. Didn't like him working with these kids—with GANG."

Skye caught her breath. "Did she ask him to leave? Try other work?"

Nina snorted. "Like that would ever happen. He's devoted to these kids. Committed. To be honest, he needs to ease up or he's going to end up in the loony bin."

Disappointment mingled with concern. Images crowded in her head of Danny escorting a woman to the theater, fancy restaurants. She hated the thought that he'd been hurt, but she understood the woman's fears.

Nina finished the last of her coffee, set the cup down, and pinned Skye with her gaze. "He's different since meeting you. We were hoping your relationship might be serious. Permanent."

"We?"

Nina grinned. "The staff. When he relaxes, things are easier for us."

Skye struggled to smile. "I suppose that, because he's driven, he feels like you should be also?"

"That's it in a nutshell."

Skye rubbed her finger around the top of the mug, the small amount of coffee inside cold and unappealing. "I'd like to help you out, but things are complicated. We have issues."

Nina nodded. "Danny's words exactly. But hang in there. He's a dynamite person. Worth the effort."

.

The day dragged long and hard for Danny. One phone call after another. A long, stressful meeting and then the pile of caseloads on his desk. Two new boys were inducted into GANG. He'd gone to their homes, talked to their parents. He'd felt good about the prospects for the two, but three other teens had walked out, leaving a burden of guilt on his shoulders.

Topping the usual tension at work was a growing impatience to get home. To see Skye. He'd called twice and been relieved to hear her voice, calm and confident. No longer terrified. He never wanted to hear her sound like that again. Ever. He shuddered just thinking of it.

His assistant walked into his office, thankfully interrupting his thoughts. "A friend of mine has a bedroom set she wants to get rid of."

He rubbed at his aching temple and smiled for the first time in an hour. "Is it decent?" He thought of Skye's eclectic tastes.

"It was her daughter's. She's off to college. Her son can deliver it this afternoon." Joyce grinned. "I can hardly wait to meet Skye. I'm sorry I was out yesterday when you came in. Nina says she's a gem. You two getting serious?"

He saw Joyce studying him as she leaned against the bookcase. He shifted uncomfortably in his chair. "If I can convince her to stay in Seattle. She doesn't like the city."

"That could be a good thing if she drags you away. The only time I've seen you looking relaxed was after you'd been with her on the island. You work too hard. It's about time you took some moments for yourself."

He gestured toward the pile of files sitting on his desk and sighed. "And which case shall I toss out to do that?"

Joyce walked over and tapped the pile of folders. "The Bible makes it clear that there will always be the poor among us. You do what you can. Stop taking their needs so personally, Boss."

"You sound like Skye. Always telling me it's enough to be doing my best."

"I think I'm going to like her."

"Speaking of Skye, did you find out the name of Johnson's grandson?"

Joyce paused at the door. "I left a message with the realtor. He should be calling back anytime now."

"Let me know as soon as you hear."

Danny opened the next file before she made it out the door.

Danny's heart raced as he drove around the curved driveway. His house sat like a jewel in a bed of emeralds—the grass lush, the trees thick. Surely Skye could find peace here. Anxious to see how she had fared during the day, he drove into the garage and jumped out of the car, gripping a bag of assorted Chinese takeout boxes.

The minute he stepped inside the door, he sensed the difference. No longer did loneliness exude from every corner. Bo charged down the hall, tail wagging, a puppy grin splitting his chops. Wonderful smells greeted him as he neared the kitchen, something sweet with cinnamon. Skye's voice carried a folk song from the seventies, probably one she'd learned from her parents.

A lump formed in his throat when he rounded the corner into the kitchen and saw her standing there at the counter, looking out the window, her voice rising and falling in song. Her braided hair draped across her shoulders, and her skirt flowed around long legs. He wanted to gather her in his arms, but held off, drinking in the sight and sound of her in his home.

Pictures hung on the walls, lending the room a warmth that was lacking before. Linen and candles graced the table. A bottle of Martinelli's Apple-Cranberry sat chilling on the butcher block island. Gone were the stacks of unopened mail, the grocery bags, and other odds and ends he'd left sitting on the counter.

Whining for attention, Bo jumped on him. Skye turned, a smile forming when she saw him. "I thought I smelled something yummy. Figured I was dreaming. What did you bring us?" She reached for the bag.

He wrapped his arms around her, bag and all. "Not anything as delicious as you." He nibbled on her ear, chuckling at her squeals.

Stepping back, he handed her the bag. "Chinese. I hope I didn't spoil whatever that is I smell cooking in the oven."

Setting the bag down, she peered inside and started lifting out cartons. "I thought a cake might taste good later on this evening. I found a mix in your cupboard."

Glancing around the room, he noticed she'd placed pots of greenery in front of the windows, which worked to bring the gardens inside. He wanted to tell her what it meant to come home to the warmth, the delicious smells, her. Instead, he waited beside her. "What song were you singing?"

She glanced up, her eyes locking with his. "Some song my mother used to sing." She shrugged. "I don't know the name of it."

How sad that her mother wasn't alive now, would never know her grandchildren. He ached for Skye. He should take her to meet his mother soon.

"You were busy today." She smiled at him as she set the cartons out on the counter and found spoons for them. "Bedroom furniture arrived. You should have warned me. I had to think fast as to which room to put it in."

"Did you stick with the one looking out over the backyard?"

She chuckled. "That's the one."

He wanted to stop her from puttering and wrap his arms around her. "Do you like it?" He traced his finger up her arm, pleased to see his action had the same tingling effect on her as it did on him. "Joyce, my assistant, found it for me. A friend of hers was giving it away. If you don't like it, we can find something else later. I couldn't have you sleeping on the couch and—"

She placed the tip of her finger on his lips. "It's perfect. Ever since I was a child, I wanted a canopy bed."

His heart swelled with relief and tenderness. "Great! I want you to be comfortable here. So you'll come more often." Her expression closed, and he could have kicked himself. He'd vowed to go slow with her, and here he was jumping ahead. Again. "Don't panic." He dropped his forehead to hers. "I'm not going to rush you into anything. I'm not naturally a very patient man. But I can be."

She leaned her head against his but then abruptly pulled back. "Don't waste time on me. Or your hopes."

"You can't stop me from dreaming, Skye."

She lowered her head, staring at the floor. "What about

Nina? Will she be staying tonight?"

"She said to go ahead and eat. She's coming later." He reached for a glass and filled it with water. "Said you were great with Natasha."

"We got along fine." Skye nodded. "Do you want to go upstairs and take a look now, or have dinner?"

Torn, he studied her features, hoping he hadn't scared her off with his talk. "I want to see what you've done with the bedroom, but then the food would get cold."

"You have a microwave."

"If you're hungry, I can wait."

She took his hand in hers and led him into the hall. "The food will come later. I want you to see the living room, too."

As Danny walked through the house, he realized that Skye had transformed the whole place into a home. In the living room, she'd placed the couch and chairs into a sitting area in front of the fireplace. Instead of spreading out across the room, making it look under-furnished, the positioning brought warmth and coziness. "I can't believe the difference you've made," he commented.

"I didn't do that much, just rearranged the furniture and hung the pictures. Some large plants and trees are all you need to fill these spaces." She pointed to the area behind the couch. "An area rug would add warmth."

"Amazing." He pictured the two of them sitting in front of the fire on a rainy night. Like last night. "Too bad I don't have any firewood. I'll have to order some."

"It's too warm, really. But by winter, you'll want to order in a supply. Come see the rest." She led the way down the hall, where she had hung more paintings. "You have some nice pieces of art."

"Most of them are gifts, with a story to go along with each one. I'll have to tell you all about them."

"I'd like that," she said, sounding sincere. Taking his hand, she led him up the spiral staircase. "Here's the best part."

He glanced at the canopy and the matching comforter piled high with bright-colored pillows. Teal, blue, yellow, purple, and gold. Yes, they looked exactly like something Skye would feel at home in. Bo pounced on one of the pillows that had fallen on the floor. Skye laughed.

He sighed. If Skye were to move in here permanently, he could never stay at the office and work the long hours he did now. He would learn to relax, play with the dog, and talk about his day, letting the stress fall away with her smiles. Tempted to bring up the subject of permanency, he bit his tongue and walked out the door. "We'd better get to that food. I bet you're as hungry as I am."

She turned off the light and followed him down the stairs. "Did you find anything out about Johnson's grandson?"

He slapped his forehead. He'd been so caught up in the warmth of his home that he'd completely forgotten to tell her. "You'll never guess. I know the man. Quite well in fact."

CHAPTER 12

SATURDAY MORNING, Skye followed Danny into the church with mixed feelings of anticipation and apprehension. She wanted to meet Johnson's grandson. Have the opportunity to talk to him about the land he'd inherited. Yet she also worried. Would he listen? She looked at Danny as he walked, obviously very comfortable in the surroundings. Danny knew this man. Said he was honorable. Pastor Ron Evans. A minister.

She paused at the door. Topping off the anxiety regarding Johnson's grandson was trepidation about entering the church. She'd never been inside one before. Her parents had been anti-establishment of any kind. Especially organized religion. Entering a church seemed like a betrayal to her mother and father. Yet Janie belonged and believed. But then, Janie was so different than Skye. Her sister was at home in church, where she could find action to overcome the horror of their parents' deaths.

Glancing into the building, the first thing Skye noticed was the silence. Then color. Shafts of sunlight filtered through stained glass windows depicting scenes with a man as the main focal point. Jesus. She stared, feeling peace like she found in the forest, but deeper. A candle burned at the altar, scenting the room with a sweet floral aroma. Skye breathed in, closing her eyes and drinking in the calm ambiance.

A door opened and closed to her left. A man in his early forties walked toward them, a smile of welcome breaking across his face. "Good to see you." He clapped Danny on the back and then turned to Skye. "And who is this lovely young lady you've brought with you?"

Danny introduced her. "Skye Larsen. She's the one I told you about, who owns land next to your grandfather's on Leeza Island."

"Ahhh, yes. I used to go there as a child with my parents, before your family moved in, but sadly I haven't had time to return since I started my ministry."

Skye held his steady gaze, marveling at the family resemblance. "I'm sorry about your grandfather. He was a wonderful man. Loved by all of us."

"I can believe that." Pastor Evans led them to some benches situated in an alcove. "He's the one who instilled in me the love of God."

"Then you'll understand my request. You see, it was your grandfather's wish as well," she said. Danny clasped her hand, and she held on to it as if to a lifeline.

Pastor Evans frowned. "I don't recall any stipulations to the will. What is the nature of your request, Miss Larsen?"

Skye stared in surprise. "You didn't receive my letter from the realtor? I sent it several weeks ago."

He shook his head. "I'm trying to recall, but we've been so busy with plans for a new gymnasium for the youth programs. I'm afraid I left the details to the realtor."

Her shoulders sagged, but she snapped them back up. No need to give up, not with this man in front of her, listening attentively. "The land borders a preserve for the eagles. Your grandfather promised never to build on it. He loved the eagles and the island. He could see all the new houses going up. He wanted part of the island preserved naturally."

"It is a prime piece of land, Ron. Very peaceful. Pristine," Danny added.

Pastor Evans rubbed at his jaw, clearly stressed over this news. "Wish I'd known about this sooner. I've already agreed to sell to—"

"No!" Skye jumped up. "You can't sell. Who knows what the new owners will do with the property?"

Danny stood and clasped his arm around her shoulder. "Take it easy, Skye." He turned to Pastor Evans. "Is the offer firm? Could you back out and change your mind?"

Pastor Evans, standing with them, shifted from one foot to another. "I'd like to say I would." He shrugged and held out his hands. "If it were just me, I'd agree in a heartbeat, but I have the church board to consider."

"The church board? How are they involved?" Danny asked.

"My dad and uncle offered to donate the money from the sale to finance a house that will be a church-sponsored safe house for abused women. The rest will be the down payment on the gymnasium we're building."

Skye sank against Danny's chest, despair washing through her. He tightened his arm around her. "Don't give up yet," he whispered, but she could hear a hint of the same despair in his voice.

"The buyers are only interested in the undeveloped property. There's still the house for sale. Would it help to have that?" Pastor Evans asked, a look of hope easing some of the strain from his face. "I haven't had a chance to get over there yet to see the condition of the place."

Skye shook her head, forcing back the tears threatening to fall. "It's the land we need for a preserve."

"I'm sorry. So many people need the food and housing we plan to buy with the money from the sale."

She could tell the pastor truly was sorry. She could understand his position. He was involved with the needy. She, with the eagles and the land. A conflict of interests.

Danny talked with the pastor for several more minutes about GANG, but she tuned out their conversation, her mind racing. What was she going to do? How could she live without the land to meditate on and with yuppies next door? How could the eagles survive a building project? What would happen to her beloved island?

In a daze, she followed Danny back to the car. The crowded streets blurred as she forced back tears. He stopped at a mall, but she refused to leave the car. "I'm sorry. I can't face the crowds right now. Please understand."

Danny gripped the steering wheel, obviously debating whether to leave her alone.

"I'll be all right. There aren't too many people here." She gestured toward the parking lot. "I know you need to buy some things for your house."

He traced a finger down her cheek. "I was hoping you'd help me pick them out. You have much better taste than I. Besides, if you stay here, you'll mope. Shopping will take your mind off the situation."

She looked at him. At the tenderness in his eyes. She wanted to lash out. To scream. But not at Danny. Against her better judgment, she opened the car door and climbed out.

He came around the front of the car. Smiling, he took her hand, tucking it into the crook of his arm. "Want to get a bite to eat first?"

The thought of food turned her stomach. "No. What exactly are we looking for?"

"Furniture."

Walking through the parking lot wasn't bad. The cars were simply machines waiting for their owners. But inside the mall, people milled, music dinned from every storefront, all blending into a cacophony of noises. Teens with spiked hair of every color of the rainbow, accented with rings through ears, noses, and belly buttons. Some dressed in gothic black, metal chains hanging from their jeans and around their necks. Images flashed of the teens who had murdered her parents. It took every bit of self-control to keep from running back outdoors. To stay at Danny's side.

Shaking off the thought, she focused on the displays in the windows. Her nostrils flared with the smells of popcorn, cookies, and scented candles mixed into a sickening sweet mélange. Her head beginning to ache, she squeezed Danny's arm tighter and tighter as they strolled deeper into the mall.

Danny stopped at a furniture store and looked at the dining table in the display window. "What do you think? Wouldn't it fit in the breakfast nook?"

"What you have is fine, since it's only you," she snapped, her head pounding.

Danny stopped and turned to face her. "What's wrong? You look like a ghost."

She took a deep breath, fighting for control of her emotions. "I have to get out of here," she gritted between clenched teeth. "Take me. Please."

Without argument, he grasped her elbow and turned around to head back toward the mall entrance. "I'll have you home in no time. We're only about twenty minutes away."

"No." She stopped, barely missing a run-in with a stroller. She stepped around the smiling child while Danny apologized to the harried mother.

Danny looked at Skye, a question in his eyes. "What do you mean? Do you want to stay?"

She shook her head, fighting the tears brimming in her eyes. "I want to go home. To Leeza."

Air whooshed from his lungs as he raked fingers through his hair. "Saturday isn't a good shopping day. Too many people. You're upset about the sale of the land. You'll feel better at the house, with a hot cup of tea and a romp with Bo."

A tear ran down her cheek. Danny brushed it with his

thumb, his touch tender and sweet. She didn't want to hurt him, but... "I can't stay here in the city, Danny. I don't belong." Not here with all of these people. With him—a man who worked with these kids.

To her relief, he didn't argue. Wrapping his arm around her waist, he guided her out of the mall and opened the car door for her. Once inside, another tear fell as she watched him walk around the front of the car. How could she leave him? But how could she stay? If only there was some kind of work for him to do on the island. Something to get him away from working with gangs.

They drove in silence. At the house, he pulled up the curved drive to the front door and handed her a set of keys. "Get your things ready. I have to get gas for the car and arrange for the plane."

"You're t...taking me back to the island?"

He gently wiped a tear from under her eye. "Isn't that what you wanted?"

"Yes." She stared into his eyes and leaned her cheek into the palm of his hand. "And no. I want to be with you, Danny, but the city..." She trembled.

He smiled. "I'll be with you. Until Sunday evening, anyway. You've made a big move coming here. We'll take this one step at a time."

Another tear slipped down her cheek. "I don't deserve you. And you certainly can do better than me."

He laughed. "Let's say we deserve each other and let it go at that. Go on in now and pack your things. You might want to take Bo for a romp before we put him in the carrier. I'll be back in about a half-hour."

Slipping from the car, she took a deep breath. The peaceful surroundings mocked her fear. Didn't she want to have a relationship with love and commitment? How silly to be so afraid.

How could she overcome these crazy panic reactions—this fear?

While Bo ran around in the yard, she put her things in her backpack. Silently, she descended the stairs and went into the living room, where she had arranged the furniture yesterday. Trailing her fingers over the picture frames, she fought the yearnings welling inside of her. Her family had never collected works of art, nor had they ever had a home in which to display them. Her father had painted, but just as quickly sold the pieces for money to buy pot. She'd always said that if she had children, she would want them to have a permanent home. A place where they could hang pictures on the wall—pictures of their childhood, special events, their own works of art. Something she didn't have room for in her small cabin on the island.

She smiled, thinking of a wall plastered with bright-colored finger paintings, photos of laughing faces, and little sayings like she'd seen from Lenny's grandchildren hanging on her refrigerator.

Skye went to the end table where she'd placed Danny's Bible and a pewter cross mounted on a redwood burl. She trailed her fingers over the cross. Janie said God could help her overcome her fear. Could He? Janie was never afraid. Of course, she hadn't been there when their parents were murdered. Not like Skye had been. But still, maybe she should ask Danny about it. He knew. He believed.

Danny glanced at his watch, knowing he would be late getting back to Skye if he made another call. But she was at his home and Bo was with her. She'd be all right. Punching the cell phone, he called Pastor Ron.

"Danny, what's up?" Ron sounded surprised to hear from

him so soon.

"I wanted to ask about that land on Leeza Island we discussed. If I can swing a loan, could I outbid the offer you have on the table now?"

It would mean he'd have to give up his option to buy the house he was renting, but he'd rather not have it anyway if Skye wasn't going to be able to live there. "I'd like to bid on your grandfather's house, too."

Ron paused. "The house is no problem. But the land..." Danny could hear papers shuffling in the background. "I'm looking at the contract. We signed the paperwork already."

Danny's shoulders slumped in defeat. "Let me know if they back out on the deal, would you?"

"You got it. And Danny, thanks for bringing Skye by this morning. From the looks of you, you're serious about her."

Danny smiled. "I'm working on it, Pastor. We have some problems to hurdle. She has some history and doesn't want anything to do with the city."

"Can't blame her there. I'd choose Leeza Island over Seattle any day." His chuckle carried deep across the line.

"But my job is here in Seattle. You know what my work schedule is like. I couldn't commute from Leeza Island, even with a plane. The commute from the airport is worse than from my house."

"Hmmm, well, let me know if there's anything I can do to help her. The Lord has gifted me with counseling skills."

Danny shifted the phone to his other ear, thinking. "I might take you up on that. Any chance you can get out to the island?"

"As much as I'd love to, no. But bring her by anytime."

"That's another problem. Seems to be resisting church, as far as I can tell. Her sister's a believer, but Skye doesn't seem interested."

"Take heart, Danny. Sounds like people are praying for her."

"That's encouraging. Anything I should do?"

"You're probably already doing it."

"That's a heavy responsibility. I've never been strong on evangelizing."

"Don't try, my friend. Just be yourself."

About to hang up the phone, Danny paused when he heard Ron's voice. "And, Danny?"

"Yeah?"

"Don't rush things. Your time and God's time are entirely different."

"You'd think I'd have learned that one by now." Danny chuckled and clicked off the phone. He shifted the car into gear and headed for his house. Could Ron be right? Warmth crept into his body. Now if only he could manage to say the right words, be patient and prayerful.

When he arrived at the house, he called out for Skye, but she was nowhere to be found. For a second, he panicked. Could she have called a cab and left without him? He glanced out the window and saw her playing with Bo. He heaved a sigh of relief and went outside. "Sorry I'm late. My errand took more time than I planned." Bo charged over with a stick in his mouth. "But it doesn't look like you missed me that much." He bent over and patted the pup.

"Yes, we did," she said, smiling. The tension and fear had disappeared from her eyes. "But we figured you were tied up."

"That's one thing about Leeza Island. No phones. No demands. Are you ready to head out?"

She hurried to his side, calling Bo. "It's a beautiful day. You can tell summer is on its way."

Danny clenched his fists, resisting the urge to kiss her. Resisting the urge to grab her and force her to stay here in Seattle with him. Instead, he held out his hand and treasured the feel of hers in his.

The weather was perfect for flying. Sunny and calm. He watched as Skye stared out the window, exclaiming over the scenery. Rainier stood like a sentinel, towering over the other mountains, Seattle sprawled at its base. To the south, other volcanoes rose above the horizon—Mt. Adams, slightly to the east of Mount St. Helens. Farther up the coast, they could see Baker, the northernmost volcano in the Pacific chain looking like an upside-down snow cone with its ice cap and glaciers.

Islands dotted Puget Sound like emeralds set in crystal glass. He pointed out Deception Point on Whidbey Island across from the town of Anacortes, jutting out on a mainland peninsula. He chuckled as Skye practically glued her nose to the glass window.

"I can't believe how much forest has been cut for industry and housing," she exclaimed. "It was raining when Fred flew me over. We couldn't see all of this."

Danny banked so she could view the Olympic Peninsula. "The area along the coast is pretty well-developed, but over there on the Peninsula there's still virgin forest, thanks to the National Park System."

"How long does it take to fly to Leeza Island from Seattle?"

"About an hour is all, depending on the traffic and the weather."

"Couldn't you live on Leeza Island and commute?"

He leveled the plane and pointed north. "Sounds feasible. Most Americans have a longer commute in their cars. But it isn't just the flight. I have to get to the office from the airport, which is another hour."

"You could find another job. One in Bellingham."

He took a deep breath and looked her in the eye. "I love my job, Skye. I couldn't leave."

She nodded, but he could see the disappointment in her eyes. Good. At least she wanted to be with him. Would that desire be enough, though, to overcome her fear of the city?

"I could probably manage to spend a lot of time on the island during the summer, but not the winters." He shrugged. "The winds and storms are too dangerous for a small landing strip like the one on the island." Danny glanced at her, loving the crinkles around her eyes when she smiled, the golden hair framing her tanned cheeks. He shook his head. He'd find a way. He had to. He couldn't go through another month like the last one, yearning to be with her. Thinking of her every spare moment. Even during the moments he couldn't spare, which made concentrating on work an endeavor in and of itself.

"Ted's planning to go to Europe off and on during the summer. I'm sure he'd let me use his house." How was he going to find the time to get over there every weekend? Gripping the controls, he banked to the right. "Ron said his house is still for sale. Maybe I'll look into buying it."

She shifted position to face him. "Two realtors came by the other day offering to trade the house for mine."

Danny tightened his grip. The plane dove. He quickly pulled it up. "What are you talking about?"

Skye explained her encounter with the realtors. "I was stunned. I can't imagine what they would want with my cockeyed house instead of Johnson's house. I mean, his place is huge."

It didn't take much math for Danny to figure it out. "Do you have their names?"

"They gave me their card."

"Good. Give it to me when we get to the island. I think I'll give them a call."

"You can't think I want to trade my house?"

It would be perfect. He couldn't see himself in her cracker box house. But he'd bet dollars to donuts that her house wouldn't be standing long once the realtors got a hold of it. "They didn't say what they were planning to do with the land, did they?"

"No. They just wanted more property."

Danny's knuckles whitened as he gripped the controls. He could picture it now. A condominium complex. Timeshares. The perfect setting for a huge resort offering seaside views, fishing, sailboats, probably a tennis court, maybe even a golf course. He slid a glance at Skye. It would break her heart.

An ache tore at his heart—not for the land, but for her. He wanted to protect her. Keep her world safe. But the wheels of progress were grinding down on her. Maybe taking her away would be a good thing. She wouldn't have to see her beloved island desecrated by development, crowded with tourists.

"I'll ask them when I call. Always good to know who your neighbors are."

He saw her shudder and reached out for her hand. She clasped it, her fingers tight and trembling. "I don't want new neighbors. I like things the way they are."

"I know, but sometimes things change. We can't always prevent that." Though he would try. For her sake. "We have to trust that God will make good out of the circumstances. He promises to give us the strength to carry on."

"I'd rather your God just stopped the whole mess."

He laughed. He couldn't help it. Not with the indignant pout and the quirk on her lips. "Honey, if God would do that for us, then we'd all be believers. No, it's faith He wants to develop in us."

She folded her arms across her chest. "Humph. Ruining an

island seems like an odd way to get someone to have faith in you."

His stomach lurched when an air bump lifted the plane and dropped it. He looked at Skye and saw the worried look on her face. An idea of how he could teach her about faith occurred to him. He throttled down the engine, let go of the controls, and sat back.

Alarmed, she stared, her eyes wide. "What are you doing?"

"Kicking back. Why don't you fly the plane?"

Straightening upright, she squealed, "Me? I don't know how to fly this thing."

He put his hands behind his head in an exaggerated pose of relaxation. "Nothing to it. Simply grab the controls and keep her level."

Her look of panic almost made him give in. Then she grasped the controls and leveled the plane. He smiled and pointed to one of the gauges. "That line represents the wings. Keep it parallel to that other line. When you do, we're flying horizontal and straight."

"Danny, this is not funny. You take back the controls right this minute."

He faked a yawn. "It feels good to relax."

"Okay, but just for a minute. I mean it. I can barely drive a car, let alone a plane."

"Know why I'm not worried?" He cast her a sideways glance, fighting the temptation to lean over and plant a quick kiss on her worried lips.

"Because you're crazy."

"Nope. Because I have faith."

"You think God's going to fly this plane? Fine." She lifted her hands off the controls and held them in the air. "That I want to see."

Chuckling, he caught hold of one of her hands and placed

it back on the controls. "No, God isn't going to fly this plane. But I have faith that it will not crash. You want to know why?"

A look of exasperated humor began twinkling in her eyes as she stared at the gauge and worked to keep the plane level. "I'm sure you'll tell me."

"Because I know the nature of flying. I studied aerodynamics. I know that we are gliding and will continue to do so with very little or no effort on our part."

She crossed her arms across her chest again. "The point of this lesson being...?"

"I know God's nature. I have studied His Word, learned His character. That is how I can have faith, even when it looks like my world is falling apart."

She studied his face for several long seconds. Danny held her gaze, unflinching. "I've got to hand it to you," she finally said. "You're better at explaining faith than Janie is."

Laughing, he reached his arm across her shoulders and nuzzled her neck, the closest to a hug he could give in the cramped quarters. Her shoulders shook with her own laughter.

Straightening, he glanced out the window. "There's the island." He took over the controls.

"And there's the lighthouse." She pointed.

Hope welled within as he eyed the beacon. Skye had not dismissed his lesson. "Get ready to land," he said.

In minutes, he had touched down and taxied across the grassy runway to his parking place. He grabbed the carrier from the back, then climbed out to tie down the plane. Bo took off the second they let him out, sniffing and exploring his territory. Danny ached when he saw the look of joy on Skye's face as she set foot on her beloved island.

"I have to pick up the keys to Ted's house. Want to go on ahead to your place?"

She shook her head. "I'll walk with you. It feels good to get some exercise."

As they walked toward the Harris residence, Jack and Lenny came running out of their house, both talking at the same time.

"Skye. We're so glad to see you."

"We're so sorry."

Skye halted when she saw the looks of horror cutting across their faces. "Sorry? What's wrong?"

CHAPTER 13

JACK REACHED HER FIRST. "Your house caught on fire. It burned to the ground. There's nothing left."

Skye froze, stunned. Fingers tightening into fists, her heart pumped at an alarming rate. "What are you saying? No. It can't be."

Lenny caught up to Jack and gave Skye a bear hug. "I'm sorry, honey. The whole island showed up. We tried to put it out, but we were too late. It's been so dry this year." She released Skye and stepped back. "I tried calling you at Janie's, but she wasn't there, and the woman who answered the phone had no clue where you were."

Still stunned, Skye stood immobile, struggling to breathe, to speak. "H…how did it start?"

Jack lifted his baseball cap and ran his fingers through his hair before he set it back on top of his head. "Don't know. You'd already taken off with Fred. A couple hours later, we noticed the smoke. Didn't think much of it. Thought you'd left a fire in your stove."

Lenny hooked her arm through Jack's. "The smoke kept getting thicker and darker. We knew something was wrong. But by the time we got there, the fire had taken hold."

"I didn't leave a fire going."

"The sheriff found a jar that smelled of gasoline. He thinks it was vandals."

Skye tensed. Vandals? Setting fires on her island? No, there had to be another explanation.

Danny stepped close beside her, gently reminding her of his

presence. "Did she lose the whole house? Everything?" he asked.

Images raced through her mind. Her father pounding nails, her mother hanging curtains, her grandmother sitting by the stove. Gone. Her whole life gone. The afghans she'd crocheted, one for each year of her self-imposed exile. The few photos she had of her parents. The books of poetry her grandmother cherished. Irreplaceable.

A deep sorrow engulfed her. The heartache of loss, similar to the grief she'd felt when her parents were killed. When her grandmother had died. Tears streamed down her cheeks.

Lenny left Jack's side and wrapped her arm around Skye's shoulders. "Go ahead and cry, honey. Come on inside the kitchen. I'll make you some tea."

She went with Lenny but was relieved that Danny followed close. Inside the house, she looked around, absorbing the familiar surroundings, the closest to a home she had now. She lowered her head and sobbed. "What am I going to do? Where am I going to live?"

Lenny patted her shoulder. "You're staying here with us for the time being."

She raised her head. Through her tears, she could see the concern, the love of the older woman. "I can't impose on you like that. Besides, aren't you heading for Vendovi Island?"

"We leave tomorrow. Since you'll be staying here, we'll leave Mutt for you to take care of. That'll make it easier on us."

Skye wiped at her eyes, blew her nose. "You're sure?"

"I won't hear otherwise. At least until you sort out some plans of your own." She glanced at Danny.

"I'll call Ted. He's going to be gone all summer. My guess is he'll let you stay there until your house is rebuilt."

Skye gasped.

He studied her face. "You do have insurance, don't you?"

Knowing he'd seen her look of horror, she shook her head.

"Didn't have the money for it."

Lenny and Jack groaned in unison.

"Oh, sweetheart." Danny reached out and pulled her into his arms.

"I never thought I'd need it out here," she murmured against his chest.

Lenny continued to pat her shoulder. "Honey, we'll figure something out. We won't let you down. I bet with everyone on the island pulling together, we can find a way to build something."

She snuggled close to Danny and lowered her head, hiding the tears pouring down her face. The cost of construction was prohibitive, especially on the island. She knew because she'd had some estimates for enlarging her house. No way could they dig up enough funds for a whole building starting from scratch.

Tucking a finger beneath her chin, Danny raised her head until her eyes met his. He brushed her cheeks, wiping the tears with his handkerchief. "There's Johnson's house. You said those realtors offered to trade."

Jack sat across from her, excitement lighting his gray eyes. "You're right about that. Those dudes wanted your land. I bet their offer is still good."

A ray of hope flickered then died. "They aren't going to want to trade now, with the house gone."

Danny traced his thumb across her cheek. "They didn't want the house. They'll probably be glad it's gone."

Horrified, she gasped at the cold reality. "You mean they just want the land? You don't think they set the fire, do you, thinking then I would trade?"

Jack shifted. "No, I doubt they would go to that extreme. Besides, they weren't here on the island."

"I think they just want a bigger lot for their house." Danny clasped her hand.

She'd suspected that, but to hear the stark truth sent her heart pounding. "I can't let them build a bigger house so close to the eagles."

Danny entwined his fingers through hers. "They're going to build anyway. If they have more land, they'll build where your house was since it's cleared. That will save the other piece from being cut back. There'll still be trees left for the eagles."

His logic, unsettling as it was, made sense. In a way, her house had become the ultimate sacrifice to save the lot next to the eagles. Her sanctuary. She might still be able to go there. But she wouldn't have her house. Her home. Gone. Impossible. She pulled away from Danny. "I've got to go see."

Lenny clasped her arm. "Honey, it's not a good idea. Stay here. With us."

Skye jerked away from Lenny's hand and walked out the door. "I'll be back. I need to see for myself."

Danny held up his hand before Lenny could protest further. "I'll go with her. She needs to witness the site. We both do."

Lenny nodded in acquiescence. "We'll keep Bo here with Mutt. Otherwise, he'll be covered with soot."

Skye put Bo in the pen and closed the gate. The fresh breeze blew across her face, drying the remnants of her tears. She hurried across the runway and up the hill, Danny close behind her. There had to be something left. Some pieces of pottery. Her shovel. Her loom.

She smelled the acrid odor of burnt fabrics, plastics, and other man-made items even before they reached her lot. Not the clean, woodsy smell of logs burning in a fireplace. She halted at the edge of the path to her house and stared at the scorched trees, the pile of black charcoal and ashes, the empty space where her house had stood.

She took a step toward the rubble. "Gone! Everything's burned to the ground."

Danny reached for her hand. "Be careful. There'll be broken glass and nails."

"How did this start, Danny? I'm sure I turned off the propane. The stove only had a few small coals from the night before. Not enough to light a fire, even if I did leave the door open."

"No candles?" He pulled her close as if wanting to protect her from her anguish and pain.

She snuggled against him and shook her head, racking her brain, going over every detail of every minute before she left. Nothing. She could think of nothing to cause the fire. But Lenny said the sheriff had found a gas can. She hated the doubts and fears threatening to consume her. "Do you really think someone started the fire on purpose? Why would they? What would they have to gain?" Her property?

"It was raining the day you arrived in the city. Perhaps lightning struck."

"It had to be. I don't want to think of anything else." She shifted away from him and wandered into the pile of ashes. "I'll ask Jack if he heard any thunder because it seems to me it was a steady rain."

Tears streaked down her cheeks as she picked through the pile of ruins. The glassware had melted. Some pieces of metal could still be used, but not for their original intent. She would have to start all over. Overwhelmed by the thought, she sat on the scorched ground. "I can't do this," she murmured.

Danny hunkered down beside her. "Leave it. There's nothing here you're going to be able to use."

"Not that." Elbows braced on her knees, she cupped her head between her palms. "I can't start over."

"You don't have to. Come to Seattle. We'll start a new life. Together." He reached his arm around her shoulders.

She frowned, yearning to say yes, but knowing she had to

say no. "In Seattle? I can't do that, either." She wanted to. She wanted to stay curled in the safety of his arms and remain there forever. But it wouldn't be fair to give him that hope.

He sat on the charred ground beside her and tucked her closer against his chest. "Don't close your mind. Let the idea gel for a while. In the meantime, I'll get in touch with those realtors on the mainland. See if they still want to trade the property."

"You don't think they could have been involved? Did this to force me to trade?"

"Jack doesn't think so, but I'll look into it when I get back to Seattle. In the meantime, a trade will give you a house. At least then you'll be set."

Would she? Yes, she'd have a roof over her head, but what about a life with Danny? Was that what she really wanted?

Longings welled. Images flashed. Children ran in the yard in Seattle, but another montage appeared—images of children running here on the island. Healthy children. Normal children. Not gangbangers. Not children afraid of their shadows like her.

She shook her head. Her yearnings were not only for Danny, but also yearnings for love, a husband, a family. She pushed them down. Determination grinding through her, she stood and brushed off the soot. "Let's ask Jack if he has keys to Mr. Johnson's place. We might as well go take a look." She hadn't been in the house since Johnson had left.

Danny walked with her down the trail. "Sounds like a good idea. Even if the realtors aren't interested in a trade any-more, we might be able to make some arrangement with Ron." He picked up his pace to keep up with her. "Sure am glad you have your backpack with a few clothes in it."

"And my money. I'll have to go shopping." She shuddered at the thought.

"Come back with me to Seattle. We'll go shopping there."

Images of the crowded mall cropped up—the strong

scents, the noise, and the hordes of people. "No. Danny, I know you want a relationship, but, you've made it clear you won't leave your job."

"We can find a place outside of Seattle. I'll commute."

"It isn't that. I can't be with you, knowing you'll be spending every day with those kids."

Stopping mid-stride, he grasped her hand and pulled her around to face him. "You mean the problem isn't Seattle; it's my job?"

Color crept up her cheeks as she lowered her head. "Nina told me about Virginia. I can't do the same thing to you as she did."

He dropped her hand as if it were on fire. Spinning around, he stared out to sea where the lighthouse stood, a mockery to their hopes and dreams. His jaw muscles twitching, he gritted his teeth. "You couldn't possibly do the same thing as Virginia. You're as different as night and day."

Recoiling, Skye straightened her shoulders. "But we do feel the same way about your job." She stepped toward him and placed her hand on his arm. His muscles flexed under her fingers as he turned to face her. "I would be terrified that one day you wouldn't come home."

Placing his other hand over hers, he squeezed her fingers. "I'm in no danger. Not really. The kids respect me."

She stepped back. "I know what they can do, Danny. I've seen it."

Tracing his finger down her cheek, he remained silent, but she could see the pity in his eyes. She jerked away and started toward the dock. "I need to go to Bellingham. Get some food and some more clothes."

Undaunted by her rejection, he kept in step beside her. "We could fly over there right now, rent a car, and be back before dinner."

Her mind raced. They hadn't brought groceries because she had planned on using what she had at her place. But surely he didn't want to spend more time with her after what she had just said. "You don't mind?"

"I don't give up easily, Skye. I'm here to help."

She cast a sideways look at his set features, somehow not minding the fact that he was so determined. "Fred Davis has flown Janie and me over. There's a superstore close to the airport. We can take a taxi when we get there. They have food, clothes, everything I'll need."

"We'll leave Bo with Mutt and head over right now. Let's go tell Lenny and Jack our plans so they won't worry." Danny led her across the airstrip, back to the Harris's house.

In less than an hour, the taxi swung into the parking lot of the large store. It took another hour for Skye to find the clothes she wanted. Not much—some extra underwear, a pair of shorts for warm days, another skirt and blouse.

"Don't forget sundries." Danny guided her into the pharmacy section of the store. "You don't think about all the small things you take for granted every day—toothpaste, brush and comb, hand cream, and..." He fidgeted, his face scrunched and a hint of red creeping up his neck. "You know, personal things you women need."

Skye smiled at his discomfiture. "Fortunately, I have some of those things in my backpack. I do need to get soap and some towels though."

Danny stacked the items in the cart as she handed them to him. "Do you want to have a bite to eat before we shop for food?"

She nodded. "It's best not to shop while you're hungry."

He grinned back at her. "Since space is limited on the plane, it's probably a good idea."

Danny rolled the full cart outside the store's coffee shop and told the clerk they would be back to pick it up. Skye found an empty booth and slid into it while she waited for him. What a wonderful man, she mused, thankful for all of his attention and glad he was with her. She could easily picture a life with him. But he was a counselor, and he worked with gangs. Could she ever trust that he was safe and feel at peace in a relationship with him?

Danny sat across from her and fidgeted with the menu before opening it. Finally, he grabbed her menu, putting it down with his, and clasped her hands. "That fire shook me up. What if you'd been home? Been inside when it started?" He shuddered.

Skye turned her hand in his and squeezed. "I'm all right. That's the main thing."

Her winsome smile tore at his heart. Thankfully she had been with him instead of on the island. Alone. Afraid. "You're right." He patted her arm. "When I think of what could have happened to you, the material things become unimportant. They can be replaced."

"Most can," she agreed. "But things like Granny's belongings, the chair my father carved, the pillows my mom made, those are precious because of the memories. They're a part of me."

"I can't even imagine what you are going through, Skye." He traced the delicate veins on her hand and looked deep into her eyes. "You've suffered a traumatic loss. I don't know how to replace those things."

"We can't."

The sadness he saw tore at his gut. "Can we start a new set of memories, a new set of keepsakes?"

A tear streaked down her cheek, but she nodded.

The waitress arrived to take their order. After they downed hamburgers and fries, Danny helped Skye out of the booth. "Why don't you start on the groceries? I'm going to take advantage of being in cell-phone range and call Ted, the pastor, and the realtors." He wanted to be sure Skye had a place to stay before he returned to Seattle tomorrow.

Watching her push the cart away, he felt the now familiar tug at his heart. Her flowered skirt, so typical of her style, swayed around her legs as she walked straight and tall. So strong. Yet so vulnerable. He yearned to love her. Protect her. And, yes, eventually marry her.

But how? Images of Virginia swamped him. Her disapproval of his work had never waned in spite of all he'd done to try to impress her. Would he have any better luck with Skye? Doubt curled in his stomach, but he replaced it with a deep breath of determination. He would try.

Sighing, he turned and went outside where he could get better cell reception. Ted had no problem with Skye staying at his house. "I made arrangements to spend the Fourth of July at the cabin with friends, but I can easily cancel those plans."

Relieved, Danny called the pastor next. "Tell her we can find a place here in the city for her to stay," Ron offered.

Danny shook his head while he paced the sidewalk outside the store. "I tried that. She wants to stay on the island. Could she stay in your grandfather's house? Ted offered his, but it's only a temporary arrangement."

Ron paused, responding to his secretary in the background. "There has been some interest in it. She's welcome to stay, but if it sells, she'll be forced to move again."

Danny stopped mid-stride. "Don't sign any papers yet. I'm thinking of making an offer on it myself." First, he'd check with the realtors. He'd let them buy Johnson's place if they would trade the property with Skye. "Unless it's an offer from Sawyer Realtors. They offered to trade the house for Skye's property. I'm hoping they still want her land." He explained the situation.

"Keep me posted. I'll check with you before I sign anything," Ron said. "And Danny, you know I'd offer her the place, but I've committed the money to the church."

"She understands that." He thought of her resolve, her pride. "I doubt she'd take a handout anyway." Which was why he hoped the realtors hadn't been involved in the fire and still wanted to trade. She would be just as reluctant to accept the house from him.

"I think you're right."

His fingers tightened around the phone. "She's gone through so much. God is watching out for her, isn't He?" He tried to rein in the edge of anger threatening.

"Could be God's way of nudging her in the right direction. You know His ways."

Danny closed his eyes, knowing he couldn't marry Skye until she had found peace with his line of work. "Guess this could be a positive thing. Just seems rather drastic," he admitted.

"Keep the faith. I'll do my part with the prayers."

"Thanks. We need it." Danny clicked off and punched in the number Skye had given him.

"Sawyer Realtors. Jed speaking. If we don't have what you want, we'll find it for you."

"That's what I'm counting on." Danny explained the situation and was relieved to know that the realtor was still interested in Skye's property. He had to restrain himself from responding to Sawyer's obvious delight in the fact that he wouldn't have to tear down the house. Had they been behind the fire after all? If they had been, would he want Skye out there on the island with them? What were they planning anyway?

"You going to develop the area?" Danny asked.

"We're still in the planning stages, but we think the area is perfect for timeshare condominiums."

Danny had to agree, even though the news would devastate Skye. And it didn't alleviate his doubts about their involvement in the fire. "You know there's a couple of lots that are protected. A pair of eagles nest there."

"So we were told. At first we thought it might be a problem, but now see it as an asset."

"How so?"

"We advertise it as one of the features. Our target market will be outdoor enthusiasts. They'll love the environmental element."

Smart man. Danny had to admire his astute business sense. It would bring up the value of the property. If the Sawyers traded the house with Skye and she found out the realtors were involved in the fire, she could at least sell and have money to buy somewhere else. "So how soon do you think you can act on the property? Can Skye stay in the house now?" He explained that Ron Evans wouldn't have any objection.

Sawyer paused amid the rustle of papers. "I don't think there should be a problem. We'll get in touch with Evans and get the paperwork out there next week sometime. She can take possession as soon as she signs. We'll write that into the agreement."

A load lifted from Danny's shoulders. He would have moved back into an apartment in order to buy Johnson's place, but he knew she wouldn't accept the house from him as a gift. Besides, he wanted to keep his house in Seattle. He still had hopes that Skye would at least want to visit him there. From the house, he could ease her into the mainstream of the city at a slow pace. Not like he'd done this morning, taking her to the mall right off the bat. Foolish. He cringed, thinking about her unusual reaction.

Then there was the issue of GANG. If he could convince her to come to Seattle, he could show her that there was no more danger working there than anywhere. After all, he had a bigger chance of getting nailed on the freeway than at work. Wouldn't be a wise argument, though. But if he could talk Nina into bringing more girls over, Skye would see for herself.

He felt better leaving her on the island, knowing she had a place to stay. Quickly he called Ted again to inform him he didn't have to cancel his Independence Day plans. "Sounds like your trip to the island did you good in more ways than one," his benefactor teased.

Danny smiled. "Thanks to you."

Ted's chuckle rang in Danny's ear. "Can't wait until the Fourth. I know Skye, but not well. She always kept to herself. Barb and I are anxious to get to know her better."

When Ted's secretary interrupted the call. Danny signed off and returned to the store to locate Skye. He found her selecting fresh fruit in the produce section.

She smiled when she spotted him. "Do you like strawberries? They're coming into season."

He stepped beside her and reached for the luscious fruit. "Depends on what you're going to do with them. Now a strawberry shortcake—"

"Is easy to make." She grinned as she swatted his hand away. "Behave yourself and pick out some apples while I finish here."

After selecting the fruit, he followed her around the store, admiring the frugal and efficient way she shopped. He told her about his phone conversations and delighted in the way her eyes lit up when he said Jed Sawyer still wanted to trade her property for Johnson's house.

"It's hard to believe he wants to make the trade just to have a bigger lot."

"He'll have a bigger lot, and you'll have a bigger house."

She paused, a jug of milk dangling from her fingers. "I didn't need a bigger house."

He slipped the jug from her hand and put it in the basket. She started to push the cart down the aisle, but he stood in her way and leaned over the basket toward her. "It will never replace the house your father built, Skye. I know that. I'm trying to help you see the positive side of this."

She took a deep breath. "You're right. I'll still have the memories, even without the material things."

His heart ached when he saw the tears brimming in her eyes. "Remember, you'll be able to make new memories. With me."

She rolled her eyes and nudged him out of the way. "Now that we know the realtors want to trade, I can hardly wait to return to the island and check out the house—see what I need."

Danny didn't tell her about the development the realtor planned. She'd had enough traumatic news for one day. "How much more shopping do you have?"

"Getting restless, Flyboy?"

"Looking forward to a walk on the beach."

Her face fell. "I'm ruining your weekend. Your only time off."

He reached across the cart and cupped her cheek. "Nothing is ruined as long as I'm with you." He smiled. "I just want you all to myself."

He watched the play of emotions flit across her face. Knowing he had to get away from her for a moment or make a spectacle of himself by kissing her in the middle of the store, he pulled his hand back to his side. "I'll meet you by the checkout stand. I want to pick out something to drink for dinner tonight."

She nodded and continued down the aisle. Reluctantly, he turned and walked to the shelves sporting various selections of juice. How he wanted to make this domestic chore an everyday habit. How he longed to plan meals they would share. To carve out a new life as a couple. It might take a year or two of only having summers with each other. But hopefully she would overcome her fears and he could convince her they needed to be together. She was worth the wait.

It took another hour to check out of the store, load the plane, and unload it again on the grass runway of the island. Danny insisted on getting Ted's cart and hauling the supplies to Ted's place. "You'll be sleeping at Lenny's, but you'll be spending the day and eating your meals with me, won't you?"

She didn't argue. In fact, she seemed pleased. "But I'll need some of these things at Lenny's." She pointed to the flannel pajamas and other personal items.

"You're right about that. Why don't you make two piles while I go get the cart? We'll take the food to Ted's and then the other things to Lenny's. While we're there, we'll get the key and go over to the Johnson house. We'll make a list of the things you'll need that I can bring next week from Seattle."

Pausing with an armload of grocery bags, she smiled at him. "You're coming back next weekend?"

Understanding the trauma of losing one's house and the emotional aftermath that would surely come, he knew he had to return. He couldn't leave her here to face that alone. He didn't know how he was going to work out his schedule, but he'd do it, if for no other reason than to see her smile. "I'll fly out Friday night. Weather permitting."

An hour later, Danny worked the old-fashioned key into the lock. The door creaked as it swung open. Stale air rushed out. Skye opened the drapes, causing shafts of sunlight to brighten the room. Dust motes rose around them as they stepped onto the hardwood floor.

The rockwork of the fireplace covered the opposite wall from the door. Danny could picture the welcoming warmth of a fire. To the left, sliding glass doors opened onto a deck that looked out over Puget Sound. Behind him to the right was a large kitchen set apart from the main room by a bar. He could see a door leading down a hall, presumably to the three bedrooms.

The living room itself was bigger than Skye's old house, sporting a couch and two leather recliners. The coffee table was a slab of burl, cut and polished to a shiny hue. Danny liked the old-fashioned look and could picture Skye at home here. "Do you like it?"

Nodding, she traced her finger along a dusty bookcase filled with books. "Most of Mr. Johnson's things are still here. Doesn't his family want them?"

Danny went into the kitchen and opened cupboards, seeing that it was well-stocked with cooking utensils, pots and pans. Another cupboard contained a set of matching plates and cups, glassware and bowls. "If they don't, you'll be fixed for setting up house. There're even some canned goods in the pantry."

She walked down the hall toward the bedrooms, wringing

her hands. "Seems too good to be real."

Danny followed, noting the worried look in her eyes. Each room had beds, dressers, and chairs. The master bedroom had a desk and lamp that matched the heavy oak furniture. He opened cupboards and saw they were supplied with linens and blankets.

Skye opened another closet and found Johnson's clothes. Sneezing from the dust, she pulled out the drawer of the armoire. "They haven't taken anything. Here's old photographs, his rings, and what looks like personal papers."

"I'm surprised they haven't cleaned those things out, especially since they have the place for sale." He opened the top drawer of the nightstand and found reading glasses, some loose papers, and a couple of books. "I'll talk to Ron when I get back to Seattle and find out what they want to do with all this stuff."

Skye walked over to the bedroom window and looked wistfully up the hill. Toward her property. "How ironic. I'm here, yet all of my belongings are gone." Turning, she scanned the room where Mr. Johnson's personal articles taunted with their lonely, dust-covered tranquility. "And here are all of his belongings, yet he is gone." A tear streaked down her cheek.

Danny rushed to her side.

"I feel like I'm intruding in someone else's home. I don't know if I can stay here."

CHAPTER 14

SKYE LOOKED OUT THE WINDOW, wishing she could run up the hill to her house. Wishing she could open the door and once again see her granny's things. The rocking chair. The table where she'd learned to read. The bed Ace had slept in for thirteen years.

Danny shifted as he stood beside her. She yearned to lean into his chest, savor the warmth. The strength. He brushed at a strand of her hair. "Stay at Lenny's this week as planned. Then we'll move you over to Ted's. I'll talk to Ron and bring him over to clear out his grandfather's personal items so they'll be gone before you move in."

"He has to come. I don't want to have to sort his things. I couldn't. I would feel like I'm going through them for my own gain."

"What about some of the household items? You lost everything, Skye." He pulled her into his arms, surrounding her with warmth and comfort. "You could use the kitchenware. The bedding and towels. I can't imagine Ron would want those things."

Stepping out of his embrace, she shrugged. "I suppose those household things will be all right. I can wash them."

He followed her down the hall and out the door where Bo and Mutt romped in the yard. "I'll take some of the linens with me tomorrow. I have a new washer and dryer at the house."

The sea breeze lifted her hair and skirt as she stepped onto the porch. Shuddering at the thought of washing all of that bedding by hand, she nodded. "Thanks. I'd appreciate that."

He took her hand in his. "The dogs are restless. Let's go for that walk on the beach. We can pick out which room you want tomorrow."

She glanced at him, her expression questioning. "Why do I have to select a room now? Couldn't we wait until I actually move in?"

"So I'll know which bedding to take first. I won't be able to take it all in one flight, especially if I'm going to bring Ron back next weekend."

Struggling with the daunting job of starting over, she headed toward the beach. Bo jumped up, kicking sand on her skirt. Mutt plowed into him. She laughed, glad for the break from her thoughts. "Get down, silly boy. You and Mutt go chase some seagulls."

Danny let go of her hand and threw a stick up the beach for the dogs. He turned to Skye. "Race you to the point."

"No fair. You have to give me a head start," she squealed as she gathered her skirt and charged past him.

Instead of overtaking her, he caught up and slipped a strong arm around her waist. She tried to twist out of his grasp. "Oh, no you don't," he said as he wrapped his arm around her shoulder and pulled her in to curl against him. "I don't have much time to be with you. Let me hold you."

Her laughter died in her throat at his words. She stood still, feeling his heartbeat against her hand. "You're good for me. You make me laugh. Help me to see beyond myself." But wasn't that what counselors were supposed to do?

He wrapped her fingers in his warm hand and brought them up to his lips. "We're good for each other, Pocahontas. We need each other." He bent and brushed his lips across her forehead. "And we're going to figure out a way to make this work."

She studied his eyes, seeing determination and promise in the dark depths. "I want that, Danny. I want that very much." The truth of those words startled her. Would she be able to overcome her revulsion of what he did for a living? Could she learn to live in the city? She had to try, because one thing was certain: She didn't want the lonely existence she had before she met Danny.

He brushed strands of loose hair behind her ear. "Fortunately, it's summer. I'll try and fly out every weekend. We'll deal with winter when it gets here."

She studied the furrows in his brow. "Coming to the island will be good for you. You don't relax when you're home alone. You work long hours."

He let her go and continued walking up the beach, her hand in his. "I wouldn't work long hours if you were at my house."

Keeping in step with him, she smiled. "You say that, but I think your heart keeps you at work. You want to help those kids."

Gravel crunched underfoot. Bo and Mutt ran ahead, forgetting the stick as they chased a seagull. "You've got me pegged, Miss Sunny Skye." He paused and eyed her. "You're going to need help fixing up Johnson's house. We could do that together. For now."

She could picture them together in Johnson's house. She could imagine the happiness and joy she'd experience every time he flew in. But when he left...could she handle the loneliness? Could he? Wouldn't that pain eventually tear them apart?

He stopped walking and pulled her around to face him. "I love you. I know you have issues with city life. My work. But we can work on them together."

"I don't want to hurt you."

"What hurts me is being separated from you. I can stand time away from you as long as I know I'll be seeing you soon. That there'll be times when we'll be as one."

Sincerity shone from his eyes. In his smile. He'd said he was a patient man, and she believed him. Could she overcome her fears and find peace in Seattle? Images of his home swept through her mind. Spacious. Peaceful. Surely she could manage the house and the local wooded area. She could learn to handle the crowds in the stores, especially with Danny at her side. Couldn't she?

And what about children? She was beginning to realize she wanted Danny's babies. But they would need to live on the mainland so they could go to school. Hadn't she pictured them sitting around the table in his roomy but cozy kitchen? Hadn't she seen them in her mind's eye, running across the lush grass of his backyard?

She could visualize them in Johnson's home, too. The large house wouldn't seem so overwhelming if she could think of her children flying from one room to another. They wouldn't have to go to school on the mainland. She could teach them. But would she want them to be as lonely as she was? And would they want to be here while their father was on the mainland working? She shivered. What if gang members killed Danny? Their children would grow up like she had.

Danny smoothed his thumb over her brow. "Don't fret about it now. I'm hungry. Let's head for Ted's and round up some dinner."

Glad for the change of subject, she cocked her head and studied him. "Are men always hungry? I seem to remember my father being that way."

Dropping his arms, he chuckled ruefully. "It's the fresh air."

She placed her hand in his outstretched palm. "Then we better hustle, Flyboy. I don't want you to starve."

The next day, Danny suggested they go sailing before he left. "We can take some wood and build a fire on one of the beaches across the Sound. Maybe head toward the lighthouse."

She nodded. "At least I haven't lost my boats. Do you want to fish? I think I left my fishing tackle in the sailboat."

"Sounds like a plan. I'll get Ted's pole out of his shed."

While Danny ran up the wooden steps to get his gear, Skye tucked the ends of her long skirt into her waistband, then shoved her skiff toward the water. "Come on, pups. Time to get in. We're going sailing." The puppy and Mutt bounced beside her, kicking sand in her face and hair as she pushed on the skiff.

It only took one trip in the small rowboat to load the twenty-foot sailboat and be on their way. Once the sails were unfurled, they swept across the bay, bobbing up and down in the choppy water.

The wind filled the sails and whipped the nylon fabric. Skye maneuvered the bow toward the opposite shore, the wind tugging her hair, pushing away the doubts and concerns of so many changes. Time enough later to mull over the complications of their relationship and the difficulty of setting up a new house. For now, the wind lifted her spirits. Danny's laughter filled her heart.

He climbed from the bow of the boat and sat down beside her. "Great breeze today. We're making good time."

She lifted her face to the sun. "It feels good to get away. To enjoy this weather."

He leaned over and grinned. "And enjoy you."

She looked up at him, liking the mischievous smile and the lines crinkling around his eyes. "You could charm the birds off the trees."

"So my mother told me."

At the mention of his mother, she sobered. "Tell me about your mom. Your childhood."

At her question, the smile disappeared. He shrugged. "My mom lives in Los Angeles."

"Is that where you grew up?"

He nodded. "I don't remember much about Pa except he was abusive. Rough. He ran off when I was ten or so."

She studied his handsome features—the straight nose, squared jaw—and wondered which parent he took after. "I'm sorry to hear that. It's never easy to lose a parent."

"Mom and I were relieved when he left."

She straightened and pulled on the sail. "Oh."

He shook his head. "More pleasant around the house after he was gone. Mom could relax. Laugh."

"You were close, then."

He paused, scrunching his brow. "Not close. She worked long hours. Was rarely home. Which is probably why I got into trouble."

Skye held her breath, not anxious to fill in the picture forming.

"I started hanging out with a gang. Got in trouble for robbing a convenience store. Ended up in juvenile detention."

Her eyes widened. She pulled on the lines, bringing the boat about. After setting the sail, she stared out to sea, wondering if she wanted to hear more. "How long were you there?"

He leaned back and stretched his long legs out in front of him. "Most of my early teen years. I was a mean kid. Until I met Manuel."

"Another inmate?"

"Former." He shook his head. "Man of God who came every week to talk to us boys. Tried to convince us there was a better alternative than a life of crime."

"Obviously he succeeded."

"With a couple of us."

"And the others?"

He shrugged. "Didn't stay in touch."

Skye could imagine what they were doing now. From the look on Danny's face, she figured he was thinking the same thing. The flapping sails captured her attention. She tightened the line and turned the bow a few degrees out of the wind. When she focused back on Danny, he was leaning forward, rubbing his jaw, his forehead lined in a frown.

"Your mother must have been relieved that you changed direction."

He straightened, a smile forming to chase away the creases. "The difference in me brought changes in her as well. Now we're both believers."

"Does she work in a community project like you?"

He shook his head. "No, but she volunteers in her church."

Skye tried to picture the woman but couldn't. Images of her own mother came to mind. She wondered if his mom would be warm and chatty like her own had been. She missed the banter and the projects she and her mother used to work on together. She supposed Danny's mother would be too busy for joint undertakings. Too involved in church. Like Janie.

Turning his head, he grinned. "I'll introduce you to Mom when you visit Seattle again. Later this summer, when we have the Johnson house fixed up, I'll invite her up for a visit. Give you a chance to get to know each other."

She nodded. "I'd like that. I miss my parents."

Danny smiled. "She'll love meeting you."

Skye thought of her flaws and shuddered. "I hope I won't disappoint her."

He put his arm around her and gave her a hug. "I have complete confidence she will care for you as much as I do."

His words helped smooth away some of the trepidation.

"I didn't have much of a childhood." He cupped his hand over hers and looked deep into her eyes as he spoke. "I always wanted a big family. A house filled with laughter and noise. Family picnics and outings."

"I wanted that, too." She broke eye contact and shifted position on the bench. "I just don't know if I can handle the change of living in the city." She harrumphed. "I'm not doing so good at the moment. Even the changes here on the island are throwing me off-kilter."

"Losing a house is a major catastrophe. You're handling it very well."

Was she? Avoiding the scene. Putting the fact she was homeless completely out of her mind. "I fell apart at the mall in Seattle. Can you picture me driving around town, shopping for all the things we would need?" She laughed aloud, thinking of the sight.

Danny studied her, enjoying her laughter, relieved that she could poke fun at herself. "It's a good sign when you can joke about your problems. That means you have control of them instead of the other way around."

"Oh, believe me, I have no control over my fears. You have a lot more faith than I."

He sobered. "Faith helps. If I hadn't formed a relationship with God, who knows how I would have turned out? A hell-raiser for sure. Probably in prison. I was left alone so much, I had plenty of opportunity for trouble. My faith kept me on the straight and narrow."

"You learned your faith in juvie?" Skepticism sounded in her voice. "How did you keep it going when you were released?"

He shrugged and reached in the cooler for a bottle of water. "Sunday school youth activities and service projects—an involved group in the inner city." He handed Skye a water bottle, remembering the weekends booked solid with church. "That's when I met up with Ron. His dad was a youth pastor at the time."

"And you've been friends ever since?"

"When I moved north we lost touch, but when he arrived in Seattle he looked me up. He's been one of our sponsors for GANG."

"So your activities in church kept you out of trouble."

He wanted to believe he kept active for philanthropic reasons, but now, sitting here with Skye, talking about his childhood, he could see that he kept busy to hold loneliness at bay. "You're probably right. The house was empty. Silent. Unbearable, really."

Her gaze penetrated his façade. "Ahh, so that's why you keep so busy. So you won't notice how lonely you are?"

The arrow of truth pierced. What could he say? "We're peas in a pod." He took her free hand in his. "You're lonely, too. Isolated. We're both trying to escape the same thing in our own unique way."

She laughed, the sound easing the pain of the truth. "You're much too observant. I can see that there're not going to be any secrets if we stick to this relationship." She pulled on the line and warned him she was coming about.

He ducked when the boom swung toward him as she changed direction. "It won't be boring."

She trimmed the sail and pointed the bow forty-five degrees into the wind. "We're almost to the island. Do you want to land and walk around the beach, or anchor and try for some fish?"

He glanced at the rocky shore, up at the lighthouse, and then back at her. Her hair glistened in the bright sun, her cheeks turning a delightful shade of pink. "I like sitting next to you. Sharing our thoughts. Let's stay on board and catch some whoppers."

She handed him the line. "Watch the sail. I'll get our picnic lunch ready to eat before we start fishing. Can't have a hungry fisherman."

He watched her dig through the ice chest, placing packages of food on the bench while the breeze teased at her skirt, pulling the striped fabric around her legs. Yes, he could see himself giving his heart and life over to this wood nymph. He could see himself flying to the island on summer weekends. Hopefully, she would want to come home to Seattle with him during the winter. He would never be lonely as long as she was at his side.

But what about the times when she wouldn't be there? Would he be able to handle that? After being with Skye, the solitude would only be worse. He could attest to that already. His large and empty house echoed. But he did have the memories of when she was there. Her touch still lingered in the way she had arranged his furniture, hung his pictures, filled the kitchen with tempting aromas and song.

And what about his work? If he did get involved with Skye—so much so that he couldn't break away—would he be able to give up his work? What would he do? The thought chilled him.

He took the plate she handed him. Yes, it would be tough without her, but they still had many things to work out.

When Danny returned to Seattle, the ache of loneliness pressed, but not to the point where he needed to work long hours. The week flew. The knowledge that he would see Skye on the weekend kept his spirits uplifted. Kept him charged. In fact, to the surprise of his assistant and associates, he left the office on time every night. He needed to shop, wash the linens he'd brought from the island, and order the oak table and chairs he and Skye had seen at the mall.

Hope soared as he did these chores. Hope, and plans that included Skye. He pictured her look of delight when he brought her the paint to redo the inside of Johnson's cabin. He smiled, picturing Skye pressing her face into the clean linens, relishing the fresh laundry-soap smell. When he sat at the new kitchen table, he kept alive the hope that she would join him there.

Finally, Friday arrived. Like a horse chomping at the bit, he picked up Ron and drove to the airport before the rush-hour traffic set in. Impatient with the red light, he looked at the pastor. "Sorry about the short notice, but I'm glad you could cut loose from the church this weekend."

Ron smiled. "Everything fell into place. A visiting pastor showed up, needing a place to stay." He slapped his knee and grinned. "He'll earn his bed and dinner with his preaching, that's for sure."

The light turned green, and Danny turned onto the freeway. Fortunately, the traffic hadn't built up yet, and they made it to the airport in record time. Ron helped him transfer his boxes from the car to the plane and then stood back, eyeing the small aircraft. "I want you to know I'm not overly comfortable flying in one of these."

Danny studied the skeptical look on his friend's face. "Where's your faith?"

"If God wanted us to fly, he would have given us wings like the birds. And if he'd wanted us in the water, he'd have given us gills."

Danny laughed as he opened the passenger door and gestured Ron in. "Must be the reason you didn't get out to the island much."

"Smart man." Ron climbed onto the passenger seat and buckled his seat belt. "I want you to know that it's only because of our friendship and my love for my granddaddy that I'm venturing out to this piece of land in the middle of Puget Sound."

Danny shut the door and walked around to the other side of the plane, checking the propeller and struts on the way. He hoisted himself into his seat and grinned at Ron before checking his instrument panel. "I promise not to pull any tricks like I did with Skye."

Ron quirked his eyebrow. "Do I dare ask?"

In between talking to the tower as he taxied down the runway, he told Ron about letting Skye fly the plane. "It turned out to be a great witness about faith."

"My faith is fine. Don't you be trying any lessons on me."

Waiting their turn for takeoff, Danny faced Ron, his expression serious. "I'm counting on your faith. I want you to talk to Skye." He explained the root of her problems. Witnessing the violent murder of her parents. The near rape by the same men. Her self-imposed escape to the island and her chosen isolated lifestyle.

"That's deep." Ron rubbed his brow. "I doubt I can help

her overcome all of that in one weekend."

"You can start. Plant the seeds. I'm hoping I can talk her into coming to Seattle before winter sets in. If she knew she could go to you for counseling, she might consider taking the step."

A slow smile creased Ron's face. "That's a good plan. I'll take every opportunity to talk to her."

"That'll be great."

"I'll make a point of inviting her to visit me in the city."

The air traffic control tower interrupted by announcing they were clear for takeoff. Danny positioned the plane and, before pulling on the throttle, looked at Ron and smiled. "That's where my faith comes in. I know God will use you to touch her heart."

The engine roared as they lifted off the ground and into the gray skies over Seattle. It wasn't raining yet, but precipitation had been predicted. "While you're at it, pray that the rain holds off until we get this stuff unloaded and into the house."

Ron raised his hands in the air. "We're not asking much here," he exclaimed, with a facetious grin.

Danny shook his head as he leveled the plane and headed north. "I put all of my stuff in boxes. I'll empty them, and you can fill them with the things you want to keep and bring back with you."

"I'm not planning on taking much."

"You'll be surprised at what you decide you want to save. There're a lot of things that are part of your granddad."

Later that weekend, Danny had to laugh as he saw how the boxes were packing up. In a few short hours, the three of them had made rapid progress through the house. Skye ended up accepting many of the household items Ron offered. Danny attributed her ready acceptance to her immediate rapport with his friend. Danny shook his head in wonder as he saw the two of them getting teary-eyed over one of Mr. Johnson's woodcarvings. Danny had been correct in his assessment that the pastor's counseling would help Skye. Careful not to disturb them, he moved beside Skye.

Ron smoothed his hand over the surface of the carved wood. "You see, this is now a piece of art. It started out as a tree, growing beautiful and strong in the forest. But someone chopped it down." He handed the replica of the sea lion to Skye.

She cradled the wood in her hands. "The tree was damaged, destroyed, in pain."

"But with much carving, cutting, and care, this piece of wood became something beautiful."

"And you're saying my life is like this sculpture?"

"You've had more than your share of grief and pain. It tore away the life you knew. But over the years, here on this island, life has been whittling away at your fears. You don't see it yet, but with the love and care of the Lord, you'll find that you're a new person. A beautiful work of art."

Danny wanted to tuck her into his arms now and show her that love and care. He clenched his fists at his side, knowing better than to break into the moment of revelation. Caressing the aged wood, she stood deep in thought. Would she understand—accept the truth offered to her?

Ron placed his hand on top of hers, stopping the smoothing action. "One of God's promises is that He will never give you more than you can handle. He must think you are a very strong woman as you have handled much."

A tear slid down her cheek. Danny's breath caught in his throat. He wanted to prevent any more tears in her life, yet he knew there would be others. He silently vowed she wouldn't have to face them alone.

She glanced at Danny, questions reflecting in the blue

depths of her eyes. "I want to believe."

Ron lifted his hand, gesturing Danny to be still. Skye turned back to the pastor. "Will you help me to understand how?"

Danny nodded at Ron and slipped away into the kitchen. He watched as Ron settled Skye in a chair on the front porch. Rain pattered on the roof. He leaned against the counter and took a deep breath.

CHAPTER 15

SKYE STARED PAST the rain dripping off the porch to the sea, gray and calm. If only her spirit could be as peaceful. Squirming on the wooden bench, she glanced at the pastor, wishing she could take everything he said to heart. But so many doubts swam in her head.

Ron moved his chair closer to Skye. "I can see in your eyes that questions are burning."

Sheepish about her obvious reaction, she blushed. "It would take a month of Sundays to answer all of them."

He leaned back, crossed his legs, and laughed. "You've got that right."

Sighing, she smoothed the flowered material of her skirt over her knees. "You've been very patient with me. I appreciate that." She gestured at the house behind them. "I'm sorry about the circumstances that brought you here, but I'm glad you came. I needed to hear what you're telling me."

"Will you come to Seattle? I would love to talk more with you." He uncrossed his legs and leaned his elbows on his knees. "I think I could help you overcome your fears."

"Many counselors and therapists have tried, but I become unglued in a crowd. I prefer the solitude of the island."

Ron smiled. "There's nothing wrong with seeking solitude. But we are no help to anyone if we stay there."

Skye shifted again. "What do I have that anyone could possibly need?"

"Love." He paused and rubbed the palms of his hands together. "Danny needs love."

Her heart ached with the truth of those words.

"And Natasha. The girl from GANG."

She jerked her head up and stared at him. What did he know of that visit?

Ron nodded. "You did wonders for that child. She'd been so angry, resistant. Nina didn't know how she was ever going to reach her. One morning spent with you and she's made a dramatic change."

"I didn't do anything."

Ron lifted his hand to silence her. "She's talking now. Not much, but it's a big start."

"But all we did was talk. Mostly me."

"One thing I've learned while working in this business is you never know how you are going to be used. You help others and you might think you're helping with one issue, but you find out later it was another issue altogether." He grinned. "That's what keeps me working with troubled people. That puzzle. That thrill of the unknown."

She stared at his relaxed features, the contentment in his eyes. Could peace be that easy? "That was one incident. A fluke."

Ron shook his head and continued, "I think you're closer to God than you realize. I can tell from how you've treated me, a complete stranger, that you're full of tenderness and caring." Bo sat in front of her and placed a paw into her lap. Ron reached over and rubbed behind the puppy's ears. "And you have a fondness for animals."

Skye shivered, not wanting the responsibility, yet she did care for others. She was no help to anyone isolated on this island. She must face the fact she did love Danny and wanted to be with him.

Bo tossed his head up and down.

Well, she could care for animals out here. But she would have summers to do that. Hadn't Danny promised he would bring her? She glanced around at the cabin. The place would be hers. She would always have the house to come to whenever the city got to be too much. "You've given me a lot to think about." She smiled, studying the pastor's caring eyes. "And you've promised to be there if I need you. I assure you that I'll think on this during the weeks ahead."

Ron held out his palm and enfolded her small hand into his large one. "Keep your heart open and you'll see there's nothing to be afraid of."

She lightly squeezed his fingers. "You make it sound easy."

He stood. Lines creased his face as he gave her a warning glance. "It's going to be tough. You'll have a battle going on in your head. Just let it rage. Try to sit quiet and listen to your heart. That helps."

She told him about her special place located on his property. "You can see across the water for miles." She explained about the view of the lighthouse and about the eagles that flew overhead. "Under the large cedar trees, it's peaceful and calming. If it stops raining I'll show you."

"I'm sure it's breathtaking. Remember, though, that you don't need a special place to pray. It helps, but God hears you wherever you are."

She smiled. "Even in the mall?"

"Especially in the mall. Or in a crowd."

"Whew." She shook her head. "It'll be a miracle indeed if I learn to handle the throngs."

Ron stood and stretched, then gestured toward the sea. "Look at how beautiful it is out here, even with the rain coming down."

Skye stood and leaned against the post by the steps. A strange peace settled over her. Her eyelids drooped. A nap sounded inviting. She glanced back into the house, searching for Danny. He was sorting through the cupboards in the kitchen.

She smiled. He enjoyed working with her. This summer could be very interesting. And fun.

"How about if I cook us something to eat? We've been working hard and we need a break."

Ron nodded as he followed her into the cabin. "Sitting here on the island, even for those few minutes, made me realize how exhausted I am."

Concerned, she studied him closely. "You loved your grandfather. Being here has to be draining, not only physically, but emotionally." She threw up her hands in dismay. "And here I am laying all my problems on your shoulders, as well."

Ron stepped close and gave her arm a light pat. "This weekend has been a blessing. Reminded me of how much my grandfather meant to me." He lowered his head. "I should have made the effort to come out here more often." Straightening, he rolled his shoulders. "I needed to get away from the church. All this fresh air has done wonders for me. I can see why Danny wants to come out here on the weekends."

"You're welcome to visit anytime. We'll always have a room for you."

Danny came out from the kitchen and joined them. "Don't wait too long to come back, though."

Skye hurried into the kitchen and began opening cupboards, looking for cans of soup for lunch. Pleasure rippled through her as she pictured the two of them entertaining together in this house. The idea brought a warmth all its own.

Thoughts of Danny and their life together kept going through her mind after the two men flew back to Seattle on Monday morning. The house, full of voices and laughter earlier, echoed with loneliness now. Unable to stand the silence, Skye decided to stay another week with Lenny and Jack. They understood.

"There's no sense moving over to the Randalls' place when you're going to take possession of Johnson's house soon," Lenny said as she piled the boxes she'd unloaded from their boat. "You're like a daughter to us. You know we love having you here."

Skye helped her unpack a carton, putting the food items in Lenny's pantry. "The pastor said the realtors will be signing the papers this week. As soon as the property closes escrow, they'll deed the place to me."

Lenny handed her another carton. "Seems like a miracle. You'll be much happier in Johnson's house. It's roomy and has a great view of the sea."

"And I can see the lighthouse too."

A knock on the door interrupted their conversation. Fred Davis entered with a stack of boxes in his hands. "Jack asked me to bring these in. Where do you want them?"

Lenny pointed to an empty corner of the kitchen. "Over there's fine. Help yourself to a cup of coffee if you want."

Fred nodded at Skye and poured a cup. "Heard about the fire. I'm surprised you didn't return to Seattle."

"I have to take care of things here." Skye handed him some packets of sugar.

He tore one open and dumped the contents into his cup. "Where you staying?"

"With us." Lenny opened the top box Fred had brought in. "Did you hear the good news about Johnson's place?"

Fred shook his head and then sipped on his coffee.

"The realtors that are buying Johnson's land want Skye's place."

Fred looked up. "You selling?"

Skye shook her head. "No."

Fred frowned. "Why not? You won't be able to rebuild that house."

Lenny walked over and handed Skye several cereal boxes to put in the cupboard. "They're going through with the trade. Johnson's house for her land. Can you imagine that?"

Fred choked. Skye rushed over and patted him on the back. "Be careful. That coffee's hot."

Footsteps sounded on the porch. "Skye, are you in there?"

Skye hurried to the door. "Janie. What are you doing here?"

Janie swept in, scooping Skye into her arms. "Oh, my poor dear. I heard about the house. I just had to see for myself." Tears streamed down Janie's face. "I begged Fred to fly me over."

Skye wrapped her arms around her sister. "Have you seen the ruins already?"

Janie nodded. "What a mess. All those memories. Gone forever."

Skye rubbed Janie's arms. "All that was left of our family."

Janie lifted her head and sniffed. "That was my haven, too. Whenever I was down, I knew I could come here and you would cheer me up. What are we going to do?"

She reached in her skirt pocket and handed Janie a tissue. "I'll still be here."

Lenny pulled a chair out from the table. "Come over here and sit. I'll make some tea." She motioned to an empty chair between Janie's and Fred's. "Join your sister, Skye, and tell her and Fred your news about the house."

After Lenny made the tea, they drank the herbal brew while Skye explained to Janie and Fred the details of the trade.

Janie jumped up and raised her arms, skipping around the room. "It's an answer to my prayer. Oh my. A miracle."

Sighing, Skye cleared the cups. Thank goodness Danny wasn't here to witness her sister's theatrics. But then again, if they were going to see much of each other, he would have to get used to Janie. She watched Janie dance around the room, then smiled. At least her sister was happy. Maybe Skye would be dancing and laughing soon, too. With Danny.

Fred stood and caught Janie's hand, pulling her to a standstill. "I don't know what the fuss is about." He turned to Skye. "I would think you'd be glad for an excuse to get off this island. Don't you want some social life?"

"Yes, I want a social life, but not in the city."

Lenny poured more tea. "She's met Danny. That's enough for now. Give her time."

Janie and Fred turned to stare at Lenny with questioning gazes.

Lenny pointed a finger at Janie. "You weren't home when Skye went to Seattle. Danny Fraser took her in. He brought her back to the island in his plane."

Skye squirmed, embarrassed and uncomfortable with their curious stares. "Well, it's just that Danny found Johnson's grandson and helped arrange for the trade."

Fred stood and paced the small kitchen, his footsteps echoing in Janie's stunned silence. "Amazing," he muttered. "You lose your house and wham,"—he slapped his hands together— "another one appears like magic." He crossed the room and bent down to stare into Skye's face. "It's as if the fates are keeping you here."

Janie reached for his arm and tugged. "There are no fates, Fred. More like answers to my prayers to watch out for her."

Fred rolled his eyes. "You and your prayers," he said as he walked out the door. "I'm going up to see Pop. You know where to find me."

Janie turned to Skye. "Don't pay him any mind. He told

me he's having a difficult time with his dad."

Lenny sat in Fred's place at the table. "His father has made his life tough. Harling Davis has always been too controlling."

Skye sipped her tea. "You have to give Fred credit. Despite the past, he stays in touch with the man. Cares for his mother."

Lenny plunked her cup on the table, sloshing tea. "More like groveling for attention."

Janie swept down into her chair. She turned to Skye. "Enough about Fred. Tell me your plans. I'm here to stay for the week. Your every wish is my command."

Skye smiled at her sister. "I'm glad you're staying, Sis. I could use some of your positive outlook, as well as the help."

"Pining for Danny?"

"You don't miss much." Skye ducked her head, hoping her blush wasn't too bright. "How are you at painting? Danny brought over several gallons of 'oyster white' to do the inside of the house."

Lenny raised her hand. "Are you sure it's okay with the pastor? The house isn't yours yet."

"From the way Ron was talking, it's as good as mine already. And even if he changes his mind, the place needs a new coat. He did approve of the paint. In fact, I think he was with Danny when he picked it up."

"I'll help too," said Lenny.

Janie stood. "Then let's go, girl. Time's a wasting."

"Won't Danny be surprised when he arrives next weekend and the painting is all finished?"

Walking into the house, Danny's nose twinged at the smell of fresh paint. He stepped inside and looked in amazement at the walls. Turning to Skye, he raised his arms. "You've finished.

How'd you get all this done in one week?"

"Janie stayed to help. Lenny came over, too. We finished in no time at all." Skye gestured around the room. "Do you like it?"

His footsteps echoed as he walked down the wood floor of the hall, peeking in each bedroom. "I'm impressed." He turned to Skye with a nod of approval. "Love it. Guess that means I won't be painting this weekend." He lowered his voice and added a hint of mock disappointment. "What a shame."

Skye put her hands on her hips, the paisley skirt she'd bought in Bellingham swishing around her legs. "Don't worry, Flyboy. We have plenty of other projects for you."

He groaned, then laughed.

Janie bounded in the door. "What's this I hear about more help?" She pulled on Skye's arm. "You're not putting him to work already, are you? The man's come all this way to see you."

Danny studied Skye's expression. "I want to know the answer to that question myself."

Blushing, Skye glanced up at him. She glared meaningfully at her sister through lowered lids. "Don't worry. I'll make sure he has time to relax."

Janie's squawk bounced off the walls. "I should hope so."

"We've planned to work on the house together." Danny took pity on her and stepped next to Skye in her defense. "It's a change of pace from work. No problem."

Janie studied him and then turned to Skye, a twinkle of mischief in her eye. "Tell me all the details. We have so much to plan. You'll have to come back with me to Seattle. We have to shop. Buy new things for the house."

Skye glanced at Danny and rolled her eyes. "Now do you see why I don't tell her anything?"

He laughed. "I'll let you handle this, Pocahontas. I'm no match for her."

Paying no attention to their comments, Janie continued

dancing around the room, singing songs and making outrageous plans.

Danny slipped Skye's hand in his and guided her out the front door where he could be heard. "This is a good time to go get the gear I brought with me. I'll head over to Ted's and get his cart."

Skye tugged on his hand. "Coward," she whispered, standing on tiptoe so he could hear.

Tempted to pull her into his arms, he leaned over and brushed his lips across her forehead. Janie's squeals carried out the door to hurry him along. He chuckled. "Get her settled down while I'm gone."

"You're always expecting miracles."

"Faith, my dear. Remember what I taught you about faith."

He left her on the porch shaking her head, her blond hair flying across her shoulders. Bo tumbled down the steps to follow. Danny smiled. Life with Skye would never be boring.

Taking the trail, he passed the charred remains of Skye's house. He shuddered, thankful that Skye and Bo hadn't been home when the fire started. He was certain now that he didn't want to live without her sunny smile and her love.

About to turn into Ted's driveway, he spotted Jack farther down the road. "Hellooo." He yelled and waved his arms.

Jack waved back and motioned him over.

Bo immediately loped on gangly legs toward Jack. Danny followed. "What's up?"

Jack patted Bo. Adjusting his ball cap, he nodded toward the cabin on the other side of the Randalls'. "I was checking out the place. Seems Sawyer Realtors offered to buy it."

Danny frowned. If Sawyer Realtors wanted so many lots, they were planning a bigger development than he had originally thought. "Are they going to sell?"

"They were offered a good price. They're getting older. Haven't been around that much lately." Jack tossed a stick for Bo. "They had to make unplanned trips when the windows were broken and the place vandalized. They're concerned about keeping the place up."

Sounded like the realtors wanted the whole peninsular section of the island. Again he wondered if they could be responsible for the vandalism. "Did Sawyer make an offer for Ted's place?"

Bo pranced back with the stick in his mouth and dropped it at Jack's feet. "I wouldn't be surprised." He picked up the piece of wood and threw it again. "They've made me an offer."

His gut constricting, Danny grabbed another stick for Bo. "You thinking of selling?"

Jack nodded. "Lenny was saying it might be nice to be closer to the children. She loves those grandkids."

Danny raked his fingers through his hair. How would Skye react? She loved Lenny and Jack. Would she want to stay on the island with them gone?

Danny watched Bo run through the trees. "Did Sawyer mention what he intends to do with all this land? He told me he was going to build condos. He has plenty of land for that without buying up more."

Jack rubbed at his jaw. "That's another reason we're thinking of leaving. He showed me the plans. Wants to build a large condominium timeshare resort. Wanted me to manage it."

Surely Skye didn't know about any of this. She would have told him. The news was going to break her heart. Danny straightened his shoulders. She was going to need him more than ever. "Sounds like a good opportunity for you."

Jack harrumphed. "If I'd wanted ulcers and high blood pressure, I would've found work on the mainland." He patted Bo's head when the dog plopped down, out of breath, at his feet. "I wasn't interested in the job. I'm sure that's why they offered to buy me out. My property is a key location with the dock and airstrip."

Pictures flashed in Danny's mind. Trees toppling to make room for two- and three-story buildings. They would have to build a larger fresh-water facility as well as provide electric power. "They told me they were gearing the complex for the outdoor enthusiasts."

"Sure, they'll have hiking and bicycling trails, sites to observe the marine life. But they're planning to enlarge the dock and build a marina, not to mention an eighteen-hole golf course."

"That's going to make a big change on the island. How are the locals handling it?"

"Some—like me and Lenny—are appalled. That's why we're thinking of selling out." He took off his hat and slapped it on his leg. "But others will think it's wonderful."

"The yuppies." Danny had to smile.

"They're going to like having the electricity and other amenities."

"Their property value will skyrocket."

Jack nodded and placed his hat back on his head. "Don't get me wrong. The plans are good. They'll build a fantastic resort. But it'll still change the look and feel of the island."

"Skye doesn't know about this, does she? She hasn't mentioned it to me."

"I wanted to tell her, but Lenny said to wait until she'd regrouped after the fire."

Danny nodded. "This'll have a big impact on her." He shuddered to think of her reaction, but she needed to know.

Bo stood and wagged his tail, begging for more attention. Jack tossed the pup another stick. "Could be the best thing to happen to her."

"How's that?" Danny watched Bo sniff in the ferns for the stick.

"She needs to get off this island. Find friends." He peered at Danny, his blue eyes piercing. "Get married."

Danny smiled. "My sentiments exactly. I was going to give her time to get used to the idea, but this news changes things. She's going to have to know. Soon."

Jack shook his head. "She's been through so much. I hate to think what this is going to do to her."

Danny clapped Jack's shoulder in reassurance. "You can't protect her forever. She has to face the changes."

"I'm glad you'll be there for her."

Danny's shoulders sagged. Sighing, he straightened them again. "I came to get Ted's cart. I have to unload some gear from the plane. Then I'll tell her the news. I'd really like you to be there for moral support."

"Let's take her and Janie over to our place. Both girls rely on Lenny."

Danny hoped Skye would rely on him, but he could see Jack's point. Lenny was like a mother to her and Janie.

Jack gestured toward the Randalls' house. "Let's get that cart. I'll help you unload the gear."

Danny hurried down the path, thankful for Jack and Lenny. This was going to be a tough blow for Skye.

Unloading the plane didn't take long. Skye and Janie weren't at the house. He followed Jack home and heard their laughter as he mounted the steps of the caretaker's porch.

Jack paused before opening the door. "It's a shame to ruin their good mood."

Danny reached around Jack and opened the door. "I'll tell her."

Inside, Lenny was pulling out some material from her closet. "These will go great in the kitchen." She unfolded bright yellow curtains.

Janie hopped out of her chair and hugged the material to

her. "Oooooh, Skye. This'll be perfect. Like sunshine. I'll look for matching towels in Seattle."

Fred sat on the couch, his left leg crossed over his knee, grinning at Janie. He winked at Danny when he entered the room. "Glad to see you two. I need male support. All these female hormones are dangerous to face alone."

Skye shook her head, laughing. "Do you like these curtains for the kitchen?"

Danny sat on the stool at the kitchen breakfast counter, dreading what he was going to have to say. He shoved his sunglasses on top of his head and shrugged. "Before you get all excited, you better hear the news."

His gut tightened when her face sobered at his tone. He hated taking away that smile. He hated seeing her suffer.

CHAPTER 16

SKYE STARED IN A COMBINATION of horror and disbelief at Lenny and then Jack. Her body heated, her pulse quickened, and tears stung the back of her eyelids. She reached for Danny's hand and squeezed, hoping he'd shake her out of this nightmare. "You're moving away? Why?"

As Jack explained Sawyer's offer, a stunned silence filled the room.

Lenny stepped forward. "We went to Vendovi Island to look for property."

Jack nodded. "We're going to Bellingham next week. There are some nice homes along Lake Whatcom."

Lenny wrung her hands, obviously upset with Skye's reaction. "We'll probably go there since it's closer to the kids."

Skye's chest constricted. Gasping for breath, she staggered.

Danny guided her to a chair and sat her down, pushing on her shoulders to place her head between her knees. "Take deep, slow breaths," he ordered.

Loud sobs filled the room, and Skye realized Janie was crying, as well. She looked up to see Fred pulling her down on the couch and into his arms. "There, there. Everything will be all right."

Skye blocked out his words. She didn't want progress. She didn't want change. Hadn't she had enough of both? Anger welled at the unfairness and her helplessness. She straightened and gulped. "We're not giving in to this. I'm going to contact every environmental group there is. I'm going to protest this development. They can't build with the eagle nest here. Can they?" She turned to Jack.

He shrugged. "As long as they leave some space for the birds, they can."

Janie shifted out of Fred's arms. "Who would want to come here? There's no electricity. Nothing."

Fred reached for Janie's hand and patted it. "That's the point. The developers will provide all of the amenities."

Janie glared at Fred. "Is that all you can think of? The material conveniences?"

Skye pictured hordes of people jogging around the island, sailing offshore, wanting more conveniences until the island looked like the city they had left behind. An ache grew in her heart.

Fred broke into her thoughts. "Think of the property values. Your place will be worth a fortune."

"You *would* think of that." Janie yanked her hand out of Fred's. "Not everyone needs glitz and glitter to be happy."

"Who's talking about glitz and glitter?" Fred lifted his hands. "They plan to keep the place environmentally attractive. They hope to market to the outdoor types."

Skye riveted a glare on Fred. "You knew about this, didn't you?"

Fred lowered his hands. "They're making offers to everyone on the island. I'm selling my lots."

That news didn't surprise her at all. "What about your folks?"

"They made Dad an offer."

"Is he moving, too?" Janie asked.

Fred shrugged. "Don't know. He's a stubborn ol' goat. I'm trying to talk him into selling. He'll probably stay just to be cantankerous."

Skye mentally applauded the man. "Maybe he'll help me

form a committee."

Danny tapped her arm. "Do you want to stay if Sawyer goes through with these plans? We can always look around for a quieter island."

"We saw some nice places on Vendovi." Jack thumped his baseball cap on the counter.

Skye stood and began pacing the crowded room. "I'm not giving up without a fight. If I lose, then I'll think about moving. Nothing is set in stone yet. We have at least some opportunity to change this around." She stopped in front of Lenny and Jack. "Are you with me? Will you help me form a committee?"

"We'll try," Jack said. But from the look on his face, she realized he thought her efforts futile.

Lenny clasped Skye's hands in hers. "But, honey, you have to be prepared for the worst. That's an awful big corporation you plan to fight."

"It doesn't matter. Small guys have brought big guys to heel before." She fisted her hands at her sides. "All I know is that they can't build a resort here. It would change everything." Yet many things had changed already. Vandalism, explosions, the fire. The island was never going to be the same anyway. Maybe they were right and she should stop fighting.

Danny stood. "There's nothing we can do here, so let's go back to the house and think up some strategy."

"You're backing her up?" Fred swung around to stare at Danny in surprise. "You of all people should want more modern conveniences. Look how you acted when you first arrived."

Danny flushed. "Well…"

Skye jumped up to defend him. "Danny had a hard time at first, but he learned to appreciate what we have here. Peace. Quiet. Solitude."

Fred scowled, obviously unimpressed.

Danny stepped forward. "Skye's happiness is my major concern. The changes don't bother me. But if they make her unhappy, I don't want them."

Skye stepped by Danny's side and clasped his fingers. "Come on." She reached a hand to Janie. "Let's go back to the house and discuss this. We've imposed enough on Jack and Lenny."

Lenny protested that they were no bother, but Skye could see the strain on her face. She ushered everyone out the door, including Fred. "We're going to start planning. Do you want to join us or not?" she asked, figuring Fred would be glad for an excuse to hightail it out of there.

Fred shook his head. "No, I have to get back to Seattle. I came to check and see if Janie was ready to fly home."

Janie stopped in her tracks. "You're leaving now? This morning? I thought you said we could stay until next week. I took two weeks off work."

He shuffled his feet in the sand. "Some business came up. I have to get back today." Fred rubbed his jaw. "If you want to stay the week, I can come back next weekend and pick you up."

Janie flew to Fred's side and gave him a hug. "Would you? That would be great. Skye and I have much more to do."

Danny stepped forward. "Don't make a special trip. I'll be back next Friday or Saturday." Danny turned from Fred to Janie. "I can take you home next week."

Janie raised her hands in the air. "Thank you. See how everything works out?"

Skye led the way back to the house. She had wanted to take advantage of the sunny day to work outdoors and clear the yard of weeds and the trash that had become entwined in the long grass. But more pressing matters captured her attention. "Let's make a list of who we can contact. I think the pastor left some paper and pens in the top drawer of the kitchen counter."

She riffled through the drawer and found a partially used tablet of yellow, lined paper. Janie took it from her and sat at the table. "Fix us some tea, Skye. I'll start on the list." She looked up at Danny. "You know a lot of influential people. Who should we contact first?"

The afternoon flew. By four o'clock, they had a letter drafted and a list of possible supporters. Skye pushed her chair out from under the table and stood. Stretching, she glanced over at Danny. Lines of tension carved his cheeks. His eyes looked dark and stressed. Immediate remorse filled her.

"You came over here to relax, and look what we have you doing." She walked to his side. "You should have been outside enjoying the warm spring sunshine."

Janie jumped up. "We can still do that. Let's go for a walk on the beach."

"We can dig for some clams." Skye straightened and looked out the window. The long sea grass swayed in the light breeze. She turned in time to catch the grimace on Janie's face, matched by that on Danny's. "Okay. Forget the clams. Let's just walk," she conceded with a grin.

At the mention of the word "walk," Bo pranced to the door. Danny stood and stretched. "Come on, pooch. You need a romp as much as we do."

Small waves lapped the shore, tiny rocks rattling as the water receded. Seagulls squawked overhead, fighting over morsels brought in from the tide. The salty odor of seaweed filled the air. Skye breathed deep, trying not to dim the peaceful setting by imagining huge condominiums along the slopes and crowds of people milling on the beach.

She closed her eyes. Not sure exactly how to pray, she whispered a silent plea.

No answer came to comfort or console. Only the sound of the gentle wind rustling in the trees. Her feet crunched on the shells and rocks. She looked down and realized they had come to the oyster beds. Smiling, she bent and started placing small shells into a sling made by gathering up her skirt.

Janie stopped and stared. "What are you doing?"

Skye straightened. "I conceded on the clams, but oysters will be easy to fix." She started toward the house. "I'm going to take these to the cabin. I'll be right back."

When she returned, she found Janie and Danny taking turns throwing sticks for Bo. She joined them, but her heart wasn't in the fun. She couldn't stop thinking about the island without Jack and Lenny. Could she bear losing such dear friends? She chided herself for being selfish. They were getting on in age. The money from the sale of their property would make a nice retirement nest egg. But still, she would miss them terribly.

Hanging back from the others, Skye glanced up at the clear blue sky. "The pastor said You wouldn't give me more than I can handle," she whispered. "It would break my heart for them to leave."

Again, silence. She shook her head. What was she doing? She had to keep her mind clear. Focused.

Maybe she should go back to Seattle with Janie. She could make phone calls, set up appointments with key people. She dreaded the thought of dealing with the city. But if she didn't make the effort, Leeza Island would end up being just like the mainland. There would be no peace and quiet where Danny could escape. Their children would be swallowed up in the crowds. They might as well stay at Danny's house in Seattle full-time rather than bother flying to an island swarming with people. At least he had a big yard. Space.

A tear slid down her cheek. She swiped at it and straightened her shoulders with resolve. "I'm not going to let anything happen to Leeza Island." Or was this fight an excuse to put off facing a life in the city? A life with Danny?

Danny dreaded leaving for Seattle. He wasn't sure Janie was such a good influence on Skye. Janie kept insisting everything would be all right. Danny had no doubt that things would work out. But he'd had enough experience to know that the circumstances Janie and Skye thought were *all right*, wouldn't necessarily be what they ended up with.

He also worried that Janie was putting too much pressure on Skye to marry him. There were a lot of changes happening in her life. She shouldn't be rushed into any of them, not even a relationship that he hoped would end in marriage.

Sunday morning dawned, and he climbed down from the loft. Sun filtered through the windows, spotting the hardwood floor with shadows from the pine trees surrounding the deck. He looked out across a calm sea at the lighthouse. Birds dotted the sky. Squinting, he spotted the pair of eagles soaring hundreds of feet above, unaware of the impending changes they would have to face. Changes that would be as difficult for the raptors as they would be for Skye.

Danny curled his bare toes on the sun-warmed floor and raked his fingers through his rumpled hair. For Skye's sake, he wished things didn't have to change. He wanted to shelter her from the events that were coming, but he knew that if the wheels of progress were rolling, there wouldn't be much she could do to stop them. He sighed. He couldn't do much either. Except stand by her side.

Stretching, he ambled into the kitchen area and looked at

the formidable coffeepot, wondering if Skye had some already made at her place. He glanced out the window again. Today, he decided, they would not write any more letters nor discuss any more strategy. They would work outside as they had planned. The sun and physical labor would be the best therapy for all three of them.

Dressing quickly, he donned his new hiking boots and went outside. Bo greeted him and charged around with all of his puppy energy. "You here to escort me to Skye's?"

The dog barked and tore down the path toward the Johnson place. Laughing, Danny followed. Skye and Janie were sitting on the porch enjoying the morning sun. He stopped at the foot of the steps and smiled. "Morning. Aren't you two a pretty sight?"

Skye blushed and smiled back. Janie rose out of her seat. "I bet you're starving. Let me fix breakfast. You two lovebirds sit out here and visit."

Skye started to rise, but Janie placed her hands on her sister's shoulders and nudged her back into the chair. "No arguments. You know I always get my way."

Skye rolled her eyes. Danny grinned as he climbed the stairs and sat next to Skye. He took her hand in his, relishing the soft feel of her skin. "Ready to tackle those weeds?" He nodded toward the field spread out in front of them.

"Might as well. They aren't going to go away by themselves."

"Too bad." He eyed the thistles, knowing he was going to be sore by the time he got back to Seattle. "Good thing I brought those thick gloves." He patted her hand. "Don't want to leave you covered with scars."

She squeezed his fingers and sighed. "Wouldn't be the first time I've scratched up my hands. There're berry bushes in there too."

"You'll have a nice lawn before summer's over."

"I'd like that."

Bo clambered up the steps and dropped a piece of drift-wood at their feet. Skye's laughter rang across the field.

"I could spend forever listening to you laugh."

She suddenly stiffened. "Shouldn't we wait and see how things develop?"

Bending toward her, he tucked a strand of hair behind her ear. "If the developers proceed, we make alternative plans. We adapt. We'll do what we have to do. That's what a relationship is about. Facing the world together."

She stared, her blue eyes capturing his. "Is it?"

"Challenges are easier when you're a team." He leaned toward her, drinking in the sweet scent of lilacs on her skin. "We're like two ragged halves of a circle. Those rough edges fit together, and we make a smooth and rounded whole. Can't beat that."

She turned her face to his, her lips a breath away. Her eyelids lowered, and he heard her breath catch. Unable to resist a moment longer, he leaned into a kiss of lips tasting of mint from her tea. His heart raced at the touch.

Slowly, she pulled away and raised her head. He could see her pulse pounding in the curve of her slender neck. He leaned his forehead against hers and sighed. He wanted to wake up together—sit out on the porch every morning, like they were now. But he knew she wasn't ready for that. Not yet.

Her eyes twinkling, she smiled. "Want some hot coffee and breakfast?"

He shrugged. "In a minute." Nuzzling her neck, he tickled her, making her laugh.

Janie called from inside the house. "Hey, you two, stop fooling around. Breakfast is ready."

Edging away, Danny stood and pulled her into his arms.

"In the nick of time," he murmured against her hair.

She ducked under his arm and entered the house, skirt swaying with each step. "I think Janie has fixed something nourishing and yummy. Smell those pancakes and maple syrup?"

Thinking he couldn't be any happier than this very second, he followed, mentally ticking off the appointments on his calendar. He'd have to talk to his assistant about helping him keep the caseload down. He needed to spend as much time with Skye as he could. He wanted to be here to calm any doubts, help her with all of the changes she faced. He wanted to help her see that they were indeed a team and could face things together.

Danny noticed Skye studying him as she sat in her chair. "What do you have on your mind? You're grinning like the cat who caught the mouse."

Danny shrugged as he pulled out his chair and reached for the plate of pancakes. He glanced up at Janie. "Looks delicious, Sis."

Skye's fork clattered to the floor. Janie almost dropped the pitcher of hot syrup.

Shaking his head, Danny took the pitcher out of her hand and motioned for her to sit. "Didn't know I could fluster you two so easily."

Skye's eyes widened. "You called her 'sis.'"

Janie narrowed her eyes.

Ignoring the disconcerted look on Skye's and Janie's faces, he took a bite of his pancakes and swallowed. "I've always wanted a sister, so I hope we'll be close."

Janie slid out of her seat and rushed over to hug him. "Oooooooh, I've always wanted a brother, too. How great is that?"

Danny refrained from putting his hand over his ear to protect his eardrum from Janie's squeals. Instead, he reached around her shoulder and returned the hug.

Skye bent to pick up her fork. "A little premature, aren't we?" The light dancing in her eyes and her smile belied the censorious words. "But it's a relief to see the two of you getting along."

Janie hurried to Skye and hugged her next. "Of course we get along."

Reacting to the excitement, Bo bounced around the kitchen, barking and wagging his tail. Skye stood and shooed him out the door. "We'd better finish breakfast and get busy."

"I agree." Danny ate the last bite of his pancakes. "I found some tools in the shed. We can start clearing the yard near the house and work our way out."

Skye shook her head. "Janie and I can weed tomorrow." She ignored Janie's pout. "I need to get this protest committee underway."

Danny narrowed his eyes at Skye. She was stalling again. "What do you have in mind?"

She pointed out the window. "I saw a couple jogging this morning. The nice weather brought in some of the weekend residents. We could go talk to them this morning before they head back to Bellingham."

Danny sighed. "I'd much rather work outside in the yard, but you're right. We need to talk to the residents while we can."

While Skye gathered her papers with the information she wanted to share, Danny helped Janie with the dishes. In less than a half-hour, he escorted the two women across the island toward the newer homes.

Skye knocked on the first door. Where had the woman who had been so frightened in Seattle disappear to? Evidently, determination and a cause helped overcome some of her fears. He stood behind her in a show of support while she introduced herself to the couple who opened the door.

"We aren't really acquainted, but you've probably seen me around since I've lived here for the past few years."

"Of course." The man smiled. "I always jog by your house. I'm sorry about the fire."

The woman straightened her pink velour sweatshirt. "We've been meaning to come by and ask if you needed anything. We heard you're moving into the Johnson place on the beach."

"Well, yes. I've traded property with Sawyer Realtors." Skye paused, her hands tightening on the papers, the only visible sign that she was nervous.

The man rubbed his jaw. "Doesn't seem like an even trade. I wonder why they would do that."

"That's what I'm here to talk about." Skye explained her proposal to the young couple.

Danny had to admit she sounded convincing. Even though he suspected she was avoiding personal issues by pursuing this project, he was proud of her for taking this step out of her self-imposed isolation. True, she was in safe and familiar surroundings, but it was a big step nevertheless.

Skye finished and smiled at the couple. "So, are you willing to join us?"

The man scratched the top of his head. "Actually, the resort sounds great." He turned to his wife. "Can you imagine what that'd do to the value of our property?"

Skye stood open-mouthed and stared at the couple. Hadn't they heard a word she'd said? Did they really want to see the island destroyed? Danny guided her and Janie from one house to another. To her amazement, she encountered the same reaction from most of the other residents on that side of the island. She stopped on the point at the end of the northern-most branch of the "Y" and looked out at the sea. "Don't they realize what a treasure they have in this place?"

Janie stepped by her side and clasped Skye's hand in hers. "Obviously they're into material conveniences, not the beauty of this place."

Danny stood behind them and dropped his arms across their shoulders, hugging them both against his sturdy chest. "I'm sure they appreciate the beauty and peace. That's what draws them here. But each of us has our own unique outlook and needs. What satisfies you may not appeal to someone else."

Skye thought of Danny's reaction when he first arrived and nodded. "I admit I like things simpler than most. But can't they find what they need on the mainland or someplace that's already developed? There are other people like me who need a quiet and peaceful place to retreat to."

But did she need the solitude? Hadn't she discovered how lonely she'd been? Hadn't she delighted in Danny's company? Change was evident. She shook her head. But not this much at once. Not like this.

Stepping aside, Janie exclaimed, "We'll continue looking for support. Let's try over there."

Skye envied the calm expression on her sister's face. Janie lived in the city and did seem at peace most of the time. Overly exuberant and zealous, yes, but rarely stressed or worried.

Pulling away, Skye walked down the path. "Let's check out the houses on the other point where the old-timers live. We might find more support from them."

Skye did find some who were interested in her point of view and promised to help. But, surprisingly, some said they were relieved that changes were coming. Skye had to admit that they were getting older, and the primitive lifestyle was probably too much work for them. They were glad to have someone interested in their property, giving them the excuse to move into Bellingham—closer to doctors, pharmacies, and stores.

Weary and discouraged, Skye led Janie and Danny back to Johnson's house. Reaching the front porch, she stared at the weathered cedar and sighed. Maybe Danny was right. Maybe they should take the money for her property instead of this trade and go find another island.

Fear curled within. No, she wasn't ready for that much change. Not yet. Not without a fight.

Janie sat down in one of the plastic molded chairs they'd found in the shed. "What do you think about Fred's dad? Did he sound like he could be persuaded to join the committee?"

Danny nodded as he sat on the bench. "Sounded that way."

Skye sat beside Danny and stared out at the islands dotting the sea. "He might opt to sell out because he's getting up in years, too."

Danny folded Skye's hand in his. "His land borders the property Sawyer has already purchased. He'll get more pressure than the others to sell."

Tired of the discussion, Skye stood and glanced down at Danny. "You don't have much time left before you have to head home. How about a quick sail in the bay? I want to drop some crab pots."

Danny stood. "Sounds like a plan. The breeze will clear our heads."

Janie leaned back in her chair and propped her feet on the rail. "You go on ahead. I hear my pillow screaming my name. I think I'll take a nap."

Skye stepped off the porch and called Bo. "Come on, pup. We're going for a sail."

After an hour in the late-spring sunshine, Danny's tan

darkened and the stress lines along his forehead disappeared. His muscles bunched as he pulled on the sails. Skye admired his handsome features, thinking she would be content to be staring at them for the rest of her life. "You look better now that you've had some fresh air to clear your brain."

Danny smiled at her. "You do, too. I wish the day wasn't ending so fast. But I suppose we'd better head back to dock. I'll need to take off for Seattle soon."

"Sure enough, Flyboy." She smiled, but the ache of loneliness started to form inside. Strange that having Janie around didn't take the feeling away.

The lonesomeness grew Monday morning. She'd rebuilt a loom to weave her blankets, but even that activity didn't take away the blues. Pulling weeds helped. The exertion distracted her from thinking too much about Danny. She tried to focus on Janie's chatter, but the issue of development on the island tugged constantly on her mind. Danny would be mailing the letters this morning.

The hoe pounded into the hard ground with as much force as the turmoil pounding through her head. Should she fight? Should she just give in to the inevitable changes? Should she focus on Danny, blocking out what went on around her?

She stopped and tossed aside the hoe. "I'm taking a break."

Janie paused and leaned on her rake. "Sounds like a good idea. Want me to fix lunch?"

Skye walked toward the path leading across the island. "Wait about an hour and I'll be back. I want to talk to Mr. Davis one more time. He pulls a lot of weight with the other old-timers."

Janie brushed her hands on her jeans. "Ask Jack to go with you. He has a lot of influence."

Skye looked back. "You're right. I won't be gone long."

Bo romped ahead of her as she strolled down the path toward the caretaker's house. She found Jack on the dock, cleaning fish he had caught that morning. "You're going to miss all of this fresh fish if you move to Bellingham."

Grinning, he wiped his brow with his forearm, careful to keep fish scales from falling in his face. "I'll miss more than the fish." With knife in hand, he gestured around the island. "This has been our home for thirty years. I can't imagine living anywhere else."

Skye leaned against the rail, her skirt brushing against her legs in the gentle breeze. She gathered the loose ends of her hair and twisted them in a knot. "You aren't that anxious to leave, are you?"

He shook his head. "No, but it would kill me to see the island change." He started filleting the bass. "Lenny will like the conveniences."

Skye bit her tongue to keep from arguing that Lenny loved it here on the island. She supposed both he and Lenny were rationalizing, trying to make the best of a bad situation.

She held the pail for Jack so he could throw in the large fillets. "I'm heading over to talk to Mr. Davis. Want to come along?"

Wiping the blade of his knife with a rag hanging from his belt, Jack scrunched his brow in thought. "Going to try and talk him into staying?"

She nodded. "He'll listen to you."

Jack hesitated. "We can try. If we get enough support, we could possibly turn this around. Discourage the developers."

Jack tucked his knife into his tackle box and closed the lid. Lifting the pail in one hand and the box in the other, he motioned for Skye to follow. "Let me put this away and we'll head on over. I saw Davis out fishing earlier." He nodded toward the bay where boats bobbed and tugged on their buoys. "His boat's here now, so he must be home."

Jack and Bo led the way across the island, while Skye silently went over what she wanted to say. By the time she knocked on Harling Davis's door, she had rehearsed her rationale until it was clear and concise.

After her spiel, Davis served them coffee on his deck, apologizing because his wife was on the mainland and wasn't there to join them. "Fred's pushing for us to leave the island." He settled into a chair, squinting against the sun shining in his eyes. "Says this place is getting too big for us. Wants us to move into one of those fancy retirement communities. Preferably in Arizona." He snorted. "He doesn't really care about us. I think he wants a place to stay so he can come down during the winter."

Skye nodded. Fred wanted the money. Bending to pet Bo's head as he lay at her feet, Skye stared out at the ocean. They were on the opposite side of the island, looking out over the open sea. She could see the industrial stacks near Anacortes. Thankful for the uncluttered view on her side of the island, she focused her attention back on Davis.

Setting his cup down, he turned to Jack. "Wouldn't you like to retire? How's Arizona sound to you?"

Jack adjusted his baseball cap and grinned. "Sounds good in the dead-cold of winter." He looked around. "But you can't beat the cool summers here in the Sound."

"Yeah, that's the problem with the Southwest. Hotter than Hades in the summer."

Skye sighed. She was wasting her time here. Fred appeared to be doing a good job of talking his parents into selling. She set her cup on the table and rose out of her chair. Bo jumped up and circled her legs. "I left Janie at work in the yard. I should get back to helping her."

Jack stood. "Go on ahead. I'm going to stay here and talk awhile."

"Sure. I'll see you later."

Bo tore down the path toward the burnt ruins of her old house. At the top of the rise, she could see Janie chopping at the weeds on the far perimeter of the lot. Skye had only been gone a short time, and Janie didn't expect her back so soon. Maybe she'd follow Bo, slip over to her special place, and meditate for a few minutes.

Under the canopy of trees, Skye breathed deeply, relishing the cool, fresh air. Her feet automatically wound their way down the path. Tears misted her eyes as she thought of the countless times she'd retreated to her sacred spot in the forest. How many of those times would she have left?

Sensing her melancholy, Bo circled and pranced, trying to persuade her to play. Halfheartedly, she threw a stick, but when he returned and dropped it at her feet she ignored the pup. Impatient and restless, the puppy took off to explore a field of ferns.

Hoisting herself onto the smooth stump, she sat cross-legged, tucking her skirt under her legs. She straightened and took a deep breath. Peace did not come. Her mind reeled with scenarios of condominiums merging with her new house. Images of Danny. Life with him. Life without him.

Shying away from the negative, she tried to focus on the good things about Danny. A husband. A father. Children roaming the island, looking for nature's treasures. She tried to picture Danny showing them the beauty found in each shell. He would teach them how to build a fire, and they would sit as a family and sing songs. Watch the stars.

She sighed. Try as she might, the images wouldn't stick. She closed her eyes again. Nothing. Realizing the futility of her efforts, she slid off the stump and called Bo. He bounded over, jumping and yapping his joy at more attention. Skye laughed and tossed a stick into the brush. Bo charged through, snapping twigs as he went. He brought the scent of fresh pine with him when he returned, stick in mouth.

She played with Bo the whole way down the path. When she emerged from the forest near the house, she wondered what Danny was doing this very minute. Was he preparing for a break? She pictured him straightening his desk and rising to leave. More than likely he was escorting a couple of punks, trying to convince them to stay out of a gang. She wished he were meeting her for lunch.

About to throw another stick, Skye paused. That's what she would do. Go to Seattle. See Danny and make one more plea to the realtors. Maybe she could convince them to find another location for their development.

Skye reached the field and called to Janie. "Come on in and pack. We're catching the ferry to Seattle."

CHAPTER 17

DANNY PUSHED HIS CHAIR BACK from his desk and stretched. Behind in his work, he frowned at the files stacked in front of him. Rolling his neck and shoulders, he sighed. Leaving for the island every weekend was taking its toll.

The door opened, and his assistant walked in carrying several more files. "Here you go, Boss. These came in today."

He groaned as she placed the new files on the bottom of the stack. She straightened but didn't leave. "You're getting quite a pile there."

He rubbed at his jaw. "Don't I know it?"

"Haven't been working those long hours on the weekends." She picked up his cup and quirked her brow. "Want more coffee?"

He nodded. "Thanks, Joyce. I feel guilty about not coming in."

She turned in surprise. "You shouldn't. You've finally cut back to a normal pace." She held out the full cup and smiled. "You look better for it, too."

"But the cases keep piling up."

She shrugged. "As long as you keep slaving overtime, your supervisors keep sending more work to you. If you let yourself get behind, then maybe they'll wake up and see that you need help. Another counselor."

Would Ted actually hire someone else? Danny had never considered that. "Another counselor would be a relief." And give him more time off. Time to be with Skye.

Joyce poured herself a cup and settled into one of the chairs in front of his desk. "I know someone who has experience.

Someone who's available."

Grinning, he eyed her over his cup. "Hmmmm. Couldn't be someone named Joyce, could it?"

She shrugged but didn't back off. "I'm almost finished with my counseling degree at Washington State, and I'm going to be looking for a job. You need the help. Sounds like a perfect solution for both of us."

"I'll bring it up next time I see Ted." Danny set his cup down on the coaster. "Now let me get back to work, or he'll be hiring you and firing me."

Laughing, Joyce stood. "Like that'll ever happen. Keep at it, Boss. I need those top two files by this afternoon."

Her laughter followed her out the door. Danny paused, pen poised in hand. Another counselor would certainly ease the load. Give him more time, he thought, smiling. He needed to tell Ted about his relationship with Skye. If they ever did marry, he would need time off for a honeymoon.

The opportunity came sooner than Danny expected. Twenty minutes later, Ted knocked on the door and entered Danny's office. Danny stood and shook Ted's hand. "What brings you down to the trenches?"

Ted glanced around the office and pointed to the pile of folders stacked precariously on the desk. "I see you have plenty of work, and judging from the lineup of kids out there, I'd say you were right about calling this place 'the trenches.'"

"Funny you should bring that up." Danny gestured toward a chair and then poured coffee for his friend and benefactor. "Joyce graduates this month."

Ted accepted the coffee and sat down. "Counseling degree, right?"

Danny nodded. "She's a great worker. Organized. Stays focused. Plenty of experience for a position in this office."

Ted straightened. "You aren't planning to resign, are you?"

Danny paused, choosing his words carefully. At least he hoped that it wouldn't come to a decision so drastic. He loved Skye, but could he give up his life's work? "No, I love this job. But Skye and I are becoming more involved. I want my weekends, and I was hoping I could use your cabin."

Setting his cup down, Ted stood and pounded Danny on the back. "You dog. It's about time you took time for yourself. I'm glad it's Skye."

Heat crept up Danny's neck. "I plan to head out to the island most weekends."

"I can understand that." Ted grinned. "Skye has been good for you. You've eased up. Started to relax. And are you redefining your priorities too?"

Danny nodded and, encouraged by Ted's enthusiasm, took a deep breath. "Which brings up the fact that I won't be able to work long hours anymore."

Ted stepped back. "I should hope not. You're going to want to be with that pretty lady." He picked up his cup and took a sip. "I've told you you've been working too hard. This is perfect. You'll be having fun instead of working yourself to death like you were doing."

And hopefully one of these days he'd become a husband and a father. Afraid Ted would bring that up too, he quickly changed the subject. "Glad to hear you're supportive. Now you know why we need another counselor."

Ted burst out laughing. "You always were a sly fox. Let me talk to the board. I'm sure we can arrange to hire one. Tell Joyce to put in her application."

Danny motioned again to the chair and waited for his benefactor to sit before he settled in his own desk chair. He leaned back. "Have you heard about the plans to develop Leeza Island? Sawyer Realtors is negotiating the deal."

Nodding, Ted's brow furrowed. "James and Jed Sawyer."

Danny nodded. "Know them?"

"They go to my church."

Surprised, Danny tapped his pen on his desk. "Do they have rock-solid values?"

"What do you mean?"

He set the pen aside. "There has been a sudden rise in vandalism. I told you about Skye's house burning down."

"You don't think the Sawyers are behind it?"

"I didn't want to say anything to Skye or the other islanders without proof. I can't help but put two and two together."

Ted rubbed his jaw. "I don't know them personally. They seem nice enough, but of course that doesn't always mean anything. I saw them the other day, and they made an offer on my island house."

Danny steepled his fingers and leaned his elbows on his desk. "Are you considering selling?"

Ted finished his coffee and set the cup on the edge of Danny's desk. "Barb wants to keep the house. What kind of development are they planning on?"

Danny explained all that he knew.

Ted rubbed his jaw, his expression thoughtful. "Can't say I object to a project like that. Would be nice to have a golf course. I could bring my clients for some R and R."

"It'll change the face of the island. No more quiet nights and peaceful days. No more time to be still and commune with God."

Ted chuckled. "You're throwing my words back at me."

Danny stretched his feet out in front of him, rocking back in his chair. "Yeah, I do seem to remember someone practically forcing me out there. You're the one who insisted I needed the peaceful retreat." He studied Ted's thoughtful expression. "I'd hate to see that change, especially if there's corruption behind the scenes. Skye and I were hoping you'd support a movement to keep the status quo."

"I can understand your point of view." Ted stood up to look out the small window at the city. "You might be right. A large project like the one they're proposing could be detrimental. I'll look into it."

"I knew you'd understand." Standing, Danny walked next to Ted and mock-slugged him on the shoulder. "So how about it? We're going for another counselor, right?"

Ted paused at the door. "Barb would kill me if I did anything to get in the way of romance. Send me a list of applicants."

The door shut behind Ted. Danny returned to his desk and sat, staring out his small window at the city without really seeing the skyscrapers silhouetted against the gray sky. Ted was a busy man. Would he follow up on researching the Sawyers?

His phone rang. He answered it and bolted out of his chair. "Skye's here? In Seattle? Why?" His heart thumped as he raced to the door, almost bumping into her and Joyce as they prepared to enter. He stepped back, relieved to see Skye's expression determined, but in control. Not panicked like the last time she was in town. "Is everything okay?"

Skye nodded as Joyce shut the door, leaving them alone.

"It's great to see you." He wanted to pull her into his arms, but he could see the hesitancy, sense her nervousness. "Come sit down."

She shook her head and remained standing. "I'm going to talk to the Sawyers. Can you come with me?"

"Now?"

Nodding, she tugged at the pockets of her sweater. He eyed the files on his desk and thought of the boys waiting to see him. "Can we do it in half an hour? I can take you on my lunch break."

A tap sounded, and the door opened. Nina stepped inside. "Hey, Skye. You staying in town?"

Sighing with relief, Danny motioned to his co-worker. "Can she wait with you while I take care of the Rodriguez boys?"

"Sure thing. Sign these for me, okay?" She set papers on his desk and whisked Skye out of the room. Raking his fingers through his hair, Danny hurried to the front desk and motioned the young brothers into his office. As promised, he finished with the boys, signed Nina's papers, and laid another folder on the finished pile.

Grabbing his jacket, Danny shrugged into it and left his office. He found Skye sitting with Nina and Natasha. "Ready to go?"

Nodding, Skye patted Natasha's hand. "We'll be there for you. Don't you worry."

Danny eyed Nina. "What's up?"

"Skye offered to chaperone Natasha at your place tonight. Her old gang's out to get her."

Danny rubbed his jaw. He knew the danger of Natasha staying in her neighborhood. She would be safe at his place. "Good. Keep her here with you until Skye and I finish up." He turned to Skye. "I'll drive you both out to my place this afternoon."

Located only a few blocks down the street, Danny didn't take long to find the offices of Sawyer Realty. James Sawyer stood and held out his hand when he spotted Danny. "Glad to see you again. I hear you're helping Miss Larsen move into the house."

Danny nodded, but considering the nature of his visit, kept his manner distant.

Skye stepped forward. "I do appreciate your generosity, which is why we want to alert you to the fact that we're going to try to stop the development you're planning for Leeza Island."

James plopped down in his chair. "I don't understand. I've been more than fair with you folks. Miss Larsen, you received a decent trade."

Danny remained standing. "Yes, but we both know you benefited more, since her property borders the other land you purchased. Rather convenient that the place burned down after she made it clear she wouldn't sell the property to you."

Skye gasped.

James straightened. "I hope you aren't implying—"

"There has been a rise in vandalism on the island."

James shot out of his chair, his face red and angry. "I am a respected businessman. I don't need to use those kind of tactics."

Danny clenched his fists at his sides. "Just so we're clear, Skye is going to protest your development, and I don't want anything happening to her because of it. Or to anyone on the island, for that matter."

Jed Sawyer entered the room, paused as if to assess the tension, and moved toward Danny and Skye with his hand outstretched. "Couldn't help but overhear the conversation, and I don't blame you one bit."

Reluctantly, Danny shook his hand, as did Skye. The look of confusion on James's face matched Skye's.

"I just got off the phone with Ted Randall. Appears we have some investigating to do." Jed motioned to the couch.

Skye's fingers trembled when Danny grasped her hand and pulled her beside him. "You talked to Ted?"

"Yes," Jed replied, then explained to his brother what had been transpiring on the island. He glanced at Danny and Skye. "We're meeting with the authorities later this afternoon to review the events."

Danny eyed Jed. Either the sincerity was real, or he was a good actor. Quirking his brow, he looked at Skye, wondering if she had more to say. She shook her head. "Glad we had a chance to clear the air."

Jed reached over to shake his hand. "We'll keep you posted

on what we find."

As Danny escorted Skye out the door, he could hear the two men's voices as they discussed their plans.

"Can we trust them?" Skye interrupted his thoughts.

"I think so."

"I about fell out of my chair when you brought up those accusations."

"There's no proof, and now that I've met them, I doubt they had anything to do with it." Danny tucked her arm in the crook of his. "But I believe we'll be finding out soon if vandals were involved." There probably hadn't been a thorough investigation. It took power from the right places to get the wheels of justice rolling on an island as small and indistinct as Leeza.

A light mist moistened his face as they stepped out the door. "How long have you been in the city? Have you eaten? Can I take you to lunch?"

The chill he felt from the damp weather and the conversation with the Sawyers dissipated when he saw her smile.

Skye eyed the tattoos trailing up Natasha's arm. The girl sat at Danny's new kitchen table, her shoulders slumped, a frown on her face. Skye could only imagine what horrible memories were sailing through the teen's mind. Again, Skye wondered why she had volunteered to chaperone. A moment of insanity, she decided. For the hundredth time, she wished she hadn't left Bo with Lenny and Jack. At least the pup would have kept Natasha occupied, and Skye wouldn't feel like she had to entertain the unhappy girl.

She shook her head. The teen was in danger. Why did Skye think she could live here and raise her children in a city riddled with crime? The Sawyers' faces came to mind, and she shuddered as Danny's accusations hit her again, reminding her there were vandals on Leeza Island. Nowhere was safe anymore.

Skye reached for two mugs for the hot chocolate she was heating. Loud banging sounded on the front door. Skye froze. Natasha jumped up.

Skye shook away the fear threatening to choke her and motioned for Natasha to sit back down. "Stay here. I'll go see who it is."

Hugging the wall, Skye inched her way down the hall, hoping no one would see her through the beveled glass in the doors. Outside in the drive, a metallic blue car sat close to the ground, loud music pumping. A lowrider. Had the gang members found out where Natasha was staying? Her heart thumped wildly in her throat. Should she call Danny? The police?

Banging sounded again. "Natasha. Are you there?" a loud male voice yelled. Impatient. Insistent.

A chair scraped in the kitchen. Skye rushed back and motioned for Natasha to follow her into the hallway. They might come around the yard to the back. Had she unlocked the door when they arrived? She couldn't remember. She'd have to go test it.

Shoving Natasha out of sight, she straightened. "Stay here. I'm going to make sure the door's locked."

Hurrying, she got to the door just as a teen rounded the corner of the house. He spotted her and started to run. Crying sounds escaped her lips as she rushed to reach the door before he did. Two more boys rounded the corner. Visions tore through her mind. The scenes of her youth. The teens forcing their way into her house. Attacking. Murdering.

Her fingers fumbled as she closed the latch. The first teen banged on the door. "Let us in. We want to see Natasha."

Her heart thumped wildly. "Please. Please help." A strange

peace settled through her as if in answer to her prayer.

The boy dropped his arms and turned to his friends, an expression of dejection on his features. "I guess she's not here."

Startled by a movement behind her, she swung around to see Natasha coming toward her.

The boys returned to the door when they spotted Natasha. Skye's heart sank. What could she do to protect the girl?

"It's all right, Miss Larsen. I know them. They're friends."

Skye prayed fervently as Natasha unlocked the door.

The first boy swept in and wrapped Natasha in a hug, swinging her onto the porch outside. "You're here. We've been so worried. Are you okay?"

Tears streamed down Natasha's face as she hugged the other two boys. Skye pressed against the door, staring in shock. These boys knew Natasha. Cared for her. Who would have known?

Natasha tore her attention from the boys and turned to her. "Can they stay?"

Now aware of Skye's discomfiture, the boys backed away from Natasha. "Hey, don't be scared, lady. We're cool."

Natasha introduced the first boy as Ramón. "And this here's Jason and Lamont."

Ramón took off his backward ball cap and brushed long fingers through his dark hair. "Sorry we scared you. We just wanted to make sure Tash was good."

They sounded normal, but chains dangling from baggy black pants brought unpleasant memories.

Natasha wiped at a tear. "How'd you find us?"

"Fraser. He told us you were here."

Skye straightened. "Danny said you could come?"

The boy backed away, his glance darting from Natasha to her. "Well, not exactly, but we're staying with Tash. No one lays another hand on her. We'll see to that."

Lamont stepped forward and put a protective arm around

Natasha. "You good with her?" He nodded toward Skye, clearly not trusting.

And why should he when Skye was obviously terrified of him?

Stepping forward, Natasha grabbed Skye's hand. "You scared us half to death, right, Miss Larsen? We didn't know who you were when you came to the door."

The boy dropped his arms and stared.

Natasha eyed Skye carefully. "She's cool, Lamont. She's the one I told you about."

Staring at the girl, Skye relaxed. So she'd told these boys about her. Judging from their reaction, Skye had indeed made a positive impact. She felt for the first time that she was a mature adult able to influence the life of a kid. That was a good thing. Wasn't it?

The boys shuffled in place, and she realized they were waiting for her to invite them in. "I was making hot chocolate for Natasha. Do you want to join us?" She motioned toward the table, glad now that Danny had purchased the larger dining set they'd seen at the mall. "Sit down and visit while I get it."

Chains clattered on the hardwood as the boys sat around the table. They took off their caps and tossed them on the floor at their feet. While she poured chocolate into the mugs, she listened to the concern and caring in their voices. What had she been so afraid of anyway? These were just teens who cared for one another.

As soon as she'd served each one a mug of steaming chocolate, she left them talking in the kitchen. She needed to be alone. To assimilate what she had discovered and learned this past hour. In the living room, she sank into the cushions of Danny's chair. His masculine scent enveloped her.

Muted light streamed through the windows, highlighting the Bible sitting open on the nearby table. She took a deep breath and touched the pages with shaking fingers. Warm peace washed over her. *Danny's work is important to these kids. He's helping them, and You're keeping him safe.*

She glanced around the room, suddenly sure of one thing. She could handle living here. She could handle the reality of Danny's job—maybe even help him with it. Surely by helping others like Natasha, Skye would lose some of her own fears. Hadn't she already?

Danny sat back in his chair and rubbed his eyes. He missed Skye. He glanced at the calendar. Wednesday. Two more days and he'd be flying out to the island. He could hardly wait to see her again. She had been amazing during her visit. Her reaction to Natasha and the others gave him hope.

He straightened and returned his attention back to his desk. The request for funds from the Baker Foundation sat on a pile of other proposals demanding action he wasn't sure he could provide. More emergency situations that needed funding. Would they never end?

He straightened. Of course not. He thought about Skye and the progress she had made during her last visit to Seattle. If she could move toward change, shouldn't he? She had scolded him many times during his stay on the island. He needed to let go of the circumstances he couldn't change. He was not responsible for providing for every cause in the city. He had to stop being so hard on himself.

Danny shoved back his chair and grabbed his jacket. He passed by Joyce and handed her the file. "I'm going to check out the Baker Foundation. I'll be back in the office after lunch."

The Baker Foundation proved legitimate. The funds they requested would be put to good use. Danny invited the director to lunch, and by the time they left the restaurant, both men were smiling.

They stood under the awning, out of the rain. Danny held out his hand. "We'll have those funds transferred by the end of the week."

The director shook his head, his ear-to-ear grin brightening up the gray day. "You don't know how hard we've been praying. Bless you, Mr. Fraser."

Feeling better, Danny walked down the wet Seattle sidewalk to his office. The misty rain formed droplets of water on his eyebrows and hair. He breathed in the clean smell of the moist air. Glancing upward, he smiled.

Weaving his way through other pedestrians, he mulled over the change in his attitude. Before meeting Skye, he brooded over the cases he couldn't help. Now he took pleasure and satisfaction in those he could. Like today with the Baker Foundation.

Whistling, he strode into the office, shedding his wet suit jacket and loosening his tie. "Don't forward any calls for the next hour, Joyce. I'm going to attack those piles you've stacked on my desk."

Joyce held up the receiver of the phone. "I don't think so, Boss. Skye is on the line. There's big trouble."

Heart pounding, he grabbed the receiver and pressed it against his ear. "What's up?" He could barely understand her words through the panicked sobs. "Are you sure? She's missing?"

"I went to collect oysters for dinner, and when I came back to the house she was gone."

CHAPTER 18

SKYE SAGGED WITH RELIEF at the sound of Danny's voice. "Janie said she was going to fix lunch for me, so I didn't think anything of it when I didn't see her in the yard."

"Are you sure she's not out walking somewhere? Maybe she went looking for you."

She gripped the CB microphone, her knuckles white. "I've looked everywhere." Her throat constricted. Her words stuck. Turning to Lenny, she held out the instrument. "You tell him," she mouthed.

Lenny took the microphone with one hand and wrapped her free arm around Skye's shoulder, pulling her close. "We've organized a search and rescue party. Jack's out in the boat, circling the island for any sign of her on the beach."

Taking deep breaths, Skye calmed the threatening panic. She could hear Danny's voice but couldn't distinguish the words due to the static. No matter. She already felt better knowing he understood what was going on.

Lenny signed off. "He's flying out as soon as he can." She returned and brushed a strand of hair off Skye's forehead. "Don't fret. Janie probably went off somewhere private to pray."

A slice of annoyance slid through the concern. But it wasn't like Janie to go off without telling anyone where she was. "She'll be horrified to know she caused us all to worry."

Heavy footsteps stomped up the steps and across Lenny's porch. She opened the door, and Harling Davis entered. He raised his hand before either woman could speak. "They haven't found her yet. We combed every inch of the island." He motioned to Lenny that he wanted a glass of water. "Young folk.

Don't have any sense of responsibility." He accepted the glass and took a swig. "Fred used to pull stunts like this all the time. Took off, never saying a word about where he was going."

Not wanting to hear another one of his rants about the younger generation, Skye clasped Davis's hand in hers. "Did you find any clues?"

He shook his head. "The fella that lives out on the point"—he nodded toward the part of the island with newer houses—"said he thought he saw a small boat take off from Arch Cove around noon. Said it looked like a man and a woman."

Thinking of the boat she'd seen earlier, Skye frowned. "Janie wouldn't go home without leaving me a note." She glanced at Lenny. "Or at least telling Lenny or Jack. It's not like her to do that."

Davis handed the empty glass to Lenny. "Maybe one of her friends arrived. You know the kind of work she does. Could have been a crisis at home, and she returned to Seattle with them."

Pouring a glass for herself, Lenny shook her head. "Nope, I've been here all morning. No one showed up at the dock."

Twisting her hands, Skye leaned against the counter. "None of her friends know about Arch Cove."

Lenny and Davis exchanged looks. Skye pressed her head against the nearby cupboard. She closed her eyes against the waves of anxiety.

Something was wrong. She felt it in the pit of her stomach. She looked up at Lenny. "How long did Danny say it would take him to get here?"

"A couple of hours." Lenny set her cup down and smoothed Skye's forehead. Her hand felt cool against her hot, clammy skin. "You look peaked. Why don't you go back to the house and stretch out on the bed. When Janie returns, the first place she'll go is back to the cabin."

Skye straightened. "I can't…"

"We'll come right over the minute we hear anything." Hands on hips and a stern expression on her face, Lenny stood in front of her. "You won't be worth a hoot when Danny arrives if you don't take care of yourself."

Sighing, Skye relented. "Promise to call me."

"Yes, yes." Lenny shooed her out the door.

Walking down the steps, she heard the worried tone in Lenny and Harling's voices as they talked. She took a deep breath. No way was she going to be able to take a nap with Janie missing. She glanced at the house and then at the sea. Arch Cove. Boats had landed there before. She spun around and hiked toward the cove. "Come on, Bo. Heel."

Seeming to sense her stress, Bo remained at her side. Skye marched across the fields and down the narrow trail. Bo leapt onto the sand ahead of her, but she called him back. "Stay here, buddy. I don't want you messing up any evidence."

After making sure that Bo would remain, she stepped carefully onto the sand. Her stomach knotted as she searched the small cove. A boat had beached—she could see the groove where they'd dragged the bow across the sand. From the height of the tidewater line, they had to have been there within the last two hours.

Footprints dotted the sand. One heavy pair. One light pair. The tracks from the forest looked normal until they reached the spot where the boat had sat. There, the sand piled as if churned by a struggle.

Her legs turned to jelly. Moaning, Skye slumped into the sand. Surely Janie had not been kidnapped. And if so, why?

Bo hurried to her side and licked her face. Skye saw the worry in his eyes. Worry that matched her own. She wrapped her arms around his neck and buried her face in the ruff of fur. Panic rose from the place deep inside—the place where she'd buried the scene of her parents' death.

Fear wrapped insidious fingers around her heart. Choking her. Punching her in the gut. Laughing at the way she cowered.

Rocking back and forth, she loosened her hold of Bo and pounded her fists into the sand.

Visions of the summer afternoon her parents had died rocketed through her mind. She'd been in her bedroom, listening to the album her father had just bought. The window had been open, letting the ocean breeze filter through the chintz curtains.

When she'd first heard the scuffle in the kitchen, she'd thought her parents were playing around like they usually did. She remembered smiling and turning the volume up to give them their privacy. Then she'd heard the scream.

Bolting upright, she'd scrambled off the bed and hurried to the door. Her mother's scream ripped through her heart. Her father's curses blasted down the hall. Then they abruptly halted.

Her heart pounding, Skye slid down the hall, bracing herself against the wall. She froze when she saw the blood gurgling from her father's slit throat. Her mother struggled in the corner as one man held her down. Another was on top of her, hitting her over and over. Skye wanted to scream. She wanted to attack the men. But she stood. Frozen. Terror gripping her body.

Skye shuddered, blocking out the images tearing through her head. She balled her hands into fists. If only she'd done something. If only she hadn't remained rooted to the spot. Maybe she could have saved her mother's life. But no, she'd cowered against the wall and watched the murderers.

When they had finished with her mother, they turned and saw Skye. At first they made fun of her fear. Then they'd come after her. The sight of the evil in their eyes jerked her back to her senses. Furious, she'd screamed and fought as they tried to pin her down. The screams must have alerted neighbors. Sirens broke into the rage. She didn't remember much after that. Except the nightmares. The horror.

And now Janie. Would someone hurt her?

"Nooooo! I will not sit by and do nothing. Not this time." She glared at the sky. "Do you hear me, God? She's all the family I have left. You can't let them take her, too."

Struggling to her feet, Skye stood and peered out across the sea. Where would they take her? Where could they go? There were hundreds of isolated islands in the Sound.

She closed her eyes and took a deep breath. A small measure of peace calmed the fury. Again, she peered around the beach. Only Bo stood nearby in the wet sand. The wind plastered her skirt to her legs, tossed her hair about her face.

Taking another deep breath, she called for Bo. A sudden urge pushed her onward, a yearning to go to the dock. Unmindful of her steps, she walked down the familiar path.

Her mind reeled with possibilities. Maybe someone on another island needed help. Janie would drop everything in an instant if she thought anyone needed her. But no, she'd tell someone before taking off. Wouldn't she? Maybe Janie knew the person in the boat and had simply gone out for a ride. No, the prints in the sand indicated a struggle.

The list ran on as Skye tossed aside one possibility after another. She paused and closed her eyes, taking in the smells of the berry bushes in bloom, the fresh grass in the field. "I need You. Help me find her."

Colors swam before her eyes, drawing her gaze toward the sea where the islands sat like giant emeralds.

Her boat. She could search the nearby islands. Urgency pressed. Running now, she rushed to the beach where her skiff sat. Bo ran beside her, barking as she dragged the small craft to the water's edge. She glanced toward Johnson's house. She should get some supplies.

Quickly, she ran across the beach, her boots straining

against the uneven rocks. Bo trotted along beside her, barking, obviously sensing her unrest. She tore up the steps and grabbed bottles of water, her jacket, and some fruit Danny had brought from the mainland. Stuffing them in the backpack, she glanced over at Lenny's house. She should run over and tell her where she was going. Danny would worry.

Frantic now, she dropped the backpack on the floor and scrambled through the drawer for a pencil and piece of paper. Quickly she wrote a note. She paused, then started writing again, telling about her suspicions of what she saw on the beach. Finished, she spun around, searching for an obvious place to hang the paper, settling on the refrigerator door with one of the seashell magnets that had belonged to Mr. Johnson.

Bo ran ahead of her and jumped into the skiff. With adrenaline pumping in her system, she pushed the craft into the water and rowed to her sailboat in record time. Hoisting the sails, she checked the direction of the wind and pointed the bow into it. She wanted the fastest speed.

"I'm coming, Janie. I'm going to find you. I promise."

Danny landed on the island and looked toward the beach, expecting to see Skye heading toward him. Instead, he saw a group of people huddled on the dock where the sheriff's boat tugged at the ropes. Mixed emotions tore through him. Had they found Janie? Was she all right? How was Skye holding up?

The gusts of wind hampered his efforts to tie down the aircraft. Struggling to hurry and get the job done, he bumped his head on the struts. Pain riveted him motionless for a second. Forcing himself to rally, he ignored the drops of blood and bent to tie the last strap.

Grabbing his handkerchief, he dabbed at the cut and shoved the cloth into his pocket. He opened the door of the craft and reached for his duffel. Hoisting it over his shoulder, he started for the dock, wondering why Bo wasn't nipping at his heels like he usually did when Danny flew in. Tension curled in his gut.

As he passed by Jack's, he tossed his bag on their porch. He could collect it later. Picking up speed, he jogged across the dock. Jack waved him over when he spotted Danny.

Puffing and out of breath, Danny approached the older man. "What's up? Where's Skye?"

The group split apart, letting Danny in. The sheriff stepped forward. "Skye's not here, but we know where she is. It's her sister, Janie, we're concerned about."

Forcing a calm he didn't feel, Danny clenched his fists. He took deep breaths, reminding himself to be patient. "Still no sign of her?"

The sheriff shook his head. "Appears she might have been kidnapped off the island in a small boat."

Bile surged up his throat. "Kidnapped." He choked. "You've got to be kidding."

Jack pounded him on the back. Danny swallowed hard.

Writing in his notebook, the sheriff continued. "Several people saw a boat leave Arch Cove around noon with a man and a woman in it. No one recognized the boat, but we've searched the island. We can only conclude that Janie was the woman in the boat."

"You've ruled out that she went voluntarily?"

The sheriff nodded his head. "There is that possibility. But one of the witnesses said they thought they saw the man pulling the woman into the boat."

Jack stepped forward. "Skye saw evidence of a struggle on the beach. She's convinced that Janie went against her will."

Danny directed his attention to Lenny. "She would have let Skye know she was leaving, wouldn't she?"

Wiping at a tear, Lenny nodded. "Nothing like this has ever happened before. I don't understand. Why would someone want to take Janie? She's such a sweet girl."

Danny refused to think of all the whys. "Where's Skye? I should be with her." Thoughts of the worry and terror she must be facing tore at his heart.

Grasping his arm, Lenny stepped toward him and led him away from the others. "You're not going to be happy." She stopped next to the rail.

Danny glanced out at the harbor. Skye's skiff bobbed up and down against her buoy. A new fear etched its way down his spine. "What do you mean? Don't tell me she went after the boat?"

Lenny nodded and pulled a piece of paper from her pocket. "She left this note."

Danny grasped the paper, reading it and forcing himself not to crumple it in his sudden fear-inspired anger. "She's searching the shoreline of the nearby islands for signs of the boat." Danny looked across the Sound, hoping to see the white sails billowing against the blue sky. He shoved his sunglasses on top of his head. "She's gone off by herself. Is she nuts?"

Jack joined them. "The sheriff's heading out toward the islands. Hopefully he'll find Skye. Want to ride with him?"

Relief surged through Danny. "Yes. When I do, I'll need him with me to keep me from wringing her pretty neck."

Jack placed his hand on Danny's back. "Now, son. You must—"

Danny interrupted. "I know. She's strong-willed and independent. But she shouldn't be out there alone. Who knows what these people want?" Fear tore through him as his imagination kicked in. Images appeared of the recent vandalism, the gunmen on the point, Skye's house burning. Surely whoever was behind the recent acts of violence wouldn't go this far. Or maybe the person had hired thugs, and who knew what they would do?

Jack grabbed his arm. "She's sensible. She won't do anything foolish."

"I'm not so sure. Janie is the only family Skye has left." She'd become very independent and self-sufficient living alone on the island. "I wouldn't put it past her to confront anyone threatening Janie. I'm worried about what will happen if Skye catches up to them."

Lenny wrung her hands.

Striding toward the sheriff, Danny dropped his sunglasses back on his nose. "Hear you're heading out. Can I hitch a ride?"

"You bet. Get whatever you need and meet me back here in ten minutes."

Without wasting time to respond, Danny hurried up the dock to Jack's house. He grabbed his duffel bag and pulled out a water bottle and a windbreaker. The temps were warm now, but the air would chill past sunset. Hopefully he wouldn't be out that long, but best to be prepared.

On the dock, Jack helped untie the lines and held them until they were ready to cast off. The boat rocked as Danny jumped on board, followed by the sheriff. The engine roared to life, but the sheriff didn't open the throttle until they had cleared the dock. Once in open water, he pushed on the stick. The boat lurched forward, creating a huge wake as they aimed for the islands across the bay.

Standing next to the sheriff, Danny searched the horizon. The wind whipped past his face with a roar, preventing any conversation. Once they rounded the island, the sheriff let up on the throttle and slowed the craft. "Jack said she'd start around these islands first." The sheriff pointed toward the small inlets. "Keep your eye out for her. There're plenty of coves around here to hide in, so look for signs of another lone boat. Even if Skye passed this way, she may have missed them."

Chewing his lip, Danny wished he could hurry the sheriff along. They could easily catch up to Skye with the engine-powered motor. "Let's look for Skye first, then search for Janie. I'm worried she'll find them before we get there."

The sheriff rubbed his jaw. "Good idea. If you joined her, we could split up and cover more territory."

He would rather take Skye back to Leeza Island where she'd be safe, but he knew she wouldn't be having any of that. She'd be desperate to find her sister.

Clouds scudded across the blue sky, casting shadows on the shoreline. Danny squinted against the glare and gripped the rail of the boat. The painful thought of something happening to Skye emphasized how much he loved her.

The boat pounded into the whitecaps, jarring Danny's body. He gritted his teeth, searching the horizon. Something flashed in the distance. He straightened and pointed. "Over there. I see something. Could be Skye's boat."

The sheriff turned toward the island. "Could be a white sail."

Danny climbed onto his seat, spreading his arms for balance. "Looks like Skye's boat."

His knees weakened as relief poured through him. Sliding into the seat, he took several deep breaths.

In minutes, they caught up to Skye, who looked as relieved to see him as he was to see her. She luffed her sails into the wind. "Have you found her?"

Danny shook his head. "I'm coming aboard."

She nodded and waited while he gathered his gear.

The sheriff held the boat steady. "I'm going through that passage." He pointed toward a channel between two large islands. "You two head east. We'll meet at the other side."

Danny agreed and then leapt across the water from the sheriff's boat to Skye's. Skye stepped into his arms. He held her close, taking in the feel and smell of her, convincing himself she was truly okay. Following the reassurance came anger. "What were you thinking? Couldn't you have waited for me?"

Bo barked and jumped on the back of his legs. Letting go of Skye, he patted the pup's head and then returned his attention to Skye.

Tears slid down her cheeks. "I didn't mean to worry you, Danny. I couldn't sit around, knowing Janie's in trouble."

He clamped his jaw, trying to stem the desire to shake sense into her. "What would you have done if you had found her? Besides compound the situation?"

She stiffened. "I have the radio. I would've called."

That news didn't reassure him in the least. Even if she'd notified them, perceiving a threat, she would have run to Janie's side.

The sheriff yelled across the water. "You two okay?"

She took a step away from him.

Danny waved. "We're good to go."

"I'm heading out then." The engine roared to life as the sheriff pushed in the throttle. Water lapped against the side of their boat, the only sound breaking the silence.

Danny turned and started to speak.

Skye raised her hand to the cut on his brow. "You're hurt. What happened?"

Embarrassed, he waved aside her concern. "Nothing. A bump on the head. I'm here now. The sheriff said to head east."

She straightened. "Let's set sail."

He rubbed his hands up and down his arms, the action calming him. "I didn't mean to yell at you."

She smoothed her palm down his cheek. "I know. You were

worried about me. I'm sorry."

He turned his face and kissed her palm. "Okay, Pocahontas. Tell me what you want me to do."

Skye issued orders as she maneuvered the sails. In minutes, they were heading at a forty-five degree angle to catch the wind. Using her binoculars, he scanned the beaches as they sailed by. Every now and then, he'd sneak a glance at Skye, marveling at her calm. After her reaction to perceived danger in the Seattle mall, he expected her to fall apart with this new danger. But like her confrontation with Natasha's friends, from what he'd heard, she appeared controlled and confident in spite of her concern. Hope flared. Was she learning to cope with her fears?

They hit a stretch of open water as they sailed toward the next island. Danny moved close to her side. "Need a break with the lines?"

She shook her head. "It's better if I stay busy. Otherwise I'd be a basket case."

He brushed back a strand of her hair. "In spite of the fact you scared me to death, I'm proud of you. You have a new inner strength."

She looked at him, her blue-eyed gaze penetrating and deep. "I'm beginning to trust in your God. Janie does. That faith will keep her strong through this."

Not wanting to cast any doubts on Skye's newfound faith, he remained silent.

She continued. "I felt so helpless." She tightened her hold on the line. "I still do. But I need to be strong for Janie. If believing helps me, helps Janie, then I believe."

Danny nodded.

She pointed toward the sail. "Duck your head. I'm coming about."

He sat beside her as she maneuvered the sails. The heavy canvases flapped noisily until they filled with wind. Skimming the water, Skye approached the next island. A flash of red caught his eye. He grabbed the binoculars and searched the shore.

Adrenaline rushed through him. He stood and pointed. "I see a red boat. On the shore over there."

CHAPTER 19

SKYE'S HEART POUNDED as she shaded her eyes against the glare. "Where?"

Danny pointed toward a group of rocks framing a small sandy cove. "Better not let them spot us, if it is them. Head over to the other side of the rocks while I radio the sheriff."

Skye quickly dropped the main sail and raised the centerboard. The boat skimmed the water, the light lapping of waves against the hull the only sound. With the change of speed, Bo started to move from his spot. Skye motioned him back down. "Shhhh, boy. Lie down and stay quiet."

The pup flattened on the deck at her feet. Skye steered the boat toward an outcropping of rock and motioned for Danny to drop the anchor. Avoiding a splash, Danny eased the heavy metal into the water. The boat secure, Skye reached for the ladder.

Danny grasped her arm and stopped her. "Stay here. I'll go ashore and see what I can find."

Skye shook her arm free. "No way. I'm going with you."

Danny leveled a stern look. "Someone needs to stay and signal the sheriff."

Frowning, Skye eyed the shore and then the sea. Janie could be there on the beach. She shook her head. "No, I…"

Danny grasped both of her arms and held her close, apprehension and determination emanating from his eyes. "Janie could be in big trouble. She could need help. I don't want to have to be worrying about you, too."

Skye opened her mouth to protest.

Danny tightened his grip. "No argument. You stay put."

Bo jumped up and barked.

Danny let go of Skye and reached for the dog.

Skye sat down and grabbed Bo's muzzle. "Quiet," she whispered.

Danny leaned over the dog and cupped Skye's cheek. "See. You need to stay here and keep Bo calm. He could scare these dudes into hurting Janie."

Knowing he was right, Skye nodded. Fear crawled up her back as she watched Danny slip over the rail, drop into the water, and wade to shore. What if something happened to him? Could she bear losing him too?

Gripping Bo's ruff, she kept an eye on Danny's progress across the beach until he disappeared into the thick forest. Spasms contracted in her stomach as fear edged her heart. The two people she loved most were in danger, and here she sat like a coward. Again.

She let go of Bo and started to rise. As if sensing her intent, Bo planted himself between her and the stainless steel railing. She pushed away from the dog. "I can't sit here doing nothing. I have to help."

She started to move, but her conscience reared. She'd promised Danny she'd stay put. She sagged back onto the seat. Hating her helplessness, she rocked back and forth. Her stomach heaved. She wrapped her arms around her waist, willing herself to remain calm, but to no avail.

"What am I doing?" she gasped as she gripped Bo's fur.

Bo cocked his head, then nuzzled her neck.

She glanced at the sky overhead. Clouds scurried across the expanse of blue. "Are You there?" She closed her eyes and sensed a strange calmness.

The breeze kicked the edges of the sail, flapping it against the boom. Cleats clattered as they hit the wood, the sound echoing in the stillness of the sea. On shore, the waves lapped the sandy beach and knocked against the outcropping of rocks.

Skye looked at the deserted shoreline. She glanced skyward. An eagle flew overhead, circling in the thermals above the Sound.

I'll give you the strength of eagles.

Danny's quote echoed in her heart. She gripped the rail and pulled herself upright. Taking deep breaths, she stared at the shoreline and willed herself to be strong. Her decision made, she locked Bo in the cabin. "Stay here, fella. The sheriff will be here soon."

Searching the boat for a weapon, she grabbed a flare gun and an oar and placed them on the outside of the rail. Pulling her skirt between her legs, she tied the ends around her waist, making pantaloons, and then took off her boots. Easing herself into the icy water, she felt for the rocky bottom and got a foothold. She grabbed the weapons, held them over her head, and carefully waded in, the cold water numbing her legs.

Sharp rocks and shells dug through her socks and into her feet. The pain penetrated the numbness. Pausing, she took a breath of salty air. Another step, and another. Pain shot up her leg. Stumbling, she waved her arms for balance. Cold water hit her chest. She gasped, but managed to stay upright.

She glanced at the sky. The eagle still circled overhead. Strength surged through her. She took another step. And another. Wet and cold, she staggered onto the sandy beach.

Bending, she panted. When she had caught her breath, she straightened and peered at her surroundings. Like sentinels, the trees outlined the rocky clearing. She clamped her teeth against the urge to yell for Danny. Silent, she followed the sets of footprints. At the edge of the forest, she froze. Fear iced her blood. Her hair prickled the back of her neck.

Closing her eyes, she inhaled slowly. Her heart rate steadied. She stepped into the dark shadows. A twig snapped underfoot, stinging her toes. Another step. Another. Her ears strained as she listened for any sound. Silence. Except for the loud pounding in her ears. Her heartbeat thundered.

Again she paused. Chewing her lip, she studied the woods. Shadows danced on the ground. Squirrels scurried up trees, then stopped to chatter at her. Skye ignored them.

Another sound caught her attention. She froze. Listened. Yes. A voice. Danny.

Fighting the urge to run to him, she forced careful steps. Twigs littered the rocky ground. Careful to avoid them, she inched forward. Closer and closer to the deep rumble of Danny's voice.

Pausing, she scanned the forest, hoping to see a sign of them. Large trunks rose from heavy underbrush. What was Danny wearing? Blue. A light blue shirt. Janie had on jeans and a brown shirt. Hardly colors that would stand out in the shrubbery.

Danny's voice droned on.

Glancing at the ground, she took another step. Then another. Her arms ached with the weight of the awkward oar. She had to be close. She could make out Danny's words.

"Come on, Fred. You aren't going to get away with this."

Fred! Had Janie gone with Fred? Her mind jumbled with relief. Here they were all worried, and Janie had only gone for a ride with Fred. Smiling, she stepped toward them.

Danny's next words stopped her cold. "Put the gun down. We can work this out."

A gun! Fred had a gun?

Bright sunlight came in shafts through the trees. A clearing. They had to be there. Taking a deep breath, she crept to the edge of the trees and peered around a large trunk. Her breath caught in her throat.

Danny stood in front of a small cabin. Janie huddled against the porch rail behind him. Fred rested one booted foot on a rock in the open, with a gun pointed at Danny's chest.

Skye leaned back out of sight and pressed against the trunk of the tree. A measure of courage steadied her legs. She studied the ground, memorizing where every stick threatened to break the silence. Closing her eyes, she breathed deep, drawing on a well of faith she prayed was there.

Danny's words soothed her fear. "It's not too late. We can work this out."

"Shut up, Danny. I'm tired of your drivel." Fred's voice cracked with tension and fear.

Janie peered from behind Danny. "Fred. Please stop this before someone gets hurt."

Fred snorted a forced laugh. "I'm in too deep now. Too much to lose. And you and your crazy sister are not going to get in my way anymore."

Skye's mind reeled. How had she gotten in Fred's way? What was he talking about?

Danny waved for Janie to get back behind him. "You're responsible for the vandalism on the island." His voice resonated with understanding. "You set Skye's house on fire." He scowled.

Fred waved the gun in the air. "I knew she wasn't there. I'm not stupid."

The fire. The vandalism. Fred? Why? Skye started to step out into the clearing, but Danny's next words warned her.

"Did Sawyer hire you?"

Fred grunted. "That man is even more stupid than you. He wasn't interested in guaranteeing his investment. But I am. I want that development to go through."

"You stand to gain from it, I gather." Danny's sarcasm carried across the clearing.

Fred shifted position. "I own the lots by my dad's. They weren't worth much, but they are now. I can sell them to Sawyer and get out of the ol' man's life." Bitterness and pent-up anger laced Fred's words.

Skye shuddered. She knew Harling Davis had been hard on his son, but she didn't realize how deep the scars ran.

"So how do you plan to keep us from telling the authorities?"

Fred waved the gun again. "They'll find you eventually. But you'll be dead by then."

Skye straightened, her sympathy replaced with renewed fear. She had to rescue Danny and Janie before Fred did anything crazy. She peered around the tree again. Fred's back was to her now. She glanced down at the flare gun. He was close enough; she couldn't miss. Her hand shook as she tightened her fingers around the metal. The flare would kill him.

No, killing was not the answer. She set the gun down and grabbed the oar. If she could get to him before he noticed, maybe she could knock him out. But if he heard her... No. She closed her mind to the thought. To the fear. Better that she was shot than Danny. The distraction would give Danny time to attack and defend himself.

She took a deep breath. Her fear disappeared, replaced by determination. She stepped from behind the tree.

Danny saw the movement. His heart froze when he realized it was Skye. He clenched his jaw. He wanted to yell at her to go back. Run for the boat. For safety.

The determined look on her face changed his mind. He shifted position and started talking to keep Fred's attention on him. "I'm not afraid to die, but spare Janie. She has nothing to do with this."

"Yeah. Right. She'll be so good as to spare my life and lie for me." His sarcastic laughter rang through the clearing, covering the sound of Skye sneaking up on him.

Skye planned to hit Fred. Danny bunched his muscles, prepared to leap. His heart raced. Fear pumped adrenaline through his body.

Skye leapt forward.

Janie screamed.

Danny jumped the second he heard the smack on Fred's arm.

Fred bellowed in pain. The gun flew in the air, and Danny dove for it, the heavy metal cold in his hand. Fred turned and started to grab Skye.

Danny bolted upright and shot a bullet into the ground. He trained the gun on Fred. "Don't move."

Fred froze.

Skye started toward Danny. He waved her aside with his free hand. "You and Janie get in the cabin."

Skye ran to Janie. Janie grabbed Skye but stared at Danny. "Don't hurt him."

Danny tightened his finger on the trigger. For an awful second, he wanted to shoot the man who had put Skye in such danger. He eased his hold and motioned to Fred. "Sit down on the ground and keep your hands on your head."

Danny nodded at Skye. "Go inside and see if you can find a rope or cord. Anything to tie him up."

Skye ran inside. Her footsteps echoed. Hope plummeted as he realized the place was empty. Deserted.

Skye coughed. "Nothing. The cabin's bare." More footsteps, then a loud clatter. "I found a blind. I'm getting the cord."

Danny glanced up when she charged through the door, a cord dangling from her hand. He reached for the rope. "Let me do it. Hold this." He handed the gun to Skye and took the cord from her. Fred twisted away.

"Don't think I won't shoot." The deadly chill in Skye's words stopped Fred's resistance.

Danny shivered as he tied the cord around Fred's hands and forced him to sit.

Janie ran to Fred and dropped to her knees in front of him. "Fred. Why?"

Danny took hold of Janie and gently pulled her upright and away from Fred. "He'll have plenty of time in jail to mull over his choices."

Tears streamed down Janie's cheeks. "I'll visit you, Fred. You'll see. I know some great prison ministers. They do wonderful work."

Danny took the gun from Skye's trembling fingers and draped his arm around her, pulling her close. "Are you okay?"

She nodded. "I left the flare gun by the tree." She pointed to the spot where she had emerged from the forest. "Let's signal the sheriff."

Danny kept Fred's gun trained on the disgruntled man. "Go ahead and shoot up the flare. We'll head for the beach."

Skye hurried toward the forest and ran back with the flare gun in her hand. Once in the open, Skye shot the flare into the air. It rocketed skyward, leaving a trail of smoke. Bright light reflected on the water when it exploded. Hopefully the sheriff would see the flare and come soon. Danny didn't want to risk Fred working his hands loose and causing any more trouble.

Motioning for Fred to stand, he nodded toward the trail. "No funny stuff. After what you've put Skye through, as well as the other islanders, I have no qualms about using this." He waved the gun at Fred.

Fred struggled upright and followed Danny's instructions, muttering to himself. "I was so close." He glared at Skye. "Why couldn't you just let things be? Why did you have to resist the project? Couldn't you see how much better off you'd be?"

Skye remained silent and slipped behind Danny, holding Janie's hand. Danny followed closely behind Fred as they made their way to the beach.

At the shore, Danny motioned for Fred to sit on one of the rocks. Head hanging, Fred sat, dejected. He wouldn't cause any more trouble. Sympathy for the man warred with Danny's anger at the danger and anxiety he had caused the women.

Shivering in her wet clothes, Skye gathered some wood for a fire. "The sheriff will be here shortly. In the meantime, we need to get dry." She pointed to Danny's wet Dockers.

He hadn't even noticed the spreading chill. Adrenaline pumped through his system, making him restless and edgy. He kept the gun trained on Fred while Janie helped her sister light the fire.

He glanced out to sea and saw a white speck coming toward them. Good. The sheriff could deal with Fred. He glanced over at Skye. And he could deal with her.

Realization of the danger hit him. Anger warred with the awe that filled his heart at Skye's unfaltering courage. Did she realize what she had done? How she had overcome her fears? He studied her, hope replacing horror.

Her hair flowed freely, loosened during the struggle. Her wet skirt clung to her legs. She'd unfastened her jacket, the edges flapping in the breeze, allowing her T-shirt to dry. She tossed another piece of driftwood on the fire. Straightening, she caught his stare.

Locked into her blue-eyed gaze, he smiled. Her lips curved. His heart thudded in his chest. "I love you," he mouthed.

She waved him to the fire. "Come over here, Flyboy."

Keeping the gun trained on Fred, Danny moved to stand next to Skye. The heat from the fire warmed his chilled skin.

She grabbed the hem of her jacket and lifted it, dabbing at the cut on his forehead. "It's bleeding again." She leaned back and studied the wound. "Looks worse than it is. Mostly blood."

"You mean I'll live?"

She smiled and stepped behind him, sliding an arm around his waist. "Let me warm you up."

Her body curled against his, soft yet strong. He leaned into it, absorbing the warmth and the love.

By the time the sheriff landed on the beach, his pants were mostly dry and his body temperature back to normal. Skye and Janie rushed toward the sheriff and explained what had happened, both talking at once. Danny kept his eye on Fred.

Within an hour, the sheriff had transported Fred onto his boat. Janie decided to ride back to Leeza Island with the officer. Danny rescued Bo from the cabin of the sailboat and brought the pup on shore. Bo took off exploring, leaving Danny and Skye alone on the beach. Silence surrounded them as they sat beside the fire on the now peaceful shore.

Skye grabbed another piece of driftwood and poked at the embers. "I can't believe Fred caused so much trouble. The vandalism. Burning my house."

Danny brushed a tendril of hair behind her ear. "Not to mention the danger he put you and Janie in."

She nodded, a sad expression in her eyes. "I'm so glad we were able to stop him before he did anything more serious."

"You were very brave." He clasped her hand in his and squeezed her fingers. "Even though you scared ten years off my life."

She squeezed back. "You were scared? What about me? I was terrified. I mean, I thought he was going to shoot you. Shoot Janie."

He wrapped his arm around her shoulder and drew her against him. "It's over now."

She lifted her head and cupped his chin with her warm hand. Then she let go of him and hugged her knees to her chest, rocking back and forth in the sand. Danny bit his tongue to keep quiet and let her talk at her own pace.

She tilted her head, glancing at him. "I prayed like you said."

Danny's heart filled. He gripped his own knees to keep from folding her into his arms. "Tell me about it."

She slid around to face him, tucking her feet into the sand beneath her as she shared with him her thoughts and feelings. "Do you know what I'm saying?"

He slid around also. "Yes. People will let you down, but God never will."

She stared into his eyes. "You wouldn't."

He reached out and cupped her cheek. "I surely won't mean to, Pocahontas. But I'm not perfect. I'll make mistakes. Sometimes I might say the wrong thing. Make the wrong move. Being with me is not going to be easy."

Chuckling, she leaned back. "Nothing's easy with me. At least you know what you're getting into."

"Like I said before, I'm a patient man."

She didn't respond, but sat staring at the flames. Sparks crackled and shot out. Gases hissed. Seagulls squawked in the distance as waves lapped the shore.

Her voice came low so that he almost didn't hear her at first. "I'm ready to face my other fears."

His heart rate quickened. "Meaning…?"

"I need to face them. Try the same strategies to overcome them."

Forcing down his excitement, he murmured, "Are you sure?"

She nodded. "But that's not all."

"What do you mean?"

She smoothed the sand with her palm, then traced designs in it with her fingers. Danny clenched his fists, willing himself to be as patient as he had promised.

Her hand stilled, and she looked at him. "I want to go back to Seattle with you."

He sat motionless, resisting the urge to jump up and dance with joy. "You still have the summer here, Skye."

She nodded. "I know. But I need to make plans. Janie can help me." She let the sand drift from her fingers. "Besides, I can't overcome my fear of the city if I'm not there."

Unable to resist another minute, he reached for her and nestled her against his chest. Resting his chin on the top of her head, he closed his eyes. "I'll be there for you. Anything you need or want, just call." He nuzzled his face by her ear.

I'm counting on that." She chuckled and lifted her face to his. "You might be sorry."

"Never." He leaned his head forward, his mouth a breath away from hers. "You will marry me, won't you, Skye?"

She nodded and smiled.

Sand sprayed. He jerked back. Bo bounced and pranced on all fours. Skye laughed.

The moment lost, he stood and brushed the sand off his clothes. Skye held her hand up. He clasped her fingers and pulled her upright. "As much as I'd like to stay and talk about loving you, we'd better head back to the island."

Skye kicked sand on the fire. "Are you flying back to Seattle tonight?"

Danny grabbed the oar and flare gun and loaded it into the red speedboat. "Yes. I left in a hurry. I need to return."

Thoughts of leaving the island didn't burn like usual. Skye was flying with him. Joy and anticipation filled his heart.

Skye helped shove the speedboat into the water. She called Bo and followed him over the side.

Danny waded into the water and hoisted himself aboard. "The sheriff asked me to bring the boat to Leeza. I'll meet you there."

Skye nodded as she grabbed the railing and pulled the craft next to her sailboat. "We won't leave for Seattle right away, will we?"

He shook his head. "I'm sure we'll have paperwork to fill out."

"Good. I need to talk to Janie."

He quirked his brow, loving the pink creeping up her cheeks. She leaned over and brushed his cheek with her lips. "She and I have to make plans."

His heart raced. "So you do. Do we have a date for dinner?"

She climbed aboard and stood tall, silhouetted against the blue sky. "I'm sure that can be arranged."

He tipped his forehead in salute and eased away from the sailboat. He glanced back and saw the sails billowing skyward. Turning toward Leeza Island, he pushed on the throttle. As the boat picked up speed, his heart filled with thanksgiving.

Suddenly the clouds appeared puffier in a clear blue sky. The air smelled fresh and crisp. He glanced around at the beauty surrounding him and spotted the lighthouse in the distance. Hope throbbed through his veins.

And Skye. She'd discovered her strength. Her peace. Her changing heart. Now, they could move forward. Together.

CHAPTER 20

TRAFFIC BUZZED UP AND DOWN Martin Luther King Boulevard. Skye looked through the raindrops sliding down the window of Janie's loft. The summer drizzle didn't stop people from rushing to and fro on the busy street. She dropped the curtain and looked at Janie. "Are you sure you can't ride the bus with me to Danny's office? He offered to take us both out to lunch."

Janie finished putting away the last dish. "I can't. I promised to work at St. Vincent de Paul's and help prepare the food." She skirted the sofa and stood beside Skye to clasp her hand. She tugged. "You can come with me and help. After the meal is served, I can ride with you."

Skye pulled her hand free. "I promised Danny I'd meet him for lunch." She picked up the bus schedule sitting on the table next to the window. "He has an appointment with Sawyer Realtors at one-thirty."

Janie leaned against the arm of the sofa. "Do you really think it will do any good to talk to them?"

"Danny wants to apologize for making accusations when you were missing." She shrugged. "Maybe they'll listen to another appeal for the eagles."

"You and those silly birds. Let it go."

It wouldn't do any good to talk about the island. Janie had other concerns. Sighing, Skye held the bus schedule out toward her sister. "Can you go over the route again?"

"Sure." She glanced up and smiled, pointing at the schedule. "You'll be okay. It's a direct shot. No transfers. Just tell the driver what street you want to get off on, and he'll announce it."

Taking a deep breath, Skye tucked the schedule in her pack, slipped on her coat, and gave Janie a goodbye kiss on the cheek. "I'll call if I won't be back for dinner."

"Don't worry about me. If Danny has plans, go for it. Be careful going down those steps. They're wet and slippery."

Outside the door, Skye slid open the umbrella. The steps were the least of her worries. She grasped the metal railing with her free hand and wound her way to the street.

Two men approached. Skye held her breath as they brushed by her. A warmth crept up her back, bringing a sense of well-being and peace. The men had smiled, hadn't they?

A teenager, his eyes dancing with mischief, sped by on a skateboard, the wheels spraying water over the tops of her boots. Skye ducked back against the wall. The bus stop was half a block down the hill.

She straightened her shoulders. Taking a deep breath, she stepped behind a woman heading toward the bus stop. Her knuckles turned white as she gripped the umbrella. At the stop, she braced against the post, trying to stay out of the path of the pedestrians.

A man in a raggedy coat, holes in his shoes, his hand out-stretched, approached. "Any spare change?" he muttered from beneath his scraggly beard.

Skye lowered her eyes and frantically dug in her pack. Relieved to find the five-dollar bill Janie had given her, she held it out to the man. Her breath whooshed out when he turned and walked down the busy street without another word. But she'd seen the loneliness in his eyes. A wave of guilt coursed through her. She hadn't helped the man out of sympathy or caring. She'd wanted him to leave.

Skye glanced at her watch, wishing she had taken Danny up on his offer to come get her with his car. She glanced at the spire sporting the window of Janie's loft. Maybe she should go call him. They would have to eat fast food for lunch, but then she wouldn't have to stand out here and wait for the bus.

She closed her eyes. Danny was busy clearing his desk in order to meet her for lunch. No, she couldn't call him.

The bus arrived, its air brakes whooshing as it stopped in front of her. Inside, she found a seat next to a young woman holding a baby. Skye focused on the innocent child, trying to ignore the rest of the passengers on the crowded bus.

Minutes dragged as the bus stopped on the corner of every block. The woman got off. A young man with purple hair and rings in his nose sat next to her. Skye gripped the handle of the umbrella and kept her eyes focused on the street.

The boy smiled, his eyes holding a searching quality. Perhaps changes had affected his life as they had hers. She returned the smile.

Finally, the driver announced her street. Jumping up, she edged past the man and hurried off the bus. Outside, she took a deep breath and eyed the doors to Danny's building. Danny stood under the awning and waved.

Her heart raced as she hurried into his waiting arms.

"You made it." He hugged her close.

Wanting to stay within the safety of his embrace, she tucked her head against his chest.

Danny laughed. "That bad, huh?"

"Let's just say I didn't really fit in." She glanced up at him, enjoying the warmth and love dancing in his eyes. "I need rings in my nose and funky-colored hair."

Danny leaned back and grasped her shoulders, giving her a slight shake. "Don't you dare."

She smoothed back hairs that had strayed from her braid. "Maybe blue would go better with my eyes."

Laughing, he tucked her hand into the crook of his arm and started down the street. He glanced upward. "What have we done? We've unleashed a wild woman."

She stopped. "I'm not afraid anymore." She paused, noticing the other pedestrians stepping around them. "I mean, I'm still afraid. But I know how to overcome that fear now."

Danny stared deep into her eyes, his love warming her to her toes. He pressed his forehead to hers. "We'll have the best of both worlds. We'll go to the island for the summers. Take our children. Teach them to love the outdoors."

She traced her forefinger down his cheek. "Then we'll spend winters in the city. You can teach our children the value of hard work. Caring for others."

He took her hand in his and pressed her fingers to his lips. "I love you."

She smiled. "I love you."

"Let's go get lunch. Make more plans."

On the day of the wedding, Skye stood on the edge of the porch, her white dress frothing around her, her veil wafting in the breeze. Her fingers tightened around the bouquet of white roses that Janie had brought from Seattle. She glanced across the grass yard where friends and family sat with their backs to her, facing the sea.

Late-summer sunlight reflected off the waters of the Sound. A light breeze rippled the tall grass surrounding the cut yard of Skye's island house. Ripe berries climbing over the southern railing scented the air, mixing with the fragrance of assorted wildflowers that lined her porch. One of Janie's friends plucked romantic music on his guitar.

Danny.

He stood in front of the gathering at the far edge of the

yard, tall and rugged in his dark suit. Bo sat at attention beside him on the left. To his right, Pastor Ron waited. She studied Danny's face. The stress lines were gone, replaced by tanned skin and a happy, expectant smile. A smile that matched her own.

Lenny and Janie walked down the aisle to the front of the small group of island residents gathered for the ceremony. Danny's mother sat beside the Randalls. Skye smiled, happy that the woman had embraced her, made her feel like a true daughter. Her hair braided with beads, Natasha sat next to Danny's mother. She waved when she saw Skye looking her way.

After Lenny and Janie reached the front of the crowd, Lenny sat in the front row. Janie kept walking to Pastor Evans's left, then paused and turned, smiling back at Skye. Changing his tune, the guitarist strummed the "Wedding March," which echoed across the meadow. Skye took a deep breath. Not of fear, but of determination. She and Danny had written their own vows, and she meant to follow them to the letter.

Jack grasped her elbow and helped her down the stairs. As Skye floated toward Danny, her heart raced with anticipation and joy. Many changes had intruded upon her life. Some good. Some not so good. But this man in front of her canceled out the fears, doubts, and misgivings. She glanced skyward. "Thank You," she whispered.

Danny held out his hand. She placed hers in his warm grasp and stepped beside him. Their friend, Pastor Evans, began the ceremony. Her heart raced as she listened to Danny recite his favorite prayer—the prayer of St. Francis of Assisi.

Yes, her husband would be an instrument of peace and love. Hadn't he already been a light in her darkness, hope in her despair, giving her faith for her doubts?

Love filled her with joy as she looked into his eyes to recite her vows. "I, Sunny Skye Larsen, do promise to love and cherish you, Daniel Fraser." Tears welled as she promised to nurture and share. To be brave in her love and to be strong in her devotion. Dabbing at her eyes, she took a deep breath and steadied her inner trembling.

Danny's kiss dissolved the tears. Her heart raced. He smiled down at her. "I love you, Mrs. Fraser."

Skye barely remembered the rest of the ceremony. When it was over, she mingled with the crowd. When she noticed a plane flying low and landing on the grassy strip, she glanced at Danny. "Are we missing anyone?"

"Everyone we invited is here." He clasped his hand in hers. "May I have this dance, Mrs. Fraser?"

She smiled, forgetting about the airplane. She danced with Danny, then with Jack. Another man cut in. She paused. "Mr. Sawyer." Behind him stood his brother, James.

"Did we miss the wedding?"

Her heart dropped. Had Danny invited the realtors? Pushing aside her apprehension, she said, "The ceremony is over, but you're welcome to join us for refreshments."

Danny stepped beside her. She welcomed his arm around her waist.

Jed clapped his hands together and rubbed them back and forth. "Good. Because we brought you a wedding present."

Her apprehension faded under his smile. "You didn't need to—"

"Oh, but we did. My brother and I were very upset when Danny told us what was going on here at Leeza, presumably on our behalf."

It had been a surprise to all of them when they had found out that Fred had been behind the vandalism.

The realtor continued, "As we told you before, we're God-fearing men. We would never jeopardize our business by knowingly threatening or cheating our clients."

Skye shifted restlessly. "We don't need to bring up the past on my wedding day."

"Ah, but we need to. I told you we had a gift for you."

Skye studied his face.

The realtor offered a secret smile. "After Danny's visit, my brother and I made a decision. We called the Forest Service and offered to make a trade."

Danny's grip around her waist tightened. "You traded your property on Leeza?"

Skye's heart raced. "Are you saying you won't be building on the island?"

He shook his head. "We'll still have a resort, but on a much smaller scale. In fact, you won't notice much difference except for a clubhouse and restaurant at the end of the dock. And we're bringing in electricity."

Did he really think that a smaller resort was a gift? She glanced at Jack and Lenny. She couldn't be upset that they had sold out. Lenny did want to be closer to her grandchildren, and she had promised to stay in touch with Skye and visit her in Seattle.

Skye turned to the realtor. "I'm sure most of the other island residents will enjoy the facilities."

"We traded all of our land out there on the point"—he gestured toward the end of the island where her house had stood—"with the understanding that the Forest Service will maintain it as a preserve for the eagles and a park for the residents."

Skye turned toward Danny. Did she hear correctly? Danny nodded. Skye grasped Jed and hugged his broad shoulders. "That's the best wedding gift ever." She hugged James.

"It's the least we can do after all that happened. You can thank Danny for setting us straight."

Tears welled. Skye hugged her new husband's arm.

A screech resounded from the blue sky. Skye shaded her eyes with her hand and watched the eagle circle above. His mate followed. "No changes for you after all," she murmured.

Danny wrapped his arm around her waist and tucked her close. "They'll be fine, Pocahontas." He bent and kissed her brow. "And so will we."

Nodding in agreement, Skye smiled. "Yes, Flyboy, marrying you is my smartest move ever."

DISCUSSION QUESTIONS

1. Why is Skye living on Leeza Island? Has she accomplished her goal?

2. Why has Danny come to Leeza Island? Has he accomplished his goal?

3. Why does Skye fight to prevent the changes on Leeza Island?

4. Why does Fred fight to make the changes on Leeza Island?

5. Skye and Danny are attracted to each other. What are the issues that make Danny think the relationship is impossible? What are the issues that make Skye think the relationship is impossible?

6. How do Skye and Danny overcome these issues?

7. What moral lessons do Skye and Danny learn? Does this change them? If so, how?

ACKNOWLEDGEMENTS

To the following writers for their insightful critiques and support:
Ruth Logan Herne
Joan Domning
Barbara Larriva
Peggy Parsons
Nancy Damato
Kelly Gerlach
Crystal Miller

About the Author

Sandra Leesmith loves to travel in her RV and explore all of nature's beauty, discover America's history, and fellowship with the wonderful people she meets while on the road. She enjoys reading, writing, hiking, swimming, and pickleball. Learn more about Sandra and her books at www.sandraleesmith.com.

You can connect with Sandra on Facebook, Twitter, and Goodreads. You can also find her and her talented writing buddies at the Seekerville blog.

If you enjoyed this book, please consider leaving a review online.

Thank you!

ALSO BY SANDRA LEESMITH

LOVE'S MIRACLES
(Amber Press—Second Edition, 2013)

"From gut-wrenching to heart-soaring, Ms. Leesmith's Love's Miracles *will not only steal your heart and your sleep, but your thoughts for literally weeks after."*
—Julie Lessman, award-winning author of the
Daughters of Boston and Winds of Change series

Only by reliving her own wounded past and helping Dominic Zanelli confront a terrible memory from the Vietnam War could Dr. Margo Devaull set them both free—and save their last chance for love.

Available in paperback, Kindle e-book, and audiobook formats

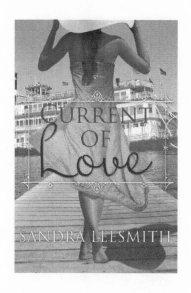

CURRENT OF LOVE
(Montlake Romance, 2012)

While on a steamboat cruise up the Mississippi, Janelle Edwards and Everett Jamison III must make a decision: continue running from their emotions—or let the current of love sweep them away.

Available in paperback and Kindle e-book formats

THE PRICE OF VICTORY
(Montlake Romance, 2011)

Can Sterling Wade help Debra Valenzuela follow her dream and in the process discover new purpose for his own life? Will they accept the price of victory?

Available in paperback and Kindle e-book formats

7505938R00176

Made in the USA
San Bernardino, CA
08 January 2014